Estelle Victory

THE OPPORTUNITY

Published by Kestrel Design Ltd
Printed by CreateSpace
ISBN-13: 978-1-5272-0655-7
ISBN-10: 1527206556
First Printing February 2017

Kestrel Design Ltd
www.kestreldesign.co.uk
mail@kestreldesign.co.uk

Ordering Information: Quantity sales. Special discounts are available on quantity purchases by corporations, associations, and others. For details, contact the publisher at the address above.

Publisher's Cataloging-in-Publication data: Victory, Estelle. The Opportunity / Estelle Victory. ISBN-13: 978-1-5272-0655-7. ISBN-10: 1527206556.
BISAC: Fiction / Dystopian and/or Fiction / Science Fiction / Apocalyptic & Post-Apocalyptic

First Edition

10 9 8 7 6 5 4 3 2 1

-PROLOGUE-

ANNOUNCEMENT: MINISTRY OF HEALTH

HELP US ERADICATE DISEASE

Following the recent demonstrations concerning public health and spending issues, we are pleased to announce the launch of a unique chance to be part of medical history.

Key to the success of this initiative is the participation of multi-generational families. Registrations of interest may be made through your allocated Health Centre. Only those individuals with an appropriate medical history will be eligible and a full range of screening tests will be mandatory for all second-round applicants.

Once screening has taken place, successful families will be relocated to a medical facility to participate in this unique experience. The facility will be the size of a small town, tailor-made to be sterile and secure, whilst abundant with pleasant leisure and social opportunities.

The selected families will live at the facility together, at no cost, and will be supplied with full accommodation, leisure, education and social facilities. There will be no obligation to be employed, and no independent source of finance is required for participants. This is a long term commitment and participants who are selected will be required to agree to remain in the program for at least fifty years, or until their last remaining child reaches twenty-one years of age. In exchange for permitting world-class scientists to monitor the effect of cutting-edge technology on their health, participants will have a golden opportunity to live an idyllic life, with the very best services provided to them in elegant surroundings.

This is the Opportunity. Your Opportunity. Become part of history. Register your interest now.

MINISTER HARTE
APRIL 2035

For more information, please contact The Opportunity hotline on 777-222

-PART ONE-

1

The day they eliminated Physicals was the worst day of my life. Physicals – the manifestations of physical illness in the human body. Cancers. Auto-immune disorders. Lung disease. Heart disease. On that day, the last incurable patient left this world, and with her, the shackles of physical illness.

It was cancer, the last Physical to take a human life in Florivale. Of course. The body literally turning on itself, cells multiplying frenetically, creating their own blood supply, and pulling the very essence of life from the body which created them. The irony. The ugliness of the language of the Physical: Neoplasm. Arrest. Carcinogen. Metastasize.

I remember all of the terms from Health class in the EduCentre, even though we were told we should never need to use them, being lucky residents of Florivale! We learnt that, with cancer, our bodies became the instruments of our own destruction. Cells endlessly dividing; ultimately cleaving life from matter.

They thought it was over as she breathed her last. That the complexity and artistry of the human mind had finally prevailed over the frailty of the body; healthcare was the final solution to all problems. They should have known better. There are some problems which just can't be solved.

Of course, none of this was apparent to me when she passed. To me she was more than an emblem of a time gone by, her death heralded as the beginning of a new chapter for humanity. She was my grandmother Sophie. I was tiny. But I remembered her. When they told me, I buried my hands in the smooth cotton hem of my jumper, curled into myself and wept hot, mystified tears.

Of course her death was news. It was touted as "world news" on the Bulletin. Whatever that world actually was. These days, I'm not really sure. Looking back, I have my doubts about whether all the people outside Florivale's boundaries knew, or cared, what we were doing here. I doubt I will ever know. Isolated in our community, our half-world. The Petri Dish of Humanity.

Don't get me wrong. I can understand how it all began. I can see it now, the hysteria, the excitement, the glimpse of an idyllic future. The excitement of her notes is infectious. I loved seeing through her eyes. But more about that later.

It's easy to imagine why people did it, considering that the Opportunity came along after years of exponentially increasing death rates, countless surgical procedures, biopsies, radiation therapy, chemical therapy, new drugs under pressurised development and devastation when these couldn't deliver the results and resilience we craved.

Faced with an escalating death toll, crippling medical costs, public outcry and widespread fear, governments had to find a solution. The official statement - that there was simply not enough funding to treat everyone - was no longer enough.

The people did not allow the government to think of them as disposable. The violence and terror of the "Value Life" riots scarred the population, and changed everything. Ironic, that a movement founded on preserving life came at such a human cost.

To a logical mind, what they did made sense. A mind trained to balance risk and reward at every opportunity would not question the Opportunity. Of course, not everyone shares that mind, that ability to calculate and measure, clinical, distanced. Perhaps it was that 'otherness' that gave Minister Harte the unique power to conduct what can only be described as the greatest experiment of human history.

The Opportunity: an experiment with wonderful, terrible, and unanticipated results.

Let's start back at the beginning. It was an easy idea to sell. Who wouldn't want to eliminate

Physicals?

The more difficult matter was how to achieve it. How to demonstrate it empirically, quickly and, most importantly, publicly.

Raised in a suburb of what was then Cambridge, Minister Harte had always aspired to more than she had; constantly striving to become more than the sum of her parts. To her, achievements were nothing if they were not public.

As her steel-tipped heels punctuated her path, Harte propelled herself into public office by sheer force of will. Knowing the capricious British spirit, and alarmed by the destruction and precarious aftermath of the Value Life movement, Harte had to act swiftly and decisively.

It is from that public office that Harte devised the Opportunity. Lauded by her peers as a visionary and a saviour, she had the nation's attention. The posters and flyers began to proliferate across the country, placed in all national and regional newspapers. The Opportunity jingle rang in ears across the nation, implanted there by the relentless radio and television broadcasts.

The saddest part is that the hook for my family, and for so many others, was the chance to live in a society which started again from scratch, without the need for money. It's like the poor families scratching their way across the Oklahoma Dust Bowl, an image straight from the pages of the old copy of The Grapes of Wrath I found in the Community Centre Library.

When they called for information, my grandparents were told that they were correct: yes, if they were selected, their debts would be written off. Yes, neither of them would have to work ever again and, yes, their entire family would be maintained in the absolute peak of health. I'm learning how many decisions came down to cold, hard cash. A concept I have limited understanding about, but don't much like the sound of. I wonder whether they ever regretted coming in here, or whether the toll of living in the Petri Dish grew over time.

Now that I know what little I do, I also know I'm in danger.

2

I suppose you're wondering where I am, who I am and why it's my story you're hearing. The first of those questions is by far the easiest to answer. The others, you'll have to figure out as we go along. Much the same as I am doing.

I'm from Florivale, which you might have heard of. Sure, the name sounds nice. The pictures, if you have any, probably look great too. There is no crime. The Physicals that plagued us Before have trickled away. Everyone in Florivale is healthy and safe. Everyone has enough food and a comfortable home.
I'm desperate to leave.

Florivale is a Community. Contained by the boundary of the Lake and manned by Carers, NutriVisors, Teachers, Protectors. I think of them all as various types of guards. Watching us, assessing us. Waiting for something wrong, something different. Something unhealthy.
The Lake used to seem to be the perfect place: tranquil, mysterious waters full of creatures and unknown dangers of the deep, something to fire our deprived imaginations. But now it's the wall of my cage. We're told the horrors of life beyond the Lake – a society populated by the diseased remainders of humanity, semi-feral in their desperation to survive. A place where even breathing the air,

drinking the water, could fill us with parasites. Somewhere no reasonable Florvite would want to go. And the Lake is our impenetrable boundary. Guards on the outer perimeter, so we are told, and our Protectors on the inner shore. Nothing goes over the Lake.

Of course, a rational human could be forgiven for seeing Florivale as a haven – free of the stresses of Before and Outside, full of healthy people living together and happy with their families. But what you would be seeing is, of course, what they want you to see. I'm certain that's a wider part of the experiment that started with the Opportunity.

I live in a large house in Florivale. We each have our own room (sanitised daily) and the main feature in our home is the huge kitchen, a legacy from Grandma Sophie, who chose the house. She loved to cook and she told me she had always dreamt of having a large kitchen and 'cooking for all of her little dinky ones'. I guess she hadn't known she would never get to do that cooking, that the large counter would never be scattered with vegetable peelings, that the range cooker would never host a bubbling pot of stew, or that the fridge would never be stocked with anything but what the NutriVisors provide.

I realise it seems pathetic to complain about not being allowed to cook. To me, the idea that people actually once cooked for themselves (perhaps they still do, Outside) is slightly ridiculous. Why would you want to peel and chop and sauté (I think that's the term) when you could just place a NutriVisor pouch in the PrepPod and have a nutritionally balanced meal in minutes? Eugh. I find myself sounding like one of them sometimes.

Moving on from the kitchen, we have our lounge, where the family does just that – we lounge. We watch the TeleCasts sometimes, but there is never much on them. Educational programmes, 'news' about Outside and the dangers beyond the Lake, channels screening classical music. You know it's bad when the most exciting thing to watch is the animated children's show about animals learning to spell. That's the level we're talking about.

So we tend to lie around, in a state of ennui. I love finding old words like that in the Library. My little brother Jack can be a blessing (for distraction) and a curse (for irritation) but he seems pretty happy here in his little microcosm. I don't think he is old enough to contemplate Outside, but sometimes I wonder if he would even care. I don't want to make him sound like a simpleton, but sometimes he seems, well... different.

If I took you to the back of the house, we'd reach the playroom behind the lounge - although nobody plays in it – Jack covers it in garishly-coloured toys, and Mum and I pick them up. Hardly what I would call leisure time. It's meant to be a room for me too, but I'm not interested in it. I'd rather be outdoors, wishing myself across the Lake and Outside, anything just to leave this island of containment. They say they are containing the illnesses, the dangers, of Before. Keeping the bad stuff Outside. My best theory at present is that, in fact, they are containing us.

To the right is the utility room - although why it is called that, I don't know. All that happens here is we place our dirty clothes in a basket and the basket is replaced with a clean set of clothes for each member of the family. We might as well just throw it all out of the window. But I guess appearances count for everything in Florivale.

Next to the utility room is the toilet. Grandma Sophie always said it was impolite to speak about the toilet, or what goes on in there, but Florivale welcomes the scatological. In the name of science. In the name of health. In the name of Elimination. So, applying that mindset, and to provide a complete tour of the house, the toilet is cream and slate grey, presumably designed to make it feel less clinical than it really is. Standing on the grey tiled floor there is, as you would imagine, a toilet, a shower stall, a sink with cupboards below and a mirror above. The mirror was probably placed there to facilitate the brushing and flossing of teeth in the most efficient manner, to eradicate bacteria and encourage gum health. Everything comes with a reason in Florivale. No detail is superfluous.

I enjoy looking in the mirror. I have heard it's vain, but I feel like there is so much to learn in a face. I spend all my life looking at the faces of others, trying to detect the differences within us and assess them by the differences manifested on the outside. I don't even know my own mind, still surprised by the thoughts that pop into it unbidden - sometimes extremely violent or dark, other times light and ridiculous. So these are the kind of things I ponder as I stare at myself.

I have dark brown, smooth hair. It's just past shoulder length. Anything longer is 'impractical', so a Carer cuts it once it gets long enough for the bouncy ponytails I see on the girls photographed in the pamphlets about Before. My skin is pale, although not translucent like some of the redhead kids in Florivale. It's more of a milky tone, with a faint flush to my cheeks; a faint flush which deepens when I'm angry, laughing or embarrassed, such a frustratingly obvious 'tell'. I have hazel eyes, the flecks of greeny-yellow set in the brown providing a link to my Grandpa Mike, and my mum. Or Annie to everyone else. I like to think of our flecked irises as defying categorisation. Jack doesn't have flecks. He has pure brown eyes.

Unlike Before - and maybe Outside - there is no make-up in Florivale. Grandma Sophie said it was better this way, reducing vanity with the added bonus that it took less time to get ready in the morning. Mum likes that it's natural and there is nothing hidden in my face, which always strikes me as an odd thing to say; can some dark pencils and creamy liquids conceal all that much of a person? The Carers are only concerned with health. Make-up harbours bacteria. Bacteria are bad. Therefore, make-up is bad. Simple.

And so the time comes to take you upstairs. The neutral beige runner over the floorboards is presumably meant to be comfortable and welcoming, but it just seems futile in the sea of beige, grey and cream that is our house. That is, save for the daring splashes of sea green in the kitchen, and Jack's bedroom, the latter having been painted at Grandma Sophie's insistence.

There's my parents' bedroom. The less

said about what might or might not happen in there, the better. As far as I'm concerned, they only did it twice – once for me and once for Jack. They have an en-suite bathroom, but (you guessed it), it follows the same colour scheme and layout as the toilet downstairs, just on a smaller scale. A couple fewer cupboards. Across the hall is Jack's bedroom. Apart from the playroom, his is the only room in the house with real, vibrant colours. I suppose children are allowed these.

He has a tiger painted on one wall, and a flock of sheep on the opposite wall. The combination makes me feel uncomfortable. Why would you put something so vulnerable with something so ferocious? It used to be my room. I was glad to leave it.

The room I now sleep in is opposite Jack's bedroom. Mine is the same muted grey and cream tones, no tigers on the walls. But I do have a couple of flourishes. The Carers kindly permitted me to keep some cuttings of pamphlets, stuck with spray glue, so it doesn't sully my hands or attract bacteria, onto a wooden panel fixed to the wall. I suspect another reason for the spray glue is so I can't peel it off, demand something else in its place. But maybe I am acting crazy. My hormones get blamed for a lot.

The upstairs bathroom is differentiated from the downstairs toilet by, you guessed it, the presence of a bath. It follows the décor of the toilet immediately below. Cream and grey, all around. We have the same sink and mirror combination, a few more cupboards, a toilet and a shower cubicle.

But there is a key difference. The

bathroom also holds a secret. Within it, there is stowed a small love heart made from reeds, washed up at the boundary of the Lake. This tiny personal touch is me and Grandma Sophie's little act of defiance. Nobody goes to the Lakeside any more. It's not really a Lake anyway. Although it looks like a sea, expanding into the horizon, we know it is, in truth, a moat. Florivale is our tiny piece of the world. Our haven, or our prison.

Nobody else knows about it, but if you pry between the boards at the bottom of the bathtub for long enough, you'll find a looser part of the panel. In there is a heart, woven from reeds taken from the Lakeside. She told me about it as she knew she was dying. I thought it was the ramblings of an old mind, slipping away from the defective body in which it was encased. I kicked myself when I found everything. But I'm so glad that I didn't dismiss her mutterings completely. Because it led me to the panel. And in that panel, along with her heart, was the first of her notes.

3

Let me walk you through an average day for me in Florivale.

I wake up, having had a carefully calculated amount of sleep – they work it out based on your age, temperature, gender, the amount of exercise you undertook, the previous few days' calorie intake; you name it, it's a factor. Grandma Sophie used to complain that she never got a 'lie in' and said she didn't care whether she'd had the (medically) correct amount of sleep – she wanted an indulgent sleep. Followed by thickly-buttered toast for breakfast. Mum remembers the toast too. She says she always hopes someone will pick that for their wedding feast. This seems silly to me, when that is the one day the couple could choose literally anything for us all to eat. Of course, the NutriVisors will ensure the following week makes up for any excess calories or imbalanced vitamins, silently undoing any naughtiness of the treat. We tend to try not to think about that, let it go. Enjoy the indulgence. Current Vic gets to let go for one day. Nutritional balance is Future Vic's problem. I hope the couple choose something different every time – something from the old recipe books. Like the hazelnut and chocolate pavlova we had last year. Nutritionally devoid of value, but utterly exquisite. I had such a high from the sugar I got a headache. But it was completely worth it. I still dream of those lightly toasted nuts and the curls of chocolate piled atop the Chantilly cream.

My breakfast, however, is a less exciting affair. I choose between 'dry' and 'moist'. Such variety! Dry is usually something like an oat biscuit (cholesterol-lowering) with cinnamon (providing sweetness, without sugar) and perhaps some almonds. Moist might be such a dizzying treat as yoghurt with special Manuka honey, or Bircher muesli made from oats soaked in fruit juice and mixed with yoghurt. It's actually slightly less revolting than it sounds. At weekends, for a treat, we can have a 'Cooked'. This includes a grilled tomato and mushroom. Pre-grilled, of course – we just put it in the PrepPod to warm it to the right temperature and eliminate any lurking germs. I also get two plant-based protein sausages (PBP to you and me, something between mushroom and soya proteins mixed with egg, no doubt genetically modified to be as energy efficient, healthy and as far from natural as possible) and some haricot beans in a thin tomato sauce. The non-vegetarian families – that's most of them - get different breakfasts. There is a lot of talk about bacon. As I've never had it, I guess there isn't much for me to miss. Something of a lifelong motto.

I get dressed. We aren't allowed to choose our own clothes in Florivale. Apparently it's part of a study into bacterial and microbial transfer, and the possibility of bio-fabrics which work with the body for optimum health. Translation: dull.

The Pioneers brought their own clothes. I

had their hand-me-downs, until our names were selected by whichever program they use to choose which families go into which test cycle. Our clothes were taken away with the washing one day, as usual, but never returned. They were slowly replaced in the utility room with the Ministry-issued stuff, given that we, the Hunters had been selected for the study. Lucky us.

In a magnanimous concession, they will permit us to choose the colour of our clothes, from a limited selection of colours, to save on cost. As 'ladies', we also have the dazzling options of knee length dresses, shorts and tops for the summer, trousers and skirts. I look like an old woman, not like I'm nearly twenty. That said, Mum was married around my age – maybe I'm older than I feel. I guess there has never been much else to do in Florivale. They're very keen on procreation here. Gross. As I said, my parents only did it twice. That's all I'll allow them. Anyway, my usual clothing combination is something along the lines of a yellow or orange tee shirt and a blue or green pair of shorts. I want to stand out and I want to be colourful. Not like boring Melanie or wimpy Jenna in their 'elegant, subdued' choices of dark blues, greys and beiges. Eugh.

After I've breakfasted and dressed in my snappy ensemble, I head out. I used to have to go to the EduCentre for the daily boredom of 'enlightenment'. We covered all the main topics. These are: (i) Health - don't do anything other than what we tell you to, or you will get cancer and die and the whole of Florivale will be a wasted Opportunity, you are the future, etc. etc.; (ii) History - everything they did Before, on the

Outside was dangerous and foolish, be glad you are here and safe in Florivale; (iii) Social - get to understand your Gen and the other Gens, and help develop Florivale and build on the lessons learned here by creating the next Gen; and (iv) General education - anything else, always reinforcing all of the other subjects, but with the odd TeleCast from Outside to update us on the astonishing progress at Florivale and the terrors of Outside.

Now I'm older, I choose to continue with 'free study' at the Community Centre, which means I basically hang around the Library most days. Most of my Gen finish learning at 16. My Gen is full of idiots. Considering how few of us there are, and how regulated our lives are, you'd think we'd get along, that we would all have similar tastes. But you'd be wrong. If it weren't for Clem and Josh, I think I'd completely lose it. I think some of the others already have.

I use most of my free study time to try to find answers. I'm always searching, and I feel like something is out there, just beyond my grasp. It's like creeping after a cat for hours, only for it to evade me even as I steal a touch of its tail. I'm not going to let my mind go to unquestioning jelly like the others though. I want to know about Outside. And Before. Of course, this is difficult, given the Carers' seemingly endless ways to frustrate this pursuit of knowledge. As I get most of the way through one of the dog-eared books, to the crescendo of a news article or the blanked out space where a photograph should be, I'll find a note: 'Redaction: content may be upsetting'. They don't want us knowing what might harm us.

They don't want us knowing what might be Outside, save for what they tell us, what they decide is worth knowing. How harmful can the truth be? And why don't many people in here care that we only know what someone wants us to know. Doesn't it make them itch? Like their skin is too tight, and like there's an expanding bubble of questions, crushing them from within? Well, now you know how I feel.

Anyway, I digress. I love old Outside words like that. They keep me reading, hunting for more. As long as we have done our mandatory education, we can do pretty much what we like. There's the Craft Centre full of dreadful pottery, abandoned artworks and half-stitched cushion covers. The Community Centre and FitHub are always open for your leisure time and daily exercise. Getting your daily exercise quota is mandatory. Our BioBands float around our wrists, with corresponding chips implanted just under the skin when we're born and upgraded every few years until we stop growing (gross, right). They monitor everything we do. Their little red lights blink if we fall short of our daily regimen and turn green when we have eaten enough or done the required amount of movement. The good thing about this system is that you can run at full pelt, feel the sweat beading on your brow and across your chest, and nobody can stop you. That is, until the green light goes and you get the brief electric shock to remind you to slow your pace and avoid over-exertion. That's not such a great aspect of the BioBand's design. You could cycle round the perimeter of Florivale. Well, almost all the way round. Never quite reaching the end, as the green light and the shock always stop you making a full circuit on any given run. You're just running and getting nowhere. Like the lab rats in the old books. The FitHub also runs yoga and pilates sessions, which take way longer to turn the light on your BioBand from red to green. Sometimes that can be a good choice. Fills up more time. Swimming is forbidden. Get into any body of water larger than a bathtub and we're out of bounds.

I like to exercise before free study, now that I'm not tied to the EduCentre time table. Get the red light switched to green at the start of the day, signalling that it's now okay for me to do things on my own time. The lazier kids in my Gen have been known to leave it to the last minute, and end up being forced into FitSessions at night. They're made to run on a treadmill until their lights go green, in front of a screen extolling (another good Before word) the virtues of daily exercise for health and reminding them of their role in Florivale, to further the human condition through the pursuit of medical and physical excellence.

As long as my exercise and free study are done, I have the day to do as I like. I eat my lunch (something as fascinating as breakfast) and often carry on reading in the Community Centre, chat with Clem or Josh - the only other sane ones in here - or go and daydream.

I sit as close to the boundary of the Lake as I can, and imagine getting Outside. Or about Before. Or what it's like now, out there. The weirder things get in here, the more I search for that knowledge. The faint shimmer of the edge of the Lake on the horizon is tantalising; the Protectors at the Florivale perimeter eternally menacing.

I re-read Grandma Sophie's notes as often as I can get to them, safely stashed under the floorboards in a little drinks flask, so nobody will find them. Because they are mine. They are all I have to connect me to her, and through her, to Outside. In them, I find more truth than I could in a lifetime of study at the EduCentre. I find a friend.

4

From: <u>Sophie.stone1994@freemailuk.co.uk</u>

To: <u>Sophie.stone1994@freemailuk.co.uk</u>
Date: 16 February 2035; 09.48.

I'm not quite sure what compelled me to write this... but that's how I feel. Compelled. As though I can't resist it. So here I am, bashing out my thoughts on a computer at work. I guess I shouldn't be doing this on work time, but if we actually go through with this, and get in to the program, then it won't matter anyway. And if we don't... well, I will just have to hope the boss doesn't catch me! I figure putting it down in an email means I can always amend it later on if I decide I am literally deranged to even think about this.

I'm also not sure who I'm writing to. I guess it's to whoever might ever get this. If we get in, I'll print this out and try and find somewhere to stow this note. Maybe under a mattress like people did to protect her savings in the old days, back when they couldn't trust the banks! Anyway, I have no idea what it will look like inside the facility, if we make it, so we will have to wait and see where this ends up. I'll try to leave some notes inside - if we get in - so maybe someone will read them, some day.

So, where to start!? Like I said, I feel I have to write something. But I'm not sure what to say. I'll try to start in the beginning and take a vaguely logical approach. However, if you've read the section above, you'll appreciate that logic is not my forté. So bear with me!

It started with all the flyers and posters, the adverts which peppered their way across the radio broadcasts. Scattered everywhere, across both the BBC and the commercial stations. You'd go from listening to the news or the breakfast show and find yourself plonked straight into an advert to apply for information about The Opportunity. It was the same on the TV. At first I thought it was some crazy over-reaction or a medical trial, like a flu camp where you get paid two grand in exchange for a week's accommodation and trial treatment for a strain of flu. Obviously I thought it was crazy. Who would be crazy enough to do that!?

But then I thought, perhaps I am that crazy. Perhaps I need to find out more about this...

I wonder how many people called the information line. I bet it was a lot.

Anyway. My reasons were largely down to intrigue at first. So little information was given in those adverts, clearly just a vehicle to get people on the phone to the information line to register their interest. However, the more I thought about it, the more I thought about what it could mean for me, for us.

Mike and I could take the kids into a safe and happy place, knowing no harm could come to them there. They wouldn't be at risk of all the disease we've seen proliferating. The rising death tolls. And money wouldn't be a problem. Not only would they have free medical care, we wouldn't need to work and our debts would disappear! We had been saving so hard for a house, a home. We were elated when we got the keys – no more renting and no more batshit crazy landlady. But our mortgage has turned out to be so expensive. It just kept hiking up and up, after the introductory rate expired. There's always something else the kids need. Just try looking into the eyes of your four year old daughter and saying, 'no, Annie. You can't have new shoes. I don't care if your old ones are buckling at the straps because of your lovely, podgy, little feet growing so fast. We are saving up instead!' It's ridiculous. Why are we so obsessed with owning a home? In France and Germany most people don't seem to give a toss about home ownership, so why do we?

Anyway, back to the rationale. We could essentially live somewhere happy, clean and safe, for free, with no jobs, and our kids would be healthy. To be honest, having worked as a secretary - or 'PA' in the classier establishments in which I have been so fortunate as to work - for years, with very little enjoyment, that sounds pretty good. I know, fat lot of good my degree gained me.

Mike's been slaving away too, on the road at all hours of the day and night in his crappy sales job. Don't tell him I said it was crappy – he is very proud and I know how hard he works to look after us. But I barely see him and when I do, he is so tired he hardly speaks. He lights up when he sees the kids, but sometimes I think they take up all of his glow and by the time he comes to me, it's faded. I know it's still there, just obscured by exhaustion and stress.

I mentioned the Opportunity to in passing when he crept in late one night, trying not to wake me - although he always does. I don't mind, because otherwise I'd rarely see him. In a state of semi-sleep, I made a throwaway comment, something like 'you know, this Opportunity thing? It would mean the couples in there actually saw each other! All the bloody time. Do you think we'd still like each other if we did?' Chuckling, I thought no more of it as I drifted back to sleep.

In the morning, I woke to a very peculiar sight.

Mike was still at home. Not gone, nor was he frantically rushing around the house with one sock on, his tie loose and his cuffs un-linked, coffee in one hand and toast in the other. I imagine you are probably familiar with this sort of morning. For once, Mike was sitting right there on the edge of the bed, his sleek dark hair softly reflecting the morning light. The blinking red lights on the alarm clock informed me it was 6.48 in the morning, a good twelve minutes before the 'dawn' setting starts on the kids' grow clocks kicks in. He was half-dressed for work, his soft pink shirt tucked into his grey tailored trousers, but missing his customary belt, tie and cufflinks. Even odder was that he wasn't wearing socks. A man in a suit, without any socks on, looks bizarre at whatever time of day. But even more so before seven a.m.

I yawned and smoothed down my crazy bed hair and reached out for him. Perhaps he was unwell? Please don't let it be that, I prayed. We can't afford that, I thought. As my fingers touched his shoulder, he turned round, not in alarm, but slowly, and reached out to me, his fingertips brushing my face. As his eyes met mine, he simply said, 'let's ask about The Opportunity. I think I'd like us even more in there'. I was still trying to work out what he was talking about, my morning brain clicking into action, but there was a moment of electricity in the air. A moment of clarity, of understanding. He saw my startled nod and got up to fix his tie, belt and cufflinks before slinking out of the house. Daddy Time with the kids was not feasible when he was already running late, and if he woke them, there would be no escaping.

Sure enough, in came the kids around 7. Annie and Ella were as bright and fresh as any other morning and Bertie was as sleepy-eyed and confused as always. He's a little night owl. I went about the usual morning routine, reluctant dressing, force feeding of cereal, frantic location of lunchboxes and bundling of chattering children into the car for school and nursery before making my own way to work. That short drive, when the kids are taken care of, Mike is at work, and I am on my own, might be the most relaxed my life ever gets. I don't even put the radio on most days, I just drive. I exist. Free for a brief moment from having to communicate with anyone.

The road took me past the usual places - the supermarket and the retail park full of tat that everyone wanted to fill their homes with (purple fluffy cushion, anyone?), paid for with credit they couldn't afford to repay. Don't tell me you don't know that feeling.

However, on this drive, I started to notice other things. The softness of the grass at the side of the road, so fragile next to the huge cars that came hurtling along the tarmac. The ominous rise of the new hospital, three times the size of the fusty old community one, inundated with demand and its car park overflowing. All the people in there: ill, dying, visiting, grieving. Next, I saw an image of Annie and Ella's curly blonde heads of hair, and Bertie's dark mop, all snuggled in with us on the sofa. A wave of protectiveness overcame me. Not just for them, but for all of us. What if we really could be safe? Forget being a part of history. Safety and protection were what I was after.

Arriving at the office, it was the usual string of greetings, uttered without pausing or listening for a response. And from my boss, 'thank God you've arrived Stephanie, I have a million and one emails for you to write and a meeting at 11.'

Yes, my name is Sophie. Despite being here for months, he still doesn't remember. Perhaps there was a Stephanie before me, whose emails contained fewer typos. That seems to be the only thing he ever notices. Not the softening of his tone when he's angry about some deal or another, an adjustment of the emphasis so he doesn't come across like the asshole he actually is. Perhaps the clients don't even notice. The good thing is that he can hear and see me typing this email and he thinks I am working on his dictated monologues. Ha.

I'm feeling ridiculous again. Who is actually going to read this!?

Right. I must go and see to The Creep's emails.

5

That was the first note I found. Her words seeped into me across the years, answering questions I never knew I'd wanted to ask, compelling me to ask more.

I hoped she would be proud of how I'd grown up. I could feel her leaping from the page when I read her notes and recognised something of my capriciousness in her tone. She shared my refusal to accept things. Mum is too docile, too compliant – it takes so much to get a rise from her or Dad that I've stopped trying. Living this half-life, in this tiny world. The notes told me all I needed to confirm that I have to get out – have to do more, know more, be more. Florivale is all I know, but I also know it isn't enough. It isn't real. Somehow isn't right. Auntie Ella and Uncle Bertie are pretty useless too, like those dumb sheep in Jack's room. Shouldn't Stone-Hunters be just that, solid as stone, ferocious as hunters? Not placid sheep, but pouncing tigers, protective and fearsome, lethal and glitteringly intelligent.

I wondered: if she had lived longer, would she have ever told me everything? Or more? Her pleading reminders to take a long bath every time I saw her in those last days meant nothing until, bereft and destructive, I started picking at the floorboards beneath the bathtub.

Sat on the rug, in a towelling robe with a mounting chill stalking across my skin and Jack banging at the door to come in for his bath, I pried my fingernails between the wood and found a loose piece. The goosebumps on my arm prickled as I reached out of my robe and into the space behind the loose board, and my fingers came into touch with the crunch of paper. Crinkly from years of steam, constantly caught in a cycle of dampening and drying in the bathroom, there it was, the first note. The first step. I've since put them all in what I think must be the right order.

But back to my moment of discovery, in the bathroom. Jack's fists were pummelling the bathroom door by now and I knew there would be a scene, requiring a discussion, an explanation and an apology. So dismally formulaic. Hastily, I stowed my contraband, my pearl of knowledge, and shoved my way out past Jack. Despite his lingering protestations and irritating younger-brother rants, I barged along the corridor and into to my bedroom, where I could shut the door and be alone. With her.

From that very first line, her email address, the time stamp, it was hard to accept that she'd had a life before Florivale – Before. That her life had such hardship. That Mum had been a child! It feels to me like she was never anything but a middle-aged walking test tube, eternally compliant. That's rude, I know. But sometimes honesty means having to be rude. I love her, but she has no backbone. Maybe that's one of her Conditions - a secret one. Would explain a lot, when you compare her placidity to Grandma Sophie, a risk taker who threw herself and her young family into Florivale life.

But more unsettling, more astonishing, is

how I felt about my unknown Grandpa, Mike. A man with sparkling eyes that sound just like mine. A man of honour and love and kindness, but who also took risks. The sort of man who doesn't exist in Florivale. Almost everyone here is so boring, following their routine and obeying rules, working out the most genetically or socially advantageous match for themselves or their children within this tiny perimeter. Who were these people, these vivacious grandparents of mine? And why were they not here with me?

Of course, I couldn't stop once I had read one note – I had to find more. I must have delved into every reachable nook and cranny of the panelling beneath the bath. Broom handles, curtain poles, anything I could get my hands on – all manner of domestic items were shoved around the cavity in my hunt for more information. This story was not easy to come by.

6

From: <u>Sophie.stone1994@freemailuk.co.uk</u>

To: <u>Sophie.stone1994@freemailuk.co.uk</u>
Date: 8 May 2035; 10.32.

We are going to do it. We have registered.

A few days went by with neither me nor Mike mentioning our conversation in the bedroom. I think we both felt it there between us, a balloon filled with a few thoughts and questions that started off tiny, but then expanded with every new thing that popped into either of our heads. A shimmering expanse of the unknown, growing between us with every passing day. It reached the point where I honestly thought I would be crushed by the weight of everything we had left unspoken, and I was sure Mike felt the same.

As I slipped into the bedroom one evening, trying not to wake the just-sleeping, puffy eyed, kids, I caught my breath. Mike was sitting there again, bolt upright on the side of the bed, clearly waiting to speak to me.

'Honey. I think we have to speak about this Opportunity stuff. It's all I can think about. I find myself taking the wrong turns on my sales trips and, even worse, not caring when I turn up late and dishevelled. That's not like me.' He patted the bed; an invitation to sit.

'I'm so glad you said something,' I replied. I explained my theory about the expanding, shimmering balloon.

'Mine was more of an elastic band, constricting around us until we had to either talk about it, or accept our fate and asphyxiate,' Mike replied, laughing softly at the contrast between our imaginations.

So much for male-female psychological alignment!

Anyway, we began to speak. Softly, and nervously at first, both afraid the other would think them mad. Deranged. Who would seriously sign up for this!?

We ran through our reasons. I can't quite remember how the conversation went, and I love nothing more than a list (I still have my "I heart spreadsheets" mug from years ago), so here are most of the factors we considered and discussed:

1. The Children

The kids were, of course, an enormous factor, both in the positive and negative reasons informing our decision.

We'd be able to give them a safe place to grow up, where there would be no crime. Who would commit a crime when there was no need for money, where health was paramount and people were free to entertain themselves at their leisure? Perhaps there might be the odd teddy-bear theft, or a casual loan-sharking - repaying two sweets tomorrow for one sweet today - but we couldn't see any serious threat. Unlike our streets, which seem to be full of shady teenagers – probably doing nothing worse than loitering together in defiance of their curfews. But they might just be plotting something more, spurred on by the resentment palpably growing within society. A society which is crumbling.

And health. Imagine if this thing actually works. I know they are calling it an Opportunity, but it is also clearly an experiment of some kind. Otherwise why would they need to run all those tests, why the rigorous selection process? But balance that against ensuring that Ella, Annie and Bertie would always be safe from the horrible diseases which are felling so many. A life free of disease. Is there any better gift we could give them?

It wouldn't be like we could never see our friends or families, either. The guidance materials all say that people can visit Florivale any time. The only constraint is that they need to have booked in and to have a medical screening. So, sure – no random impromptu visits. But I think Mike would be delighted at the idea that he could screen visitors, rather than having every random person I invite in joining us for dinner without warning.

2. The House

Our house is rubbish.

We bought it hoping to do it up nicely – replace

the ageing bathroom and scuffed wallpaper. Extend. Put in a beautiful country kitchen, one which would never have worked for us anyway, but hey - a girl can dream. I had a mood board covered in ideas for each room and had even, somewhat aspirationally, budgeted how we could do it all in five years.

What actually happened was... we had the kids. You can't justify a shabby chic dresser for the sanded-floor hallway when you need to feed and clothe your children. And even if you could, you would be too exhausted to do it anyway. And after working to pay the mortgage, pay your debts, meet the cost of childcare and go to the pub for a cheap dinner a couple of times a month, my naïve 'refurbishment budget' turned out to be a sad joke.

Needless to say, we still have the damp patches we noticed the day after we moved in, six years ago. The only difference is how much bigger they are now.

3. The Debt

Of course, like pretty much everyone else, we are in debt. We've been really good at disciplining ourselves and have cut up all the store cards and we've paid almost all of them off. Almost.

Then there is the enormous mortgage, the albatross around our necks – what boring drivel they made us read at school. Anyway, I hardly need tell you how crippling that is – we took it out when interest rates were nice and low, and affordable, and everyone wanted to lend us money. Picking the bank for our mortgage was like a beauty parade! We even got free phone insurance thrown in. It was pretty great, until the interest rates rose and house prices took a nosedive. I realise the debt crisis is impossible for pretty much everyone, but it doesn't make it any less difficult for me.

I once told Mike I had considered burning the house down as an insurance job after getting the latest notice of an increase in our mortgage rates. He laughed, trying to conceal his horror once he realised I had actually contemplated it - but I know he feels just as trapped as I do.

So, instead of setting fire, we could just... sign away our freedom for ever and move into a Ministry-designed Stepford. Totally rational thought process. Right...?

4. The Jobs

Our jobs. We hate them. I'd love to leave it there, but for your information and in the interest of a full and honest account, our main complaints (and I am sure whoever might read this would be able to sympathise) include:

(i) being underpaid and overworked;

(ii) Mike's crazy hours and long drives late at night. When he is late replying to my messages or returning a late night call, and I wonder if he has died on the M25 and I'll never see him again;

(iii) the Creep giving me ridiculous tasks to do for him, changing his mind every five minutes and shouting at me when my presumed telepathy skills fail to materialise;

(iv) seeing our abysmal pension pots and realising that, even when we have worked all our lives, we will still be scraping by in our old age, dreading becoming a burden on our poor children;

(v) thinking about all the good things we could do with our time if we weren't always at work, commuting or exhausted afterwards. Like that painting class I'd promised myself. Or the sports Mike misses playing;

(vi) watching the clock hit six p.m. and knowing the after school club will fine us for being late again. The feeling of being admonished by the scowling eyes of our kids – the only ones left on the bench, waiting for us and wondering if we will ever come and collect them. Little do they realise we hate this even more than they do; and

(vii) waking up every Monday, wishing it was Saturday. Knowing this is it for the next 30 years. In which time we might be fortunate enough to scrape by a living on our meagre savings.

So, suffice to say, we hate our jobs.

5. The Opportunity

I hate to admit this. But the fact we could benefit the rest of the human race was really an afterthought, the cherry on top of the parts - which were far more important to us. Call me selfish.

There must be a pretty decent chance of success. Otherwise, why would the Ministry spend so much public money on something if they didn't see such a viable (and possibly profitable, says my inner cynic) outcome? The 'illustration purposes only' images of Florivale in the brochures make it look heavenly. Every home has its own little private garden. A bedroom for each of the children and a spare - maybe we could use it as a study, where we could write or paint, if either of us has the skill. We wouldn't know right now, considering we haven't had time for that stuff since leaving school! The homes in the photos all have tranquil colour schemes. Our mortgage would cease and we would receive an even better house to call our own, with nothing to pay to anyone. It seems like they've thought of everything.

I wonder which pharmaceutical companies are getting a cut. And what else they are getting out of it. So does Mike. But at the end of the day, how would we ever know what it really involved behind the scenes? Would anyone answer truthfully, if we asked? We also figured, without risk there is no reward - unless you're one of those fortunate families to whom only good things happen and money appears to fall from the sky and into your lap. As you may have gathered, we are not one of those families.

So we are going to go for it.

By the time we had finished our long discussion, it was halfway to morning and the stars were feebly trying to twinkle through the clouds of pollution and through our grimy window. We had planned to have them cleaned, but there seems to be no point now.

Mike pulled the cord on the bedside lamp and the darkness washed around us. He reached for my hand as he turned out the light, protectively and instinctively curled me into him in the way he always has. 'We've got this, honey. It's all going to be fine.'

I have rarely felt safer or more relaxed. We are in this together. Getting rid of our biggest problems will mean we can focus on what really matters. Us. The kids. This one life we have on earth.

7

I want to have known them, properly known them. I'm angry that I didn't get to. And now I never will.

There is so much in her email that I want to know more about. The idea of a mortgage, the stress it caused. From the French and Latin books in the Community Centre it sounds like 'mort' and 'gauge' – literally a measure of when you're going to die. Sounds horrendous. But was it really bad enough to make you give up your freedom and come in here? To Florivale, where everything is monitored. Where life is our commodity. Where our worth is calculated in relation to our health, in our own sick version of a 'mort-gauge'.

Take today, for example. I won't bore you with the same run-down of wake up, breakfast, changing the red light to green on my BioBand at the FitHub. Tedious. No, today was special. I got my period today. That special treat reserved for women which, in Florivale, means that we get an extra batch of tests, from checking our blood (yes, that blood) to the levels of hormones in our saliva. No stone is unturned, no exam is left un-done. So my usual trip to the Health Centre took three times as long and interfered in my hectic schedule of rooting around in the Community Centre Library, thirstier than ever to know everything, anything, about Before and about

Outside. About my Grandma.

They have a display section in the Library about Florivale Pioneers. The first Gen to come in here. Each of them was asked, on arrival, to write a sentence or two for the future residents of Florivale, some founding principles to live by. With a few cautionary statements, just ambiguous enough to be pointed at as either (i) an example of the atrocities outside, or (ii) an aspirational motto to live by. Case in point: 'Be wary, be healthy, survive'. Author of that one: Mike Stone. My grandfather.

Grandma Sophie's is more hopeful, and has the ring of her writing in it. 'We are all here for life. Cherish freedom.' I used to read that as a justification of everything Florivale, that we are right in being here, that society Outside needs us here, that we are the ones who are free. But reading these statements together, and knowing what I know now, something foreboding creeps in. Here for life. For ever. Subtly ominous, like sand slipping through an egg timer, which escapes one form of confinement, only to be encased in another. Does she mean here for life - to preserve life, to find a cure? Or does she mean here for life - prisoners? I feel like she didn't know the answer to that herself.

8

From: <u>Sophie.stone1994@freemailuk.co.uk</u>

To: <u>Sophie.stone1994@freemailuk.co.uk</u>
Date: 19 August 2035; 22.04.

It's been a while since I did one of these self-emails. But it's about time – the amount that's been going on is unbelievable. We've been so busy!

We've been selected.

The process was rigorous and, frankly, a pain in the arse. Classic Harte administration. We had to register our interest at the Health Centre. This involved getting some very basic information (no more than we had from the posters, adverts and information line) and giving our consent for our full criminal and any other potentially interesting records to be disclosed to The Opportunity Selection Panel and their advisors, sponsors, affiliates etc. Seriously, there was enough small print for a small novel. We skim-read most of it, focused in on some parts, and figured anything we had ignored or skipped could be re-read later, if we got in. So many people were signing up, it just felt like it would never happen. Plus, we figured our records wouldn't reveal anything we don't want them to know, so why not just sign the form and get on with it. As easy as taking out a credit card! Why would you read the small print?

Anything from the list of required medical information, which they couldn't find out from our other records, needed to be provided, which makes sense. This basically meant a few blood tests for the kids, an updated smear - the triennial delight of all women - and a fertility test for me and Mike. This involved the usual questions about when I had my last period (God knows, how am I meant to remember that?), whether I was using contraception (yes, three kids is quite enough, thanks) and how regularly Mike and I have sex (really?). It was hard to decide whether to be honest about that one - once a week - or lie, demonstrating our virility by making out like we were rampantly in love, say four times a week. We could have taken the dignified prude option - once a fortnight with an additional birthday bonk each year. That was one of the more fun interviews.

I went for the honest approach, although I'd have loved to see the typist enter 'birthday bonk' on the form. Mike had a similar interview and his sperm count measured. The usual array of glossies were provided in his interview room. No such fun for us girls. He had the same questions about sex, but he gave the answer once a fortnight. I wonder which of us had it wrong. Either way, we agreed that we would have much more sex in Florivale, if we got in, considering all the extra time we would have on our hands. Needless to say, Mike did not have a problem with that proposition.

After the medical tests, there were some psychometrics - I'm not entirely sure what answers they were after, so I had to answer honestly. Even though it was tempting to treat it like a game... Mike always says the flecks in his eyes are his giveaway, but that nothing I do is simple – I don't have the same 'tell'. Whether or not his amateur pop-psychology holds any truth, he was right in saying that I ought to take the tests seriously. The chance to start again was something worth concentrating on.

The psychometric testing room was very basic. None of the frantically beeping white and chrome machines of the medical test rooms. No test tubes. No tiny labels for sample jars. What it did contain was a woman of about my age, blonde hair in a blunt chop at shoulder length, wearing a truly heinous pink knitted gilet over a baby blue shirt. It was tasteless enough to make me doubt whether this was a serious test. That thought lasted until I saw the man to her right (her Right Hand Man? I wondered). He was carefully put together, in an old-fashioned way. A beautifully cut three piece suit in navy (the colour of sincerity, I understand – and I must say, it worked for him) and a pocket square. If laser eye surgery hadn't become so effective and commonplace, I am certain he would have worn square-framed glasses, like all the young bankers in the City used to, before it all went wrong.

He introduced himself as Mr. Greene and his assistant as Ms. Jones. I had to stop myself from laughing out loud at his attempt to be informal, one leg crossed over his opposite knee in a gesture of relaxation that did not follow through to his eyes. Ms. Jones sat stiff as a board, back completely upright and eyes straight ahead. She was like a badly dressed robot.

The test itself was just a conversation. It's hard to remember exactly what was said, but they were very interested in my take on family values, how I felt I would cope in the unit, whether I'd miss anyone on the outside (obviously, but I'd see them on scheduled visits) and what I would do with all the extra time I had inside. Although I really wanted to be selected (that way, even if we decided not to go forward, at least it was our decision!), I decided I ought to tell this pair the truth and went through the questions rather easily. I did babble on a bit, but I suppose that just gave them more material.

When I got out, Mike was sat in the corridor, impatiently tapping his feet on the polished floor.

'You took your time, Soph,' he said, standing to walk together along the corridor. 'The kids have finished their interviews and they're playing in the nursery at the end. They have no idea what's going on.' He laughed. 'I think Annie told the interviewers more about her dolls than answering their questions'.

'Yeah, sounds about right,' I said. 'Sorry I took longer than you. Maybe I just have more interesting things to say?' I smirked.

'Perhaps that's why you should say less,' said Mike.

He is an obstinate little swine sometimes. Always calculating, reading people. I just go with the flow most of the time, until something goes wrong. Then I panic. Perhaps Mike's more careful approach has some merit, after all.

Heading back to the information desk, we were asked to sign a few more forms ('all standard procedure, Mr. and Mrs. Stone') and told we would hear in a few weeks whether we would proceed to the next stage in the process.

We received our letters within a week. Separately addressed to each of us, which was weird considering we'd applied together and would have been ineligible as individuals.

The letters informed us that we had passed the various assessments required and that we had five spaces allocated for the Stone family in the new community. Blah blah ... delighted to inform you ... blah blah ... debt will be written off ... blah blah, home free of charge ... blah blah ... have to complete regular health screenings. It all seemed pretty much fine, basically the same information we had already received. There were a couple of new items in there, like the fact we were not allowed mobiles, tablets, computers or any similar device from outside Florivale (that was the name of the town! A bit twee, but better than Milton Keynes!), but that we would be issued with new FloriConnect communication devices within the community, free of charge and fully connected to allow us to talk to our friends and family both inside and outside. It was also made clear that no trips outside Florivale were permitted, for contamination avoidance reasons. We knew this part, but the letter added that we might be required to travel around and outside of Florivale as and when required by the Ministry, should such travel be important in the interest of securing Elimination and/or any other of the Ministry's objectives in operating The Opportunity.

The letter also reiterated that no unauthorised visitors would be permitted access to Florivale and that all visit would be conducted in a "sterile facility" to minimise infection risk. Jesus, they make it sound like a prison. And I thought it was a "golden opportunity to live an idyllic life". I'm sure it's all just legal arse-covering. A little germ screening for visitors on their way in.

We also had a Ministry legal advisor's summary of the terms, in idiot's English, clearly written to bore even the below-average reader to death. There was an offer to pay for us to take legal advice on the terms of The Opportunity, from a selection of lawyers who had been briefed about the project and would be able to advise us independently. I had my doubts about just how independent that advice would be. I left it up to Mike to decide whether we did that. I am too far along the process to get bogged down in little details now. I've already mentally quit my job, stopped cleaning the house, taken the kids out of school and planned our good-bye road trip around our friends and family. Half of them are jealous. The other half think we're insane.

There was the somewhat ominous statement "Any married participants who encounter marital difficulties will be required to undergo counselling and will be provided with guidance. Should the relationship become truly untenable or dangerous to one or both parties, the Ministry reserves the right to separate the couple and allocate their children among the parents or the Community in the most advantageous manner (in the reasonable opinion of the Ministry, such decision being final)." Bloody hell – a bit doom and gloom. Given we are agreeing to remain in this place for at least 50 years, Mike and I had better not fight! But, what will there be to fight about? Our money issues will have disappeared, and we'll have a beautiful home for our happy and healthy family. Sign me up.

In the envelope, along with the covering letter, was a batch of information leaflets, pictures of Florivale and so on. I was so excited to read about the house. They had made a note of the kitchen I'd asked for! A huge space in cream and teal, a long countertop and a range cooker set in an island in the middle to let me talk to people at the dinner table, or watch the kids do their homework, as I cooked a wholesome family meal. I'd better learn to cook, hadn't I? Just like in the movies, the kitchen would be the hub of our family life. The rest of the house design I could leave to the Ministry or to Mike. We can always tweak it and add our own touches here and there once we arrive. But that kitchen! Oh my god!

We sat at the table, which was plastered with

Ministry paperwork, along with a couple of bottles of merlot, some half-decent cheese left over from a dinner party and some crisps and dips (we are a very classy pair). Once the wine was finished, we went up and saw the kids, oblivious to all of this in their slumber.

'This is for them as well,' I whispered, as Mike turned Annie and Ella's nightlight to the dimmest setting. 'We need them to have a stable, healthy, happy life. We'll be around more. We'll be well rested. We'll actually have the time to play with them.'

'I know,' said Mike. 'I just wish there was a middle ground,' he said, his speech halting. 'This suddenly feels pretty final. We're giving up so much.'

I took his hand as I replied, looking into his hazel-flecked eyes, and the slightly curled hair at his brow, the soft wrinkles beginning to appear when he frowned.

'I know. But we will get ourselves back in return. Our true selves. We'll have the versions of each other from back when we first met. We'll be ourselves again.'

We crept back downstairs to the kitchen, trying to avoid the creaking steps so the kids didn't wake up.

'Like a plaster,' I said. 'Let's do it quickly. Don't overthink it.'

I gave Mike a pen, and took another from the kitchen notepad. On the count of three we signed.

Our Faustian pact is made. See, I did pay attention at school. Occasionally.

9

From: Sophie.stone1994@freemailuk.co.uk

To: Sophie.stone1994@freemailuk.co.uk
Date: 24 November 2035; 18:12.

This is the last note I'll write from outside Florivale. We move in tomorrow! We're in the first wave of participants. I don't know how many waves are planned, but I suppose that depends on how well it works. Whether they find the cures they are after, or whether it all ends up a massive mistake and a huge waste of money. They don't seem to have planned for the latter eventuality, so they must be pretty confident. Either way, that's less my issue than theirs – Mike and I have made up our minds that this is going to be <u>our</u> opportunity. We are going to make the best of it.

I'll try and write from inside Florivale – I know there will be centralised CompStreams and we will have our other FloriConnect devices, so maybe my next one will be from a new email address. Who knows?

Wish us luck.

10

The notes change after that point. She stops using emails and switches to bits of coloured children's paper, writing from within Florivale. I lie awake at night thinking about the decision they took, pondering their reasons, the outcome, what would or could have been if they had stayed Outside. For starters, I wouldn't exist. Well, I suppose my mother might have had another daughter, wandering around with the soul that was destined for me. Staring out at a different horizon. Perhaps she would live Outside. Maybe she'd be healthy. Maybe not.

For whatever reason, I am here, with Jack and the rest of my Gen, our parents and whoever remains of the Pioneers. All of the Pioneers will have had their reasons to come here, no doubt differing greatly, and all of them have to live with their decisions. I wonder what the psychiatric assessments for each of them said, what the doctors had been looking for. And what the Carers do with all the volumes of data they must have about us all, about the impact of each of our Conditions. Sure, we're told it feeds into finding a cure, the be all and end all cure. What if there is no cure? What if humans are becoming extinct and here we are, hermetically sealed away like the contents of a NutriVisor pouch - while Outside, beyond the perimeter, all that remains is death and decay.

Which, if you believe the reports on the CompStreams and TeleCasts, is already half true. We see skeletal buildings, steel frames devoid of windows and swaying in the wind, debris and litter billowing through empty streets. Cadaverous people skulking about the streets looking for help, which never comes.

Although watching the Bulletins is mandatory, the stark images jar against the radiant tones of the Carers who cut across the images, flying the flag for Florivale and the cure, always the cure. They never tell us the details of their progress, just remind us that progress is being made and that we are essential to its continuance. We never receive our test results, except where they mean we have to change something. Your cholesterol needs to be brought down: here, have an even less appetising meal.

I was watching one of the evening TeleCasts one evening, and noticed a slight flicker on the screen during the Bulletin. Momentary. But it stopped the Bulletin for a moment, and in its wake lay an image like the curtains of an old theatre, deep red velvet like on the photos from Before. Though it was gone so quickly, I am sure there were figurines on stage, a hospital scene. There was wording emblazoned above the image. Almost as soon as I'd processed it, the screen reverted to the image of the Carer, droning on about the joys of life and the safety of Florivale, the threat from those less fortunate than us, the ones who lived Outside. But I wondered. Who defines what it is to be fortunate? The ageing Pioneers are the ones who chose this life and have something to compare it to. My Gen knows no better, and have no choice in being here. What if decay and danger are truth, whereas clean, safe Florivale is synthetic? Somehow less than real?

That stage image haunts me. A second on the screen, burned into my mind. I shut my eyes and see it in the darkness. In bed, I search my memory, strain for any clue, any more information. And the words which flashed across the top of the screen - I know them. William Shakespeare. I see them in my dreams, peeling their inky selves from the pages of the heaviest book in the Library, marching unbidden into my mind: all the world's a stage, and all the men and women merely players.

Florivale cannot be my stage; "Second Gen Victoria" cannot be my role. I must get past the stage curtains. Outside.

I wonder how they must have felt when they came in here – a world of chance, a fresh start. Everything, in fact, which is denied to me, having been born into this bubble. Her notes from their first few weeks here frustrate me so much, my fingers tense as I read the pages. I wonder, if I were faced with such a threat, would I pick safety – trade the comfort of the known world, even if it was flawed - for a promise of safety, of security? And would she have made that choice if it hadn't been for Mum and her siblings? Would she have felt like I feel now, if she were in my shoes?

What role did she play, and on what stage?

11

I don't like the look of the CompStreams in here, so I'm taking this note back to the old school with one of Ella's drawing pens and some paper from her scrapbook. There's nothing to worry about, I'm sure, but I feel a bit hemmed in, too controlled, when I'm faced with a bank of CompStreams and I can only print, on request, into the room next door. I want something in here to be just mine, not shared with anyone. Not even Mike. Until you, that is.

I packed print-outs of the emails I wrote before we entered Florivale. I shoved them in between the pages of the books we brought in and they are all still there. I'll leave them where they are for now, but I want to move them around a bit. Hide them for you to find, one day. I'm enjoying writing, unlocking my thoughts and getting them out of my head and onto the page. I never had time to write anything for myself before the Opportunity came along. It started with those emails. I'd only ever written for my education, or for work. Maybe I'll end with a note on a faded, scruffy page torn from a child's scrapbook.

It's funny, how I'd lost the knack of physically writing. This is taking bloody ages! We use CompStreams and FloriConnect tablets so often, little devices connected to each other and beeping endlessly, that I suppose they've replaced old-fashioned handwriting. Even ten years ago you could see the start of the decline. Which is all very well, until you want to write something that can't be traced, found on a backup, in the cloud or otherwise dredged up and flung back in your face.

We have arrived and I thought I ought to mark down some first impressions. Maybe I'll give my notes to the kids one day. Maybe not. Nevertheless, here I am. Writing - it's cathartic.

We are in Florivale. Everything is just as we had asked. Well, almost everything.

We are in a "transitional period" to allow us to adjust from life outside Florivale into our new setting. As they told us at our orientation meeting, that means different things for different families. For me, that means being allowed to cook. Apparently this is a privilege and our health will be monitored during Transition (absurd – everything I cook is healthy. Well, apart from the odd treat). A slight hitch to this is that, for reasons known best to themselves, the Ministry has designated the Stone household as... vegetarians.

I know. Appalling, isn't it. Why would I want to have a kitchen if I can't cook things we actually want to eat? Things with meat in. Obviously. We can't live on broccoli and rice cakes, for God's sake. I will take that up with the nutritionists - sorry, NutriVisors – everything in this place has to have some conflated, Americanised name. Maybe I'll get used to it.

Maybe I won't. I know we signed all the papers (and, possibly, I could have paid more attention to them) but this is crazy. How could removing meat and fish from our diets make us healthier? We are perfectly healthy as we are!

If they need a family to be vegetarians, they should ask one of the others.

But let's get back to the subject of my kitchen! It's enormous. Just as it was in the plans and photos they sent us. When we arrived, there were fresh flowers in vases on the countertop and a huge glass bowl brimming with the most luscious fruit, rainbow colours glinting in the soft sunlight which poured through the open window. The cupboards hold crockery and glassware, and we have two or three pans and oven dishes, presumably all they think we will need during Transition. I'll see about that!

Beyond the window-pane you can see the garden, our piece of Florivale. The grass is flat and perfectly mown. It has those ridiculous manicured lines in it - Mike and I will not be maintaining those - and it looks so enticing. The kids already adore the house – a bedroom each and new places to explore. The fact that everything is so new and so shiny makes it feel like we're in a theme park or on a film set. This has to be the single most surreal experience of my life.

While we arranged to pack up our lives and head into Florivale, we had Ministry officials 'drop in' every now and again with advice and information. And rules – always more rules. As annoying as this was, they were always ready to remind us of the benefits of moving here. Which, I agree, make their silly rules worthwhile. Ripping up our mortgage statement and credit card bills and receiving the letters from the Ministry stating that they had assumed and repaid our debt was almost like being told I could fly, I felt so free. It's hard to believe something as stupid as a debt, a promise to pay someone something, could make me feel so desperate.

Right. I must go and do some more unpacking. Mike will probably have gone half mad looking after the kids. They are manic with excitement. It's quite delightful, actually.

12

We've been here a week now. It's strange, because I still feel like we will be leaving, heading back to our normal lives. But we won't ever have a "normal" life again – Florivale is certainly not normal. The feeling of being on location in film remains. Everything is so pristine, too perfect. I'm afraid to put a mug on the table in case it leaves a ring, or to spill the washing up water on the floor in case it dissolves the shiny tiles and we become known as the "bad" house.

We're still in Transition, so I am still allowed to cook – although no meat or fish. Apparently that was in the paperwork we received, but I didn't see it. The NutriVisor (this one was called Alice) said it's about examining the role of non-animal protein in the diet and identifying whether cholesterol and animal fat-derived compounds are linked to obesity and poor health. We are currently the pilot study for something they may roll out to other homes here. Alice explained there are other studies being 'implemented' (it's always very clinical with a NutriVisor) across Florivale, some based on nutrition, others on exercise, sleep pattern and so on. I supposed I'd rather give up bacon than sleep, if that's what it came down to.

That's something I am enjoying. Sleep. Quality sleep. I'd forgotten that was a real thing! During Transition there is no sleep regulation (apparently this will come later, but I'm assured it will make us feel more energised... we shall see). No sleep regulation, for me, means lie-ins. Well, to the extent the kids allow. For Mike, it means no more godawful wake up times, no more dragging his socked feet downstairs to search for the car key, which - for reasons best known to himself - he never put on the key hook designed to avoid exactly that scenario, and no more 6 a.m. caffeine-fuelled motorway cruising. What we have instead is a gentle breeze through the window and the knowledge that all we have to do today is, essentially, whatever we want. It's quite hard to believe. Well, as long as whatever we want to do falls within the never-ending list of rules. Of course, that list doesn't include leaving Florivale. No smoking, no non-prescribed drugs. As if I'd have even known where to start with either! But for now, lie-ins and family breakfasts will suit us just fine.

We're exploring Florivale, bit by bit. As part of our orientation sessions, we got to see the Community Centre, FitHub and so on. Now we have our own free time, we're working out how all of these places link up and connect, how the homes are dotted about (all with just enough garden to feel like a luxury, but not so much as to be wasteful) and where the boundaries seem to lie. There are Protector Stations around the perimeter, primarily to keep out any protesters who might dare venture onto the Lake to try and reach us (there have been a lot of protests about Florivale, and about the compulsory purchase orders used to obtain the land for it) and to ensure no pathogens, unauthorised persons or bacteria come into our Community. I find the term Protector pretty condescending, when these guys are quite clearly security guards. I mean, they have guns. Big ones. That said, so much of Florivale is sanitised (in fact and in the figurative), that I guess I will have to get over it.

The kids are desperate to swim and paddle in the Lake. With the water twinkling back at the sunshine, glittering with the promise of fun to come, it's hard to explain to them that they aren't allowed in. Ever. Especially when I don't accept the reason why it's forbidden. How can something so beautiful be so dangerous? How could I possibly explain that to them?

And what would they do to us if we did happen to go into the Lake? Given we signed a contract saying we can pretty much never leave Florivale, would they, could they, kick us out? And what would come of us if we were expelled? We have no home, no phones, and no bank account. Everything we have is here in Florivale. I don't think we'd want to go back anyway, but I do wonder sometimes.

Apart from checking out the state of our neighbours' lawns (identical to ours, of course – until ours starts to grow out of control as it inevitably will), we're still tied up unpacking the house, sorting the kids' rooms out and so on. I'm really enjoying decorating. Most of the house is plain and neutral in beige, grey and cream, with the odd touch of duck egg blue or teal to take the edge off the sterility. As a special concession for our home, I managed to negotiate permission to paint on the walls in the children's rooms. In Ella's room – although Annie still stays in there with her at the moment – they aren't used to having all this space - I've been working on a mural of a tiger and a small flock of sheep. I saw it in a dream one night and was struck by the image of juxtaposed strength and fragility; nature's harmony, maintained through a system of checks and balances. The importance of knowing who you are. Tiger or sheep, you must always know your mind - and you must know that you can change it.

I started painting while Mike distracted the kids by unpacking the play room. The second my pencil touched the coolness of the walls, I felt calm. The outline grew, and the tiger took shape first. Working and re-working the outlines, I watched her come to life before I started on the small cluster of sheep across the room. Where I'd filled in the she-tiger's outline in glossy, precise black paint, the sheep were created more gently, their frothy wool developed through layers of white sponge imprints, some parts thicker than others, with no set borders or definition. Only their wise little faces and highly-tuned ears were painted in gloss, so they could see and hear the tiger.

I love this room. I hate to admit it, but I even prefer it to the kitchen I demanded. Perhaps it's because I've spent so much time in here, working on those paintings day by day, quietening my thoughts and focusing only on the scene as it grew. Or perhaps it's because of the kids' reactions to it when we had the "great unveiling". Also known as: Mike holding off the inevitable chaos by forcing the children to wait outside the room, Mike trying to stop them scrambling off somewhere while I whisked the paints out of the way. Orange and black footprints throughout the house would have been hard to explain away. I mustered up a little drama for the occasion with a countdown, before sweeping the door open and letting them in.

Ella loves the tiger – she ran to it and stroked the stripes before they were quite dry, so, of course, I've had to re-paint the whole section... but it was worth it to see her trying to interact with it, grinning as she unwittingly left tiny hand-shaped paint smears in her wake. Annie and

Bertie can't seem to make up their minds about the animals. I asked them to walk over to their favourites. Bertie strode towards the tiger, before pausing and gazing back at the sheep. I could hear the cogs turning as he thought it through.

'Tigers bite,' he said. And with that, he pottered towards the sheep, declaring they were 'cosy sheep'.

Annie was different. She lay in the middle of the room and pointed one arm towards the tiger, the other towards the sheep.

'I don't want to choose. I want both.'

It never ceases to surprise me, how different they turned out, despite sharing a home, parents and a (rather delightful, if I do say so myself) set of genes. And I couldn't be prouder of them.

13

There you have it. Grandma Sophie, the images of my mum as a child, and of the tiger on the wall. I can't look at it the same way any more – I used to think it was silly, antiquated. A relic of a lost childhood clung to by my foolish mother… but now, it has significance. I understand it now. The tiger's eyes still sparkle like they've just been painted. The wool on the sheep looks so soft I want to reach out and touch it.

I went into that room today, lay on the floor in the same place Grandma must have lain, and scrutinised her paintwork as she must have done. She was such a perfectionist. My mind ran over a thousand of the same questions she must have had, along with hundreds of others she couldn't have even thought of. Not then, when her head was still full of Outside, of Before. Knowledge that I will never have while I'm stuck in here.

I mentioned the first notes to Clem today. We met at the FitHub, where she was pounding away on the treadmill. I guessed she had something to vent about too. Running at speed is my thing. For Clem, she's just too calm to pull it off – regardless of how fit she might be. She looked demented with her cropped red hair bobbing behind her and the strands at the front plastered to her forehead with sweat.

It would not be long at all until Clem's

BioBand went green at this rate, and it was only eight thirty. Speeding along on the eternal runway of the treadmill in her favourite workout wear of lilac (regulation style, of course – far be it from the Carers to let us have any more flexibility, choice or dynamism than choosing a colour), she was a force to be reckoned with this morning. I peered round and spotted that her FitChart suggested she only had about three minutes left of running at that speed before her FitCapacity would be exhausted and the treadmill would automatically power down. I figured I could wait that long.

'Hey Clem.' I said. 'You want some water from the cooler?'

'Sure,' came back the panting response. 'Not too cold!'

She never wants really cold water. It's something I've always found odd in her. Like most of my Gen, she doesn't like to drink or be underwater at all, really – certainly nothing more than a shallow bath and even then, not unless she has a medical need – period pain, myalgia, something like that. I guess I'm the odd one out there too. I can't get enough. Anyway. Once she finished up on the treadmill, she grabbed a sterile towel from the rack and made her way over to me on the slightly-less-uncomfortable-than-the-floor chairs in the corner. That type of furniture design is something that Florivale has totally nailed. Uncomfortable, functional, not particularly attractive. Clean. Sterile. Community buildings like this remind me how lucky I am that Grandma Sophie was so adamant that the Stone house had to be cosy. It's unlike any other place in here.

'What's up?' I asked. 'The crazy pace, I can get used to, but what's the furious face about?'

'Mum,' she said, after taking a long drink. 'She's driving me crazy. She's gone into lockdown. I asked a couple of questions about Before, about why she came in here. I don't know what got me thinking about it but something is there in the back of my mind. Since seeing that stupid stage thing on the CompStream – did you see it?'

'I did. I thought I was making it up actually – nobody else was in to ask.' I said, desperate to hear more, wanting her to tell me what she saw and validate all the crazy thoughts I had been running through. But I also knew she had to do this at her own pace. This was Clem, after all.

'Totally weird,' she replied. 'I've never seen anything like that. It looked like some dreadful old-fashioned film reel from the EduCentre or the Library, but there was something more about it. Something kind of sloppy. Amateur. Ominous. So I asked mum whether she saw it, knowing she had. But she closed up. Like she just slammed a door on that part of the day and wouldn't accept that it had happened. She made me feel like I was going crazy.'

She was getting into a classic Clem Agitation. Ever since we were little, the odd ones out in class, I've been able to spot a Clem Agitation, or "CA", on the way. Her hands won't sit still. Her feet tap on the floor. Her breath comes in quick rasps. She fidgets incessantly. I'm pretty sure Clem's NutriVisor pouches contain about three times the calories of anyone else's because they must get burnt off at an astronomical rate. But this wasn't one of her usual moments. I knew this because I'd seen that same image flash up on screen. I'd had those same niggling doubts that I couldn't shift.

'Clem, what did your mum actually say?' I asked, conscious not to put words in her mouth.

'She said nothing,' she said, pouting back at me. 'I started by asking if she saw the stage thing on the screen. She just said no, what stage thing, something like that. So I let it drop. But then, later on, I still couldn't forget about it and I knew she had seen it – something had shifted in her, she sat differently, spoke differently. I was fixing us our green tea, watching the particles swirling around in the bottom of our cups and I thought – the image was no less clear than this. I knew she saw it. I also knew discussing it was off limits, based on her reaction from earlier. So I thought I'd try something else, another tack. I asked her if she would tell me why they came in, came to Florivale. And she just closed up. The usual responses: why would I want to know about Before, where there was illness and danger, when I am here in the safety of Florivale. And I figure, I am twenty years old, god damn it! Tell me the bloody truth!'

I let her catch her breath. Another symptom of a Clem Agitation is that her words speed up to the point of being a blur – the verbal equivalent of her run this morning. She took another swig of water and looked at the reminder on her BioBand to get a green tea. Daily green tea is a Condition for Clem's family, the Petersens. She hates it. She is just as frustrated as me. And, as terrible as it sounds, I wanted her to be agitated about this. If I could get her excited, intrigued, maybe she would better understand my need for knowledge. We'd always talked about wanting to know more about Before and Outside, but we'd never come this close to piecing anything together.

'Clem. I saw it too. I have no bloody idea what that little stage means but I can't get it out of my head. I close my eyes and see it at night. And there's nobody to talk to about it except for you. And maybe Josh.' I paused. 'Actually, have you seen Josh lately?'

Josh is our other friend. The other one who, like us, didn't want to get excited about picking out regulation clothes and being the 'best behaved' in our Gen. I was hoping to see him at the FitHub but perhaps it was better to see Clem on her own this time. I carried on, not really registering whether she answered me or not.

'Clem. I need you to keep this secret.' I paused, weighing my words. 'Lean in and listen.'

Clem laughed, snorted her water out, and looked at me like I was completely mad, but eventually leaned in. I think she saw the glint in my eyes, threatening her not to laugh at me again. Not about this.

'Clemmie. You know I wouldn't lie to you, don't you,' I whispered, my urgent tones getting in the way of the calm intonation I'd have used if I had planned it properly. 'I've found some notes from my Grandma Sophie, from Before. And some from when they moved here. She left them behind, to be read sometime. You have to read them.'

Her face was blank, stunned.

'But Vic, how? Why would she even bring notes in here?' She scanned my face. 'Are you joking? Because I'm not in the mood to be lied to, or made to feel stupid again. My mum's already treating me like a head case and I know I saw something weird. I just know it.'

'Clem. You know I'm with you on this one. Come with me. Nobody's in at my parents' place. I'll show you some of the notes. And I promise, there will be absolutely no green tea.'

With a laugh to break the tension, I had normal Clem back. She threw her towel into the bin, tapped her BioBand to the treadmill monitor to confirm that her heart rate had normalised, and pulled her bobbed hair back into whatever semblance of a ponytail she could achieve with her hairclips.

'Let's go,' she said. 'I have to see this.'

14

Transition is over now.

Gone is the cookware. The food in the fridge. It's just NutriVisor pouches now. I know I'll get used to it, eventually, but it does drive home the feeling that we are in an experiment. I have to keep telling myself that it's going to work out for the best, that the kids have a wonderful home, and we are all safe. I think back to the Value Life riots, or the sense of foreboding every time we opened a bank statement or a credit card reminder. I recall the underlining threat that something malicious was building in the streets, disenfranchised people no longer willing to sit back and shut up. And I make my peace with the fact I have to eat pre-pouched meals.

The kids have started at school. Correction, the EduCentre (eugh). We are meant to adopt the terminology of Florivale (Florivese?) to help ease us and our kids into living here. There's a name for almost everything and I'm trying to stop seeing it as a stupid, temporary annoyance and to accept it. Because it's not temporary. We've been here about three weeks and it's fair to say, we have had everything we need. Although needing something is not the same as wanting it.

I want meat, freedom, an excursion, my own non

FloriConnect mobile phone. I need protein, enough area to exercise and work, temporary distractions and the ability to communicate with others in Florivale. You see the distinction. I think everyone must be having the same teething problems. And I just have to remind myself of the thoughts Mike and I were driven to having before we came here, arguing over trivialities - which restaurant to go to, which pool to take the kids to. We were so burnt out. We've been better here.

Mike's missing his long runs. Everything is so regulated here, to avoid over-exertion, over-consumption, minimise exposure to pathogens… you get the picture. Annie and Bertie are getting on pretty well at the moment – they've stopped having the enormous fights which had started in our cramped little house Outside. I think it must be down to having more space. And Ella is sleeping in longer in the mornings, which is an absolute dream. Literally, in her case. I'm a bit worried about her, though. The others seem happy here. But Ella, well Ella is different. She's constantly comparing things to life before we moved here. She wants the food she used to eat, her old schoolbooks, her friends. I know she will find it easier in time, that we all will, but I occasionally find her absent-mindedly running her fingers along the outline of the tiger on the wall. If you're quiet, you can watch her from the staircase for minutes at a time, absorbed in her thoughts. I want to know what she's thinking. What she wants, and what she needs. I want to help my little girl adjust.

I've also been meaning to paint in the other rooms – whether I'm allowed or not. Just something personal to lift the walls. But I can't do it. I lift a pencil to the wall, a brush, a finger dipped in paint. And nothing is there. No inspiration. The other room will have to do.

15

I can't believe how the years have passed since I last wrote. I kind of forgot about it. Life just gets in the way, doesn't it?

Have you ever dreamt you're trapped underwater? And in that dream, every movement you make exhausts you. Every breath you try to take just fills your lungs with more water? I feel like that when I'm awake. It only stops when I'm asleep. And my sodding BioBand waked me up when it decrees I've slept enough.

Mike and I are arguing. He is drawing away from me, closing himself off from us. In the few years we've been in here, I've never felt like this with him. It's as though his heart contains some kind of secret, one he's guarding. Something he's protecting from me, in case I break it. I used to be the one he turned to, spoke to, advised and sought answers from. And there isn't anyone else he can realistically speak to here - he wouldn't talk to a Carer because they would "adjust" his NutriVisor pouches and he wouldn't feel anything any more. We saw that happen to the Wrights, after they asked too many questions.

This morning, once the children were are the

EduCentre and we had both done our required time at the FitHub, we came back to the house. Mike's eyes were glazed over in a way I'm becoming familiar with – the threat of tears, combined with a steely determination not to let them out, or me in. He bowed his head and took a breath.

'I have to get out,' he said.

Picture me, completely stunned. 'But you can't.' I said. 'The contract, we signed up to this. You know we can't leave. And even if you could, everyone's dying out there.'

Mike lifted his hazel eyes to me, the flecks of green glinting through the glaze of tears. 'I can't take it in here,' he said. 'I'm losing my mind. My headaches are worse and I can't run them off. I didn't tell you about them because I needed to go to the Health Centre and know for myself.' He paused. 'I think I'll die in here if I can't get out.'

He didn't say, if "we" can't get out. This was just about him. I didn't know what to say. We sat in silence until he spoke again.

'The Health Centre have said they missed something on the initial tests. I'm a defective subject.' Confused tears sprang to my eyes as he continued. I was too horrified to respond. 'I was probably already getting ill when they brought us in, but they didn't see the signs. They shouldn't have let me come. Maybe it's from all the stress, the years on the road. I don't know.'

'No,' I protested. 'It's just not possible. They tested everything. Every little thing. Blood. Heart. Brain scans. And what do you mean, defective subject? You're the best person I know.' I almost spat the words at him in my disbelief. I didn't mean to shout. I meant to speak softly, but there was too much conflict, too much pain at what I was hearing. Too much fear. I pulled back from the brink of my anger, and forced out the words, calming my tone with every iota of my strength. 'If you're defective, I'm defective.'

He reached his hand across the table towards me, properly connecting to me for the first time in weeks. 'This is it Soph. It's die in here, a test subject, or try to live out there. Maybe Outside I could outrun the headaches – I could feel free. Even if I had little time left, I'd be where I belong. Outside, where I can run as fast, as hard, and in whatever direction I choose.'

I couldn't speak. It was too much information for me, too much for anyone, to process. I pulled back the wooden chair, which scraped and squeaked awkwardly along the floor. I was grateful for the noise. Sometimes, silence was not golden. How could he leave, even if I agreed? This isn't the kind of place you can just walk out of. And he'd die out there for sure. Homeelss. Penniless. Friendless. As I neared the door, I turned and paused.

'You can't leave us. Forget about their rules. This is about me. About us. I won't let you leave me.'

16

I've put the girls to bed. Bertie is still up with me, cruising his cars around the playroom floor while I sit curled on the sofa, writing this note. He hasn't been able to sleep properly since it happened, and I don't blame him. He seems fine in all other respects, no tears, no tantrums. The odd strange word thrown in with his sentences, as though he has resurrected his and Ella's childhood language from when they were little. Other than the sleep, and the babyish words, he's fine. Perhaps the difference is that the girls are a little older, so they have more memories against which to compare our lives.

There is nothing I can write that could convey how I feel without him here. These are only words, after all.

I go through the motions. Get the kids up and send them to the EduCentre. Go to the FitHub. Come back to the house and stare endlessly at the wall.

It's not just devastation. It's exhaustion. It's loneliness. It's anger.

Of course I'm angry. I'm furious. Angry at the world for letting this happen, at Mike for leaving me, for letting go, and angry at myself for the things I said, the things I didn't, and the thoughts I still can't dispel.

Mostly, I'm angry that I didn't let him leave Florivale before they completely quarantined him. I'm consumed by sadness that I used guilt as a tool to keep him here. I thought his mood would pass, that he would get better, that the Carers would somehow find a way to make things right.

They have so many drugs now, so many procedures they could try. But they wouldn't, they didn't. Every time they said it was too invasive, I found myself thinking, how? What could possibly be so invasive that it's not worth trying, when the alternative is to let the hours tick by until he is gone for ever? Death is the ultimate invasion, leaving nothing but a void.

After my last note, and that previous conversation we'd had, I made Mike promise to stay with us. I know he wanted to try and leave, but I was too selfish to let him go.

So now I sit, staring at the wall, feeling alone and wretched. And I ache, knowing I can't leave this house, which is so full of him, saturated by memories of him.

Mike stayed because I forced him to. Throughout our relationship, I had never made him do anything he didn't want to, but this was too big. I wish I had let go. Instead, we carried on with our regularised little FloriLives, although for him, the later days were punctuated with tests and appointments. They tested me too, for completeness, but they wouldn't tell me quite what was going on. I heard about plaques, clots and tumours as possible root causes, but they never specified anything. They still won't. All I know is that the headaches got worse, the glaze in his eyes increased, and I had to watch, powerless - as my best friend, the one who holds the other half of my heart, slipped away from me.

After a few weeks of complete torture at home (for both of us), they moved him into the Health Centre full time. After that, I saw him a couple of times a day, for a couple of hours at a time. I tried to read to him, to break him out of his frozen stare, but nothing worked. There was a flicker, once or twice, when I brought the kids in, but eventually it became too painful for all of us. It was like he had already died.

He had always hated saying goodbye. So we never did.

Three weeks ago, as the sun poured through the windows on a Tuesday morning, a Carer came to the door. He was sorry for our loss. No, we couldn't see the body. It had already been taken for sample testing and autopsy for contamination assessment. All part of the terms and conditions of coming in here. Funeral arrangements would be taken care of and I was to choose my preferred casket. Condolences and leaflets on bereavement were handed out. The door closed and, as they left me to my darkest thoughts, came to the dim realisation that this wasn't a dream. I sank to the floor.

It turned out I was wrong. Mike could leave me. As if to prove it, he left me the most irreversible way possible. He left forever.

17

I hadn't been ready to read that, so I knew how Clem would react when she reached that point. She'd come back to the house with me to start reading the notes. When we get to that one, she knew that I wouldn't talk about it. She just quietly left and reminded me to get to the FitHub, so I could run it out.

So I went. I ran past the green light on my BioBand. Right through the electric shock it issues when you've gone too far, when you're about to risk burnout.

My tears combined with the beads of sweat running down my cheeks. I cried my way along the path home. It was only just before the front door that I pulled myself together, knowing I'd have to face Mum and Dad, who were not familiar with the concept of me crying. I blamed my puffy eyes and red face on a punishing run. Another entry in my lifelong catalogue of half-truths.

I don't want to dwell on it. So I'll tell you about Clem. Crazy, brilliant Clem. She's my best friend. I want to say 'my best friend in here,' but that would be nonsense as I don't know anyone outside the boundary – instead, I have a yearning to meet someone else, someone new. Anyone, in fact. Unless, of course, that 'anyone' is some sort of deranged and diseased murderer. Anyway,

I'm going off track.

Clem and I have known each other pretty much all our lives. From fighting with the other kids in our Gen, and each other, in the nursery at the Community Centre, through enduring hours of brainwashing (aka education) at the EduCentre, to whiling away our afternoons together in recent years. We complement one another – my rages tend to come when she is feeling calm, her Clem Agitations often hit when I'm feeling pretty (as she would say) zen. We balance. It's uncanny. When both of us are worked up, well... let's just say you wouldn't want to be around. Or caught in the middle.

Her family's Conditions are all the sort of stuff Grandma Sophie called Hippy Mumbo Jumbo. HMJ, if you like. Grandma always thought the Petersens should have the vegetarian Condition, not us. When anyone, including Clem, pointed out that the whole idea was to be able to differentiate between the impact of the various Conditions and that putting all the HMJ Conditions together would defeat the point, Grandma would huff and puff and clatter about in the kitchen or go off to 'do some admin. What she had to administer, I'll never know.

For Clem, HMJ is a way of life. Yes, the Petersens can eat meat and fish, but it's in very prescribed amounts (exactly the right portion size every day, per adult, with fish on four of the seven days for its healthy oils etc.). Sure, she gets hot drinks, but only hot water with a slice of lemon (pre-sliced, heaven forbid a Florivite might get a cut), or green tea. And there is no choice on the green tea. Two cups a day. Bitter and, frankly, disgusting. I have tried hers many times and, I can tell you now, I'm happy with the Stone-Hunter Conditions. I don't really get the obsession with meat anyway. As I should know, sometimes not knowing what you're missing can be a blessing.

Clem also has to have a lot of unusual treatments. She and her family are the only ones I know of in here who have to have hundreds of needles stuck in them on a regular basis. It's gross. All over their body, sometimes. It's called acupuncture. It sounds medieval. The word "puncture". That part alone must count for something. It would deter anyone normal, for sure. Clem actually likes it - but she's always been pretty weird. No doubt this is the principal reason we get along.

'It's like your energy gets caught up in little knots, and the needles burst those knots, so your energy can flow around you,' she says. I'm with Grandma Sophie. No HMJ for me please. Even their toothpaste is different. It smells like a bloody herb garden and tastes of liquorice. I prefer classic mint.

But our differences have become our strength. She offsets the way my brain works. Apart from Clem Agitations, she is the counterpart to my - somewhat over-reactive - default state. I'll fly off the handle, in a flash of anger, then immediately clam down and feel better. Whereas Clem lets things build. She floats along - Clemmily - and then, out of nowhere, this thunderball of Clem is unleashed. It's like the equivalent to every one of my little outbursts has been left to germinate inside her until the tiny irritations become a mass, which has no alternative but to explode from her in a

Clem Agitation. They are hard, or impossible, to predict. And can be hilarious (if not directed at you).

Showing Clem the notes was one of the most intimate things we've shared. Sure, we know all about each other's medical details, Conditions, menstruation, toilet habits... everything Grandma Sophie always had an issue sharing. But that's just typical of our Gen. We're actively encouraged to discuss these things, to familiarise ourselves with our bodies and their differences.

But the notes are the innermost thoughts of the person with whom, apart from Clem, I feel I share the closest connection. And asking Clem to read the notes seemed like an invitation into something more. Something dangerous. Because I know she will have the same questions as me, the same temptations. Her HMJ only takes her so far, and for one of the most logical, calmest people I know, she is also – contradictorily - the one most likely to disregard all her own rules and take a gamble.

I need her to read the rest of the notes. Soon. The frustration of being in here, the daily monotony of breakfast, FitHub, weekly tests. I know something isn't right, and every day I feel more claustrophobic. And the stage image on the CompStream that day. I want to scream and shout about it! Most of all, I want to ask Grandma Sophie what it all means. And, if she could tell me, what it was, and is, like - out there.

Sometimes life begs you to unlatch the window. To smell the air outside, crisp and new. Climb onto the windowsill. Close your eyes.

And jump.

18

Josh is our other friend. He's different again, odd in another way. He doesn't have anything like a Clem Agitation. Or my flashes of temper. Josh, unlike us, is calm and collected. He actually wants to wear clothes like everyone else, toned palettes of blue and grey being his favourite – very conservative. On the outside anyway. His whole family's like that. The McLaines. Unlike Clem's lovely mum Angie, Josh's mum definitely does not approve of our friendship. She doesn't like Clem either – in fact, I think she likes Clem even less than me. Apparently, we 'derail' Josh from the norm. She actually said that to him in an argument. Unbelievable right? Mrs. Jessica McLaine does not like anything out of the ordinary. She wants everything nice and normal, regulated, compliant. Easy.

Josh's Conditions are weird. Every Florivite has vitamin injections every month, to "top up" anything revealed to be deficient from the past few weeks' blood tests, while the NutriVisors tinker with the contents of our NutriVisor pouches. But the McLaines have to have a full blood transfusion every few months. Imagine that. A replacement of your blood with someone else's – and you have no idea who provided it. Or whether it was taken with their consent. Or simply, why it was taken and given to you.

Some of the other kids at school, the prissy ones, used to call him Frankenstein (thus proving their stupidity, given Frankenstein was the creator, and not the monster) and say his blood was stolen from murderers or animals, or call him a vampire. Perhaps that's why he defaulted - outwardly at least - to conformity. Clem and I used to stick up for him at school. They'd call her "pin-cushion" and me "rabbit". Pathetic, I know. They could have done so much better than that. Clem and I didn't care, because we had long since concluded that the others were all idiots. But Josh definitely minded what people thought. The apple rarely falls far from the tree, they say – and if anyone was bothered about public perception, it was Mrs. McLaine. Josh has mentioned to us, always fleetingly, how much he dreads T-Day, how he hopes he'll get ill or have an anomalous test result so he doesn't have to go in to the Health Centre. He once said he just wanted to be the same person for another six months. We asked what he meant, how he felt, but he closed up like a half-read book. Left on the shelf to be picked up and opened another time, when it was ready for its story to be revealed.

But before you feel too sorry for him, know that Josh also has his fun. Apart from winding up Mrs. McLaine, I mean. His 'conformist' exterior belies the mischievous, sometimes Machiavellian (yes, I read books!) streak within. And that little-known streak gives him power in Florivale.

The fact he is absolutely gorgeous doesn't hurt either. It's like his T-Days were designed to make him a shade more attractive every time. I swear he gives off a pheromone. Easily the best looking guy in Florivale, hands down. His whole family is stunning, perfect - but Josh is their crowning glory. Thick, soft brown hair, with the odd dark-blond twinkle in the sun, softly curling to one side of his parting, effortlessly. I've seen him wake up when I've visited him recovering after a T-Day. He wakes up perfect. He has grey-blue eyes which shift colour in the light – no doubt the reason for his preferred wardrobe.

His skin is creamy and golden, tanning lightly in the sun, although not much – given our water is pre-impregnated with sunscreen and the Carers watch for tanning like hawks after the skin cancer crisis of Before. He's slightly taller than average, but not gangly or ungainly. Everything is in proportion, his wide shoulders slimming into narrow-but-not-too-narrow hips, his legs athletic and strong, but not too burly for the chinos he prefers to wear.

Don't get me wrong, I don't fancy Josh. At least, I don't think I do. I have the odd moment of feeling like maybe there is something behind how attractive I find him, and then I remember it's Josh, and I'd be a robot not to see his perfection. Plus, he makes everyone feel like that – it's like a super power. How he is. Even if I did want him that way, he'd never go for me. He has his pick of the Gen. Which will come in handy when the parents start their wedding plotting in earnest. We're getting near that age now. I'm pretty sure that most parents start to align themselves, planning out our lives for us when we're toddlers. Regardless of who was pulling whose hair, of which boy teased which girl.

It makes me nauseous. We are completely trapped. Everything is so prescribed. And what's worse, Clem, Josh and I seem to be the only ones vaguely bothered by this. We're stuck in a cage and thrown random tasks, Conditions, variations, all to see how we react. I've always wondered how that plays into the whole marriage concept. Because surely, if two teens have completely different Conditions and are brought together, those Conditions could mismatch? That is, unless there is some forward planning, some man-made predestination.

Take my family as an example. The Pioneer Stones had the vegetarianism Condition. That was fine. The Pioneers on my dad's side had the high calcium Condition. Those two things work together nicely. So I have a high-calcium, vegetarian combination. But what if Dad's Condition had been like the Smiths' – a high meat diet? Not that it worked out too well for the Smiths, who have so many supplements and injections it hardly seems like a good idea. But regardless, surely people's marital alliances wouldn't always work smoothly, not if human choice - and to err is human, after all - comes into it. I suppose, on that basis, Josh might need his good looks. Who'd want the McLaine transfusion Condition, even if they got the looks, the glow... the 'Joshness'.

I haven't told Josh about the notes yet. I know I'll have to, but I'm scared that, once we have, his mother will wheedle it out of him and ban us from seeing him again. She'll say the ban is because we fill his head with troubling nonsense. But it will really be because the notes reveal that things haven't always been, and still aren't, right in Florivale. He'll have seen that stage on the screen, and he won't have dismissed it like the other numbskulls in our Gen. Happy little sheep endlessly grazing away at their genetically modified grass. Nourished, but not satisfied.

I asked him if he'd seen the image of the stage while we were walking to the Community Centre the other day.

'No, I didn't,' he snapped. 'What are you talking about Vic? Have you been eating too many hemp seeds?' He laughed awkwardly at his terrible joke. Always keeping on with the vegetarian jokes. A true wit of our time. But his grey eyes wouldn't meet mine.

'Josh, I can't believe you didn't see that image, the disturbance on the screen. I know you did. You couldn't have missed it.' I scanned his face, hoping for some sort of reaction beneath the composed surface. He could be so unreadable. 'What did it look like to you?'

'Nothing. You're acting crazy, Vic. Why would it matter anyway, what's a pair of red curtains on a CompScreen?'

'I didn't mention any curtains, Josh.'

He paused. 'OK, so I imagined that part. Made it up – all theatres have red curtains. You and I both know that from the books in the EduCentre.'

'But why would you mention that specific detail, if you hadn't seen it?'

Again, he wouldn't meet my eyes. He always said the flecks in my irises were disconcerting. He once called them dangerously mesmerising - not that I'm into detail, or anything. But this studious avoidance of eye contact was Josh's tell.

'Fine, Josh. But Clem and I saw it. We know you did too. And probably everyone else in here. We're just not choosing to ignore it, and we're going to find out what it means. We have to.'

'Nothing Vic,' he shouted. 'It means nothing! Just some old image burnt into the video link. A technical glitch.' He slowed his pace, hanging back a step or two behind us. I focused on the flecks of white, bubbly saliva which were gathering at the corners of his lips, marring his perfection, the manifestation of his anger. 'Why does everything have to be so conspiratorial, so difficult with you?'

'Fine, Josh,' I said in a low voice. 'Everything's fine. Florivale is best. Whatever.'

I couldn't take any more of his evasion. In comparison to this, dealing with Clem Agitations was a doddle. He's a tough nut to crack. I guess that makes me the nutcracker.

I've read all the notes more times than I care to remember. I don't think there are any more. I've searched everywhere, but deep down, I know that's it. I'm giving them to Clem bit by bit, so she has time for each new piece of information to settle in. A tapestry of Florivale's history.

I know that my story can't end in here. In some dead-end marriage of convenience - although for whose convenience it would be, I'm not sure. The more I read and re-read the notes, the more this was affirmed. Although I've no idea how I'd get out, or what would await me on the other side. Regardless of the doubts, the shimmering edge of the Lake calls her siren song to me. Whether what's beyond is death and decay, or whether we've been fed lies on that count as well – I simply have to know.

I find myself spending longer underwater in the bath, holding my breath for peace, some time apart from Florivale in a place that's just for me. Until the air burns in my lungs and I have to force myself up into the air, stifling my gasps so my parents don't hear. Panting quietly in the shallow bath as goosebumps form along my forearms and I snap back to my four-walled reality.

19

This morning, Clem and I had arranged to meet at the FitHub. She had awful, circular bruises all over her back. Apparently last week's tests showed extra cortisol in her blood stream. Due to stress, most likely. So they made her have 'cupping' – classic HMJ. Little plastic cups were put all over her back and suction was applied to the cups, which pulled her flesh into them. This went on for minutes at a time, until it created a bruise. Then, she was oiled up by the Carer who administering the treatment, who then slipped the cups around, leaving long red tracks on her back, raised like welts. Another quasi-torture dressed up as something holistic. Clem said it wasn't bad at the time, and that hopefully it will help her feel more balanced, but she looked awful – paler than ever between the bruises. God knows what they'll think of next.

I feel guilty. I'm certain her anxiety must have been linked to everything we had discussed – the image of the stage, the notes and their insight into Outside, to Before. I couldn't stop thinking about it, and I was sure she wouldn't be able to either.

In fact, I've been thinking about it so much that I've been issued a Sleep Notice. If I don't get an extra hour's 'Quality' sleep each night this week I'll be forced into the IsoPods in the FitHub, where the misty air is filled with something unnatural, masked with the scent of lavender, which forces you to sleep. The Carers think the IsoPods provide the best Quality sleep after a period of restlessness. It's like being trapped in an enormous, metal, egg-shaped cage. But the cage is really your own sedated body and it is your mind that can't escape its confines. Which begs the question: how am I meant to naturally get myself into deep Quality sleep, when I am so stressed about being in the IsoPod itself? I hate it. Grandma used to gently trace her fingers in figures of eight around my brow to calm me – untangling the knots in my mind – and I used to feel my anger, confusion, stress, whatever it was at the time, slip away. All I can do now is visualise her doing that.

Once I'd recovered from the shock of her bruises, Clem and I got talking. Instead of running, we were doing yoga, which meant we could exercise outside without anyone else from our Gen overhearing. They'd be too worried about getting grass stains on their sports clothes. Bunch of imbeciles. I can't believe they know none of this, that they're just ploughing along.

'So what did you think of the last notes?' I asked, trying to be casual, when all I want to do is scream with frustration and anticipation, in equal measure.

'I felt uncomfortable. Reading her life like that. I know she wrote it to be read, but it's like prying into a diary.' She adjusted her position and paused as she checked her breathing. 'Perhaps there is something to be said for not knowing those things. Why else wouldn't they let us know about Outside, about Before? Unless it was harmful? Everything in here is engineered for our wellbeing. Why would they let anything fly in the face of that?' I wanted to shake her.

'Because, Clem, with that mentality comes ultimate control. Don't let them have you as well.'

'They don't have me,' she replied. 'I'm not a possession. And just because you feel one way doesn't mean I have to feel that way too.'

'Are you saying you don't care? That you don't want there to be more to this? That knowledge doesn't mean anything to you?'

'Jesus Vic. You don't have to be so black and white. You've had these notes for weeks. I've had no time to process it all. You're drip-feeding me information when it suits you and I need more of it, and more time. I have to catch up with you, and I need to make up my own mind – you're so far ahead of me, as always.'

She was right. As she often is. It was infuriating. I broke out of my downward dog and moved into child's pose, using the excuse to take a deep breath and moderate my tone so I didn't snap at her.

'I get it Clem.' I breathed to the beat of my heart's internal metronome, just like I'd been taught. 'Just keep reading. Keep questioning. And try not to get too anxious. With all the tests, I feel like we can't even have a secret without them washing it from us, or in your case, sucking it out of you by the cup. It's so gross! Let me see your back again!'

Clem tried to stay serious but gave way to laughter as I lunged for her, breaking her pose. The laughs creased her up from the straight lines required by her discipline and into a comma shape. We both knew the yoga spell was broken.

We'd have to do something else.

'Come on, Cuppy Clem. Let's ride our bikes home and have one of those revolting green teas your family is so keen on.'

'Do we have to?' she asked, laughing as we scrambled to the bike racks. 'Can't someone just get married already so we can have a party and eat something REAL!?'

20

Annie and Toby are getting married!

Finally, something to break up the daily routine of Florivale life. It's all anyone's talking about. Perhaps that's why the Carers are so happy to encourage the younger Gens to marry, to change the cycle, just for a day. Although a bigger part of me thinks it's all about the next Gen. There's always hope for another baby in Florivale, an expansion of the Community (or, if I'm being cynical, another test subject, some more information to feed their database). I have to remind myself sometimes that I must sound like a crazy conspiracy theorist, and that we all chose to come here – it was better for each of us than whatever we had on the Outside.

Everything we hear about Outside sounds pretty awful. Swathes of the country decimated by illness, violence and rioting in the cities, neglect in the countryside. If it's all true, then something fundamental has broken within society, within each of us; human bonds unwinding in adversity.

So we focus on Florivale. We focus on the wedding.

It's scheduled for a few days after Annie's 20th

birthday. I know, so young. To think I married Mike so much later than that, after university (for a degree I never used, which, although I had the time of my life, turned out to be a rather expensive three year party - thanks for the debt, student loan company).

But living here, the majority of her life dictated by NutriVisors, Carers, the FitHub, the Community, Annie's an odd combination of unnervingly naïve, and then again, so much older than her years. And I wonder what else there is for her, or for us, to look forward to. Life will continue with its daily routine, the familiarity as comforting and constricting as a swaddling blanket, and we will live out our days in sanitised comfort. Which, although boring at times, does mean we will live. No premature deaths, illness, or physical suffering. Not having to watch anything like the pain Mike went through.

I still reach for him in my sleep, waking when my arm hits the cold pillow that used to be his. He is still the first person I want to tell my crazy middle-of-the-night thoughts to, or laugh with. In my head, I hear snippets of songs that remind me of him, imagine the shared glances we can no longer have, when the kids do something funny, or make me proud. The rawness has faded, but it's a constant pain, dull and deep.

He would have been so delighted with how she turned out. How they all did. I wish he could see her, or could have been here when Toby came in to (very traditionally) seek my approval of the marriage. For someone who is so relaxed when he usually turns up, unannounced, to spend time at the house, he was shaking like a leaf. I had my suspicions immediately. No young man in his early twenties wants a private chat with the mother of his girlfriend. No chat, no interrogation. Easy. But he held his own and gave me a rather sweet, very logical, set of reasons why he was the man for Annie. He knows I have my cynical moments.

'I know you probably think there are too few men to choose from in here, that there is probably someone else better for her. But I honestly believe I am the man for Annie. And I know with all my heart that she is the woman for me,' he said, fingers slightly trembling around the glass of water he was clutching. 'I know she hasn't been Outside since she was a toddler, but she won't and she can't, not now. Not with everything going on, it's too dangerous. We can have a life here, a home of our own, children. A wedding.'

'Toby, slow down,' I said, smiling into his nervous face. 'You already have her heart. Of course you can have her hand.'

His chest, which had been puffed up in a rather endearing imitation of manly authority, sank back to its normal size. The colour returned to his cheeks. And he threw his arms around me.

'I'll make her happy, Sophie. I promise. She is all that I have, and all that I want,' he said. I could see him struggling to contain his emotion and caught myself imagining what he would do if he were less fraught with nerves. I like to think he'd have been dancing stupidly, like a drunken uncle at the end of a family wedding.

But, credit to him, he did what he clearly thought, or had been told, was right to do and "acted like a man". I had to draw the line at the handshake he offered, leaning in instead for a hug – the kind of hug you really mean, tight and close and warm, infused with feeling.

I felt for him, panicking and having to justify his reasons for love. When Mike and I married, we just fell into it. Nobody had any cause to object, nor would they have dared to. Everyone around us was doing it. We had the usual 'you'll be next' comments from tipsy relatives, and eventually it seemed like it just made more sense to marry than not to. We had been living together for years and shared everything anyway, so what was another layer of formality to our commitment? Plus, it was an amazing party. And I wanted us, with the children we had planned, to be a family unit, sharing a name and an identity. But anyway. Back to Toby. This brave, bold young man is rather sweet. His naivety, which would be dangerous on the Outside, no doubt about it, is an asset to him here. He is happy. Truly happy. Florivale gives him all that he needs, and, as he aptly put it, Annie is all that he wants. Through spending time with him, Annie's blossomed as a young woman. His contentment and sheer delight in her has seeped through her skin, a balm for her concerns, her questions. There's a part of me that thinks she should get those questions answered and learn all she could. But with that reward comes an enormous risk. If all they say about Outside is true – if they would ever let her after the latest riots - it would truly break my heart to see her go. I couldn't lose her as well.

Needless to say, she said yes. Although it's her story to tell, and I only know what she told me, given that I'm writing this and she isn't, here's how I think it went.

Toby asked her at the furthest point of the perimeter to which we can go without raising an alarm (or inviting the creepy, unwelcome presence of a Protector). This may not sound very romantic, but Annie and I have long gone to this point to look out over the forbidden water, and wonder. We hold hands and gaze, and send our love to Mike, wherever he is since being taken from us. The tranquillity of the Lake belies the dangers beyond, and hints at the unknown world Outside.

I was waiting for her to come home that afternoon, trying to appear calm and act surprised, whilst simultaneously wanting to squeeze every drop of information from her, hear her innermost thoughts and, frankly, shriek with excitement. Maintaining calm was something of a struggle, so what she actually met when she walked through the door was my 'calm' face, which I know from experience comes across as a stern, disapproving sneer. Not my intention. Little did she know how my feet were tapping away with excitement underneath the sofa cushion, or how sweaty my palms were in anticipation.

Her smile said it all. It spread from the centre of her pink lips to the apples of her cheeks, creasing the corners of her eyes and radiating love. It was a yes. It was a hell yes! As she told me of their engagement, she awkwardly held out her left hand, trying to keep the ring to herself at the same time as showing it off, her token, her signal to the Community of things to come. I suspect she was also trying to assess whether it was sparkling quite right, held at the correct angle.

We don't have much of the ostentatious in Florivale. Jewellery is kept to a minimum. But engagement rings and wedding rings receive an exception. Special treatment. Cynic moment: they are a prompt for the next Gen, something to stir up the betrothed's peers and act as a catalyst for some further matches. But the proud mother in me saw my beautiful daughter, eyes shining, holding out a hand adorned with a symbol of love and a promise of a lifetime united. The ring is simple, but stunning. I must find out how Toby acquired it – whether there is someone in the Community Centre who has been polishing up stones for weeks, in the hope of this very match. Or perhaps, of any match. Either way, it is a slim gold band with a perfect emerald the colour of the flecks in her eyes, nestling between two tiny, brilliant diamonds. Set against Annie's milky skin, the deep green of the stone hints at excitement, of love, of a future. For her, it is perfect.

21

My little Annie is married! I can hardly believe the words, even as I write them. Annie Stone-Hunter. Like the tiger which still prowls the bedroom walls, I hope she wears her new name like an amulet – strength, grace and power. Something deeper, hidden behind her beauty.

The wedding. I can't believe it's been and gone. In the wake of the years of sadness, the constant ache when I think of Mike, I'd forgotten what it felt like to lose yourself in happiness, rapt in the enjoyment of those around you. I needed it.

Of course, there were times when the wedding was the most irritating thing in Florivale. The constant planning and last minute changes, the bickering and sniping among the girls... it was exhausting. But Florivale needed a reboot. And the Stone Hunter wedding delivered. For once, the barriers were let down a little (not the actual barriers of course, there are still germs and problems and riots on the Outside, or so the CompScreens proclaim at every opportunity).

Annie and Toby - although I suspect Annie may have had something of a weighted vote - got to choose their own menu, free of the constraints of nutritional balance. The whole Community had a day off their school and fitness requirements and there was even champagne (real champagne!) for the toasts. The powers that be are really backing this wedding.

'A Florivale wedding is a day for all of us,' proclaimed Carer Stevens, who was assigned the wedding planning. I think she saw this task as the equivalent of an annual bonus! She was effervescent with excitement as she endlessly ran through lists and spreadsheets. I remember my love of planning things from Before and, my God, Stevens puts me to shame.

'The choice of flowers really is crucial, Annie dear,' she explained, as we sat in the lounge at home. 'Without sufficient notice, the planters Outside will be under prepared and you might end up having to use disgusting river reeds as a bouquet!' Cue titters all round from Annie and her girlfriends, who were grinning like idiots.

'But I don't know what kinds of flowers are out there, Miss Stevens,' said Annie. 'How can I tell which flowers to pick when I've never seen the meadow they grow in? I don't remember how they all smell, how they feel. What would you have, Miss Stevens?'

Imagine not knowing the silken inside of a rose petal. It's moments like this (of which there are an increasing number) when I wonder whether we really did the right thing coming in here. And then I think, get a grip: what the hell is a rose petal in exchange for health? Who are we to value transient beauty above life and vitality? And potentially finding new cures for those who are suffering Outside. It is - has become - our duty.

In the end, soft pink peonies and ivory roses were chosen for their texture, scent and simple beauty, with baby's breath for volume (and, no doubt, a wish from the Community that they would be an omen of future children). Of course, there was more than just flowers to think of. Weeks of planning and pontificating between the tiny details of the day became the focus of our lives. Which colour napkins would they have? How would the Main Hall be dressed? Would anyone from Outside need a video link in? Answer: no, our remaining ties have been cut, or have become so threadbare they blow freely in the breeze. But for me, and for Annie (and, I suppose, Toby), it was the food and the dress that needed the most attention. Nobody gets to choose clothes in here any more. As what we brought in our original suitcases became too small or scuffed, new 'regulation' clothes were brought in through the utility room wash baskets. A punishment for having too much originality dressed up as necessity, regulation attire sneaks into the home and infiltrates the wardrobe.

Annie, which you will know if you ever meet her, has the figure of an angel. Slim and strong from a lifetime of NutriVisor pouches and her FitHub regime, she has a slight waist and toned arms, a gently visible collarbone and a long, elegant neck. Her legs are long and her hips swell out gently from her waist to meet them. That girl could wear beach shorts and a t-shirt and look like she'd stepped out of one of the old fashion magazines. But this dress was no such outfit.

I watched her descend the stairs at her trial session. I was meant to wait for her "big reveal" (no doubt to Stevens' shrill, girlish claps and cheers) in the lounge, but I didn't want to share my first glimpse with anyone else. I lived this moment for Mike, as well as for myself. Layers of soft ivory tulle fell from each step to the one below as she walked, tentatively watching the steps in terror of a fall. She's always been clumsy. Above each layer seemed to be another, tumbling from the bodice of the gown, connected to it by a band of gleaming beads. Above the band, slim pleats covered a simple, stunning bodice, following the curve of her waist up towards her bust. And above the sweetheart neckline was Annie's radiant beauty. Love glowed from her like sunshine. This was the dress.

But let's fast-forward from that moment a few weeks ago, to the wedding. The whole of Florivale attended, residents, Carers, NutriVisors... you name it. Even the ones Annie and Toby don't much like, and of course the few other couples from their Gen who have married – no doubt comparing everything to their big day, wondering whether peonies had the edge over freesias, and whether it all really mattered in the end.

Over our NutriVisor pouches of breakfast (the free eating did not start until after the marriage, at the wedding banquet) we laughed and chatted as I tried to calm her nerves.

'But what about tonight, Mum,' she asked,

sleepy eyes gazing wide. 'What will it be like? What if he doesn't like me, like that?' Oh God, I thought. Here we go. 'What if I don't like it?'

I still find it hard to believe she was still a virgin. Sexual relationships are not technically forbidden for the unmarried of the Community, but there is a strong rhetoric throughout most of their Health and Social classes to champion the virginal, the art of abstinence. And strangely, they buy it. It's almost Victorian. That said, there's something comforting about the knowledge they aren't throwing it all away, experimenting and risking their health. Particularly with all the sexually-transmitted illness which ravages the population Outside. They say it's rife now. It's impossible to know how much of the rumours are true, but a healthy Annie is worth a little Victorian restraint, if you ask me. It certainly wouldn't have hurt me to have held back a little at her age!

'Annie, my love,' I said. 'It will be fine. Wonderful, eventually. The first time is not generally the greatest. It will probably hurt a little, and it might hurt a lot. But as your bodies become used to one another, and you both learn what you like, sex will become something you cherish. Something which brings life; a connection which deepens your love.'

'Mum, I feel kind of weird even talking to you about it, but in Health, everything about it is always so mechanical. Put this in there, move it about a bit, wait a while and then comes the baby. What if I don't want a baby straight away? What if we want to wait a while?' She looked terrified, poor thing.

'I know there are tests,' I said. 'Of course, for the Community to grow, we need the next Gen. But nature has a tricky way about her, which you may be able to use to your advantage for a while. Although not for too long. You don't want to be subjected to endless questions or fertility tests.' I sat further back in my chair, preparing myself for more of the birds and the bees stuff – trust me – that never ceases to be awkward between a parent and child.

'If you wait until the last moment, or ideally a few moments before, assuming Toby can control himself, that is,' I paused when she winced at this, but I went on – this conversation was no fun for either of us but it all had to be said. 'If he can pull out just before he finishes, you might be able to buy yourselves a few months, and put it down to teething problems. But it won't work for long. You know they will be monitoring you both. All of your tests so far have shown excellent conception probability.'

Annie flushed as I spoke, but even if all I can give her is an explanation of an unreliable Victorian withdrawal technique, I'd like to buy her some time alone with Toby. She can't imagine how much things change when there is a child. Everything changes.

'Thanks Mum,' she said, turning up her button nose. 'It sounds gross. Like animals.'

'You have no idea how like animals humans can be, sweetheart. Disgusting, magnificent, cruel, breath-taking. Everything in this world is connected somehow, even though it seems like it is only us and Outside.' I sounded pretty good, even if I do say so myself.

'Well, I don't want to be like an animal.

Especially not today. I want to look like a princess. Which is just as well, because I don't know if you remember, but I look bloody amazing in my dress! Let's go and get ready!' she exclaimed.

That morning, we had a special treat – make-up was brought in from the Outside for Annie especially, sanitised and brand new. One of the Carers who had recently transferred into Florivale turned up at the door with an uncharacteristic grin (she was new, after all) and applied it, transforming my pretty Annie into a walking, breathing work of art. Soft kohl liner surrounded her hazel eyes, the deep green drawing out the flecks in her irises so they glinted like moss-covered stones at the bottom of a river. Her cheeks were lifted with a hint of peach blush, warming her natural flush and complimenting the creamy softness of her face. Her lips were left natural, a gentle gloss being all that was required to finish the look. I remember when people used to hunt for lipsticks to achieve Annie's natural shade – 'your lips but better,' the magazines used to call it. Well, Annie couldn't be made much better.

With her make-up finished, the Carer left to help with the other preparations. I worked on Annie's hair, gently braiding the top section so that the bottom remained hanging loosely, a waterfall of soft brown hair with gently glistening golden tips and highlights from her time in the sun. Into this braided crown I slid tiny rosebuds and pieces of baby's breath to match the bouquet. What looked back at me was a fairy queen, straight from the pages of A Midsummer Night's Dream. She couldn't stop stealing glances in the mirror when she thought I wasn't looking. She knew she looked beautiful. I wouldn't have had her feel any other way.

We had a moment together, nothing left to do but for Annie to step into the dress, me to do up the pearly buttons along the back, and for us to leave for the Community Centre.

There are no religious ceremonies in Florivale – as everyone is required to attend every wedding, and the key message is procreation (seemingly at any cost), a decision was made years ago to hold only secular weddings. At the same time as this announcement, which was met with sadness by many of the families here, was the declaration that all weddings would be co-ordinated by a Carer and would be 'free days' for the Community – with the bride and groom having a choice of outfits, wedding menus and free reign to decorate and theme the Community Centre. As you can imagine, that softened the blow. The break with routine eventually became all that the younger Gens focused on. And, as it was them getting married, any religious parents had to keep their mouths shut and resolve to say their prayers privately. This suited me and Mike of course, never having been believers. One of the few things about which we saw eye to eye with the 'powers that be'.

The ceremony was succinct, with the usual Florivale promises in place of the vows of Before. Promises to stay connected, to maintain the teachings and ways of Florivale in their new home. Yes, that's another perk of getting married here, the young couple automatically receives a small house to start their married lives in – complete with furnished nursery, to hammer the point home a little more. Annie and Toby held hands throughout and she beamed as she pulled a peony from her bouquet at the end of the ceremony, to be pressed for their family book.

They begin their chapter as the Stone-Hunters.

I caught the eye of poor Jeannie and had to look away. I'm such a coward. I feel so sorry for her. She is forbidden from marriage because she can't bear children. Her tests became progressively worse throughout her adolescence and she now faces a lifetime as everyone's best friend, but nobody's partner. Nobody's 'other half'. All because Florivale needs virile men to match with fertile women. It breaks my heart. And I thank God (or whoever may be watching over us, if anyone at all) that this will not be the fate of Annie, Ella or Bertie. I couldn't bear it, and I know Mike would have been distraught at the idea of one of his children never finding love. Love is – was - so important to him. It still is to me. And I still love him, even though he is gone.

But, the wedding. Well, every good wedding needs a good party, doesn't it? And we definitely had one of those. My ankle is still swollen from toppling over during the dancing! And the food was magnificent. Again, I felt sorry for Annie and Toby, having to select options from menus and recipe books without ever having tried the real thing, only NutriVisor pouches of nutritionally balanced imitations. But they made excellent choices. Starters of crisp butter pastry filled with rich, creamy goats' cheese and caramelised red onions. During our wedding season in our late twenties (one year there were ten weddings to attend, between April and September... ridiculous), I remember telling Mike that if I had to suffer another of those tartlets I would throw myself off Tower Bridge. But after over fifteen years, bloody hell it tasted good. The main course (vegetarian again, unfortunately – that's a Stone family Condition which cannot be negotiated, purportedly for fear that we could no longer digest it, but I imagine it is more in the Carers' research interests than out of concern for our colons) was a stack of char-grilled roasted peppers, aubergine, Portobello mushrooms and courgette strips, layered with grilled halloumi and dressed with a piquant, yet sweet, warm lemon vinaigrette. This sat atop a mound of softly steamed cous cous, speckled with toasted pine nuts and succulent sultanas, with peppery rocket leaves bursting from the bottom of the dish towards the edge of the plate.

It was utterly delicious, to have all of those forgotten textures once again. No wonder everyone gets so excited about a Florivale wedding. For dessert, we had wedding cake, a sugary concoction decorated with hand-made sugar orchids tumbling down the layers of softly shimmering white icing. Maintaining one of the traditions of Before, the top layer was a dense, no doubt rather disgusting, fruit cake, to be kept for the celebration of their firstborn. The two layers below were Genoese sponge with a buttercream and raspberry jam filling, utterly delicious - all the more so for being devoid of any nutritional benefit.

Once we'd moved on from the food... and let the three (!) small glasses of wine go to our heads, we had the speeches – classically Florivale in their brevity, references to furthering the Community etc.

There was the usual speech from one of the high-ranking Carers, which is mandatory and generally mind-numbingly dull. But this one sparked an interest in me. This man was different. As he stood at the front of the Community Centre, he brushed back his dark hair, revealing thin grey streaks above his ears. I've seen him in Florivale before, usually armed with a clipboard and various flunkies flapping around him. Today, he stood alone, his Protectors lingering at either side of the stage, trying to look casual. Which is not easy when you're carrying a large gun and flanked by visibly armed Protectors. The Carer cleared his voice.

'We in Florivale don't have many occasions to gather with no common purpose other than enjoyment,' he started. He clutched his notes in an uncharacteristically nervous way, as if he was expecting to be heckled. Heckling, in Florivale? Hell would freeze over first!

'Today is a day for enjoyment. A day for laughter and happiness. But also a day to reflect on our luck in life, our health and our success as a Community. Our strength is in our acceptance of the facts, our acquiescence to do what is right for the greater good. That acquiescence brings happiness. I, and all of us Carers, know that there are difficult questions you must think about, perhaps whilst doing your daily fitness, or dark thoughts that creep up on you in the night and disturb your dreams. But there are some questions which cannot, and should not, be answered. Some things are better left for others to question, to worry about.'

'Whilst we, and the Protectors, do our best to allay any fears you may have, to protect and serve you in this tranquil place, it has come to the Committee's attention that certain rumours have started to spread. Today, it seems fitting to address these rumours while we are gathered and our hearts are light.'

'Outside, life is falling apart. Disease is rife, the Physicals are taking over. What you may have heard in that regard is true. And without health, what are we? How can the mind function without the body's support? And in the same vein, how can a Community survive when parts of it rebel, pull away, cease to do their duty. Just as a cancer kills the body from within, the people of Outside are being attacked by their own kind, mutating into something ugly, something deadly.'

'It is with this threat in mind that I speak to you today,' he continued, his voice rallying where it had previously been weak. 'We in Florivale are the last bastion of hope for a cure. For salvation. Outside may pull itself apart, but we are the antidote. It is more important than ever before to find the solutions we seek.'

The gathered crowd varied from awestruck – we so rarely receive news about Outside - to, if I'm honest, slightly pissed. Three glasses of wine after all this good behaviour was quite something. That one of our Conditions is for every Stone over sixteen years old to drink a small glass of red wine with dinner every evening is something I am eternally grateful for. God bless antioxidants. Anyway. Back to the speech.

'We are the cure. You are all the cure. No matter what news comes from Outside, remember that. Try to resist the temptation to think of yourselves as anything less than the saviours of humanity. People may try to tell you otherwise, the thoughts that plague your quietest moments may invite you to think life here is futile. But it is not. We are the cure.' He paused, breathing in the mood of the room. 'And, for this reason, all visits to and from Outside are now strictly forbidden until further notice. For no reason other than the sheer value of your safety.'

The growing mutterings among the crowd were instantly quietened by the stepping forward of his Protectors, and the lifting of their fingers to the triggers on their firearms.

'So let us spare a moment to reflect on the future ahead of young Annie and Toby,' continued the Carer. 'One of the first second Gen couples to marry in Florivale, so happy on their special day. Surrounded by those who love them and free of chores or duties, the Stone-Hunters have chosen to embrace their lives together in Florivale, to start another bloodline in this wonderful Community. Regardless of matters Outside, Annie and Toby have everything they need here. We all have everything we need.' He raised a glass and cleared his throat again. 'Everyone, please join me in a toast to bestow every fortune on the new Mr and Mrs Stone-Hunter of Florivale, to wish them many healthy children together. We. Are. The. Cure.'

Startled, we all replied with a baffled chant of 'we are the cure,' where we knew it should have been 'to the Bride and Groom,' or at least something reminiscent of a wedding from Before.

But that is what shock does. It forces an unnatural response. Sometimes fight. Sometimes flight. Sometimes blind obedience. The latter being the most insidious and dangerous of all three.

22

First of all, let me just say how disgusting it was to read about my Grandma giving my mum sex tips.

OK, so all bodily functions in Florivale are up for discussion, procreation definitely among them, but it's so animal. So basic. And where it's about your mum, who had sex with your dad, to create you… well, it's a revolting idea. That said, obviously I'm glad they eventually did it (only twice to produce me and then Jack) and that I was born. Because it seems like everyone else in here is half asleep and they need someone to shake them awake!

That speech! How have I never heard about it? That there seemed to be people on the Outside who were reaching in, contacting residents within our safe haven - trying to upset our "unnatural order" of things? Why did this never come up? The wedding gets talked about all the time – all Florivale weddings do (what did they eat? Was there dancing? How was it all decorated? How would you have yours? How would you even start to pick what to eat!?). But conversation was always in terms of the fripperies, the finishing touches and the couple's profound love for one another. Nobody mentioned the speech. The threat. The concern. Were they all drunk? Drugged? Or simply too stupid or docile to look past the immediate and see the truth: that things in their perfect world were imperfect. That they hadn't succeeded in shutting out everything and everyone on the other side.

In the evening, after reading the note about the wedding speech, I went downstairs to eat with Mum and Dad and Jack. Same old story – four NutriVisor pouches in the PrepPod together, timed to be simultaneously piping hot and suitably sterile, allowing us to eat together at the small table. We never use the big dining table Grandma Sophie was so adamant about having. There is no call for it. Four pouches, four minutes, four people. How reductionist. Perfectly balanced and nourishing meals which never satiate your hunger, never satisfy a craving. No salt to be seen. Grandma Sophie always said she missed salt the most. I have no idea how good it must have been for her to like it so much. But apparently almost everyone Outside liked it, too much, and their bodies didn't. So out it went. Off the menu. Chewing on my steamed kale, pouch-fresh, I decided to take the plunge. And what better scapegoat for my bringing up the topic than 'elegant' Melanie. Perfect Melanie. I'm sure a daughter like her would have made my parents' lives significantly easier.

'So,' I started. 'Everyone's talking about who Melanie will marry – I mean, everyone except for me because I don't care. Unless she marries Josh, in which case I'll never be able to stand being around him any more. Anyway, it made me think, I never heard much about your wedding. Just how lovely it was - so far, so boring. How was the day for you? What was it really like?' There was a pause, and Dad reached for Mum's hand like a teenager going through the complex courting rituals in some old film. Who needs courting now, when the Community can just match you up with another fertile Florivite?

'Vic-a-nic!' exclaimed Mum, suddenly animated as though someone had wound up, a clockwork doll for Florivale. 'What a funny way to phrase it. But we'd be happy to tell you more. We can show you some images too – there are hundreds more in the Community Centre, with the video and everything. No Florivale wedding goes undocumented! Oh my, I don't suppose you've even thought about what you might have – such a little tomboy. We can get you plenty of ideas!'

I wanted to vomit at the idea of my own wedding. And no. I hadn't mentioned my awful nickname. I count myself lucky that they've abbreviated it from 'Vic-a-nic-a-noodle,' although occasionally 'Noodle' slips out. Mortifying. Anyway, thankfully Dad cut in on Mum's reverie.

'Yes honey, we all ought to have a look, remind ourselves of that happy day. I can still see your mother as she entered the room, those rosy lips and her shimmering hair. A goddess. My goddess.'

'Oh Toby, stop. You're making a fool of me,' she blushed. 'But I did like getting to wear the make-up. And the dress. And that food – oh – sublime! What did we have again? That was another problem. All the wine! We were one of the first couples in our Gen to tie the knot, and definitely the happiest. So I suppose perhaps a little too much wine was consumed all round. It's a wonder anyone Outside ever remembered their weddings, the stories we heard from the Pioneers about how drunk they used to get!'

'But what about the ceremony and the speeches?' I cut in, trying not to gag when I remembered what Grandma had written about the wedding night. 'Surely there was more to the day than material things and food and excess? What was said? Who was there?'

I was met with a stilted pause, a joint intake of breath from my parents. Like when you have déja-vu and it takes your brain a moment or two to re-set.

'Speeches, Victoria? Why on earth would you want to know about the speeches?' said Dad. 'Just a bunch of old windbags talking about how great we are, usual wishes for health and children etc. All very formulaic.'

'Yes. Formulaic,' added Mum, her warmth gone. Just the run of the mill Florivale spiel. 'Now eat your food. I don't want it to go cold.'

'All the same, Mum, even if it is spiel, I'd like to know what they said.'

It was all I could do to maintain a cool exterior and prevent my fork from shaking in my hand with anger at their unwillingness to question anything, complicit in the lies by failing to probe any detail which struck them as unusual. Why wouldn't they tell me anything? I decided to use an emotional lever to try and pry more from them.

'With Grandpa Mike gone by the time of your wedding, I just wanted to know how he was made to be part of the day,' I said. 'I don't like the idea that he just disappeared because he died. I never knew him and I wish I had. The stories about him make him sound so rebellious, so funny.'

The room cooled a degree while Mum looked at the floor and Dad slowly inhaled.

'Vic-a-nic. You know your mother doesn't like talking about your Grandpa not being around. You know how it upsets her,' said Dad, suddenly stern.

'But that doesn't mean it's not worth taking about,' I replied. Just because something hurts doesn't mean you shouldn't acknowledge it. Just because you feel wrong doesn't mean you can ignore it and somehow be right. Emotions aren't tumours Dad, you can't cut them out.'

My voice was raised and I'd given up on dinner. The amber light on my BioBand was starting to flash to show my increased heart rate. I'm not even allowed to be angry!

'Vic. We aren't going to discuss this. Your Grandpa was a wonderful man. The wedding was lovely. That is all.' A hard edge came into his otherwise soft and relaxed voice. He sat straighter. Like something from a nature documentary about instilling obedience among your pack. As he spoke, Mum put her knife and fork to her plate and complained of a headache, said she was going to bed early to read.

'Well done, brains,' teased Jack. 'Great job pissing Mum and Dad off.'

He narrowly dodged a swipe to the ear for swearing from Dad. I'd lost my appetite but stayed out of stubbornness, not wanting to accept or admit that I'd caused the row, from something so innocuous. Jack didn't care. He was impervious to all this stuff. Happy little moron, like I said. Maybe everyone's like that at his age. It's exhausting.

Once I was in the relative sanctuary of my bedroom, hot, frustrated tears streamed down my face and onto my anti-microbial, hypoallergenic pillowcase. Surely my parents must know that sharing the story is more important than keeping the secret. Perhaps it's just been so long for them that they've forgotten what it's like to question anything. But they must know, deep down, that something wasn't, and isn't, right. That must be why they don't want to talk about it, don't want to admit any of the niggling doubts they've harboured for so long. Because how could a speech like that get forgotten, be left undiscussed?

I went through the motions of getting myself ready for sleep, knowing it was hours away from me. Brushing my teeth for the prescribed 3.5 minutes at the correct pressure (the lilac light on the toothbrush means you have a good brushing technique), staring at my reflection and wondering if the flecks in my pupils were in fact flecks of madness, rebellion, "otherness". How could everyone else in here live like this?

I stepped into the shower tray and selected 'relax' mode. Soft steam clouds scented with peony and vanilla billowed through the jets of water as I stretched my arms above my head and shut my eyes. I let the warm water run over me, trying to visualise it sweeping away my thoughts, like Clem tried to teach me. But every time I got to thinking, maybe it's worked, maybe I've nailed it, whatever was stressing me out came lurking back from the recesses of my mind and planted itself on my shoulders, sinking its roots into my chest. Perhaps I can't be taught to be mindful. The phrases from that speech simply can't be washed away: 'no matter what news comes from Outside,' or 'life is falling apart.' They were said; they had meaning.

I got into bed knowing I wouldn't sleep properly. That blessed relief from the thoughts which coiled themselves up in the corner of my mind like a serpent would not be mine. I've not slept enough since I found the first of the notes, but it's been on the borderline of sufficiency to escape having to go into the IsoPod.

Based in the Health Centre, each one is set up in its own room. They don't tend to be used at capacity because people tend to get enough Quality sleep here. But there are about 12 Pods in total, in a wing of the main building. They're all the same. As you walk through the door, you tap your BioBand to the monitor on the door frame and it calculates what you need in term of sleep 'assistance' and tallies everything up with your records. I try to avoid having to come in here. I've worked on mindfulness techniques and meditation, even tried to visualise Grandma Sophie doing the figure-of-eight thing around my forehead. Most of the time, for me, mindfulness is simply not enough.

The IsoPod itself looks pretty innocent. Sitting by itself in the middle of the room, the large, white, egg-shaped exterior could even seem inviting. Intriguing. To one side is a monitor, so Carers can look at you if necessary. To the other is a control panel covered in symbols and keys. Presumably they are used by the Carers to override the automatic program if anything bespoke were required - although it's almost unthinkable that the all-knowing computer systems wouldn't select the right program. There are a couple of hooks on the walls for coats and a small side table with drawers if you want to put your clothes in there when you put on the standard-issue lilac IsoPod pyjamas. I think that's to accentuate the lavender scent of the IsoPod. The pyjamas comprise some unflattering but, admittedly, extremely comfortable trousers and a loose T-shirt, like the Carers wear – although of course without the Carers' identification badges or pockets.

I undressed, taking my time to carefully fold my clothes and place them in the drawer, anything to delay the inevitable. Pulling on the pyjamas, I got the first waft of lavender. My jaw clamped together. My shoulders stiffened. How can something which makes me feel so anxious be used to put me to sleep? I sat into the open hatch of the Isopod and folded myself in, pulling the hatch of the door closed behind me with a softened, but sickening click. The BioBand had done its job and the disembodied voice of the IsoPod welcomed me by name.

'Good evening, Victoria. Welcome to your IsoPod. Together, we will make sure you get the three Quality hours of sleep you need to satisfy your quota. Did you know that, at present, you specifically need 7.2 hours of sleep in any 24-hour period to function correctly? Your cells need sleep to repair and function. Sleep makes you healthy. Enjoy your Quality sleep, Victoria.'

There are many people who enjoy IsoPod sessions. I am not among them. From the patronising voice updating me on the sleep I need but don't have, through the rigid formality of it all, to the cloying scent of lavender that haunts me, there is nothing good in this process. Once the voice had shut up, the next phase began.

When you're sealed into the IsoPod, there comes an eerie silence, which filters out all external noise. As soon as you have noticed this, the next process begins, with the dimming of the lights from their ambient golden glow, through a deep blue, like the pictures of underwater in the Community Centre (not that I'll ever see that colour for real), into perfect darkness. So dark that there is no colour to describe it. Clouds of synthetic lavender-scented chemicals begin to billow in from the vents around the inside of the IsoPod. They leave a subtle, but piercing afterburn in your nostrils. I tried to hold my breath once, but ended up gasping for air, swallowing lungfuls of the fumes as chemically-induced sleep took over. I've learnt since that time to calm myself, as much as possible, before the dreams set in. For there can be no tranquil dreams in an un-tranquil mind.

It's disorienting, confusing. Nobody else seems to feel like this, not even Clem. Most of them actually enjoy the experience, and I have no idea what is wrong with me, to make this such torture. Clem loves it. She tells me I should live for the moment and enjoy every sensation, revel in the deep sleep.

The first thing to go is always my toes. I feel them get heavy, like they're warm and swollen. My fingers start to feel the same pretty soon afterwards and the golden, heavy glow begins to spread up through my hands and feet and along my arms and legs, into my core. It's quite pleasant until that point. But as soon as it reaches my hips, my shoulders, that gentle heaviness seems to transform into chains, strapping me down against the base of the IsoPod, pressing my back into the mattress, pushing, always pushing down. I try to lift an arm, and find I can't, powerless. Panic sets in and I'm certain my heart rate increases – I can hear it pounding between my ears, but the BioBand doesn't monitor any change. The sedation is total.

I endured my last IsoPod session only by reminding myself it was only for three hours. I've trained my brain to the point that I can accept the pressure of the chains I feel around my chest, and that I will eventually be released. I calm my breathing, knowing that, on the outside, my body is already calm. Already showing all the signs of peaceful sleep.

'Victoria, congratulations on three hours of Quality sleep!' came the voice, cheery as ever. 'You have met your quota. Did you know that every animal on earth needs sleep to survive? Imagine that. Sleep is so important. Congratulations again.' I wanted to strangle that machine. Short-circuit it. Anything.

With the end of the statement came the gradual lightening of the IsoPod. Through shades of soft green into a bright yellow to the soundtrack of twittering birds, no doubt intended to remind us of crisp spring mornings, the last of the chemicals wisped away into the vents and the hatch eventually, finally, opened.

I couldn't help it, I thrust my head

through the hatch, desperately drinking in the freshness of the Health Centre air. Three hours of forced relaxation. Willing myself to accept the state I was in. Every time, I wonder how the monitors fail to light up and scream 'CODE RED' as soon as my mind takes over in the wake of my body's submission to the fumes. But yet, it never happens. Clem never feels like this. She loves the IsoPod, but she almost always gets enough sleep so she doesn't even need it. Ironic, huh?

As I stepped down from the IsoPod, the contrast of my warm feet against the cool tiles snapped me back into reality, grounding my thoughts and calming my pacing heart. I silently thanked the designers of Florivale for the cold tiles. Immediately stepping away from the IsoPod, casting off its shackles, I pulled my arms back through the pyjama top and wriggled free of the trousers. I left them where they fell on the floor. They'll be sanitised anyway. The cool air on my skin was a relief, and I slowly pulled on my clothes before tapping my BioBand on the wall to open the door, moving out of the room, down the corridor and out into the open air.

It was early evening by this time, and I went straight to lie on the grass in the Field. Melanie and some of her usual posse were there, no doubt discussing Melanie's wedding plans (for some poor, unsuspecting groom), or moaning about their Conditions. Melanie's family gets a pet. Hardly a Condition. Some people get all the luck. They currently have a sleek black cat called Spirit, 'to remind them of the spirit of humanity' and their 'purpose in finding a cure'. It truly is sick-making. Luckily,

Spirit has some ideas of her own, and I enjoy throwing her a sideways glance whenever I see her away from Melanie's house, silently apologising for the hideous life she must have to endure. The group of girls sidles over, giggling nonchalantly at some inanity of Melanie's.

'Hey, Rabbit Girl'. Great start. Such comedic prowess! 'What's up? Don't you get enough plants in your life? Aren't you happy enough eating everything that grows in the ground that you have to lie on it too?'

'Eugh,' piped up an accomplice, Sara. 'Maybe she's working on becoming part of the field? She'd have so many more friends if she was a blade of grass!'

Cue much giggling. That insult didn't even make sense! But I still wanted to hit them. Not that I've ever punched anyone. Physical abuse is not permitted in here, although of course 'playful banter' like this is absolutely fine. Especially if you happen to be Ms. Perfect.

'Guys,' said Melanie. 'Drop it. Let Sick Vic lie on the grass if she wants.' She paused, smiling sweetly in case anyone missed how magnanimous she was about to be. 'Hey Vic. Don't forget to think about what you might get to eat at my wedding. I bet you can't wait to hear all about it. Be nice to liven up you and Clem's dreary little lives. We want you to be happy. You know, you're always welcome to join in with us.'

Like hell I was. Ever since we were toddlers, it has been clear to all concerned that Melanie and I were not destined to get along. For her soft blonde curls, I have straight brown hair. My flecked eyes are too messy compared to her ice-blue glare. Where she has a lilting voice and sycophantic ways, I call it like I see it, earning me the epithet of 'disrespectful'. I just think I'm a realist. I couldn't take any more of this pretend kindness. Daily mockery forms the building blocks for deep cruelty.

'Ladies,' I began. 'I'm sure each of your weddings will surpass the last. You will be the centre of attention, finally. For one short day. Then you can all move on and realise there is nothing to your dreary little lives.' They looked at one another, aghast that their own wedding day might be superseded. I carried on. 'You're so vapid. You have no souls.'

I got up from the grass, immediately regretting what I'd said. Not because I hadn't meant it – I had. The bigger issue was that there would follow be a long admonishment and a reminder of the importance of harmony within the Community to ensure the cure is found and reinforce our purpose in Florivale. So predictable. I walked back home, fists clenched in anger at both them and at myself, for rising to them. I crept through the house, not wanting to speak to anyone and lay on my bed, trying to imagine Outside and seeing nothing, clouded by my rage. Surely this had undone any benefit of my so-called Quality sleep?

I realised, once again: this place is not real. This life is not real. Everyone must know that, but they just follow the rules. I couldn't cope much longer. As I lay in my room, trying to unfurl the knot of frustration in my belly, I knew the only person who would really understand me had gone. Grandma Sophie, whose notes are the only connection I have to reality, to Outside. Perhaps there is an After for

me, out there. Because I cannot see out my days
here.

23

I've hidden what I wrote about the wedding. I'm so sorry to whoever might never be reading this, but I almost hope it is never found. Then again, part of me knows I would have burnt it, drowned it in the Lake, kept it somehow hidden if I truly didn't want there to be even the tiniest chance someone would find it. I may very well be losing my mind.

So, the wedding. Rest assured, it was a wonderful day, beautiful Annie, flowers and food, handsome and happy Toby, much dancing and merriment by all. The speeches were a little odd. Who needs details?

I wonder whether I should have done any of this. Writing things down. Coming in here in the first place. Bringing the kids - not that we had an option of leaving them behind! Not fighting more for Mike. Not talking to him more in the last few weeks. I miss him so much, the only person to whom I could pour out my thoughts and thereby remove them from rattling about in my skull.

It gets so full, my mind, a fountain overflowing with no sign of the water running out. That's another thing; thinking too much. Maybe that's it. Overthinking. What are we here for? What is happening Outside? In fact, is anything happening Outside? And what happened to that Protector? For one who seemed so important, and made such a startling speech, why has he not maintained contact with us, a figurehead to lead Florivale?

Are we the cure?

Too many questions. They seem to be all I have these days. It's all going to be fine. Outside is fine. In here is fine. All will be well. It simply has to work out.

24

She was scared and confused, forced into accepting things. But I knew from all her other notes that she was strong and powerful. She had been a force of nature! So how did she let herself be beaten down, to succumb to Florivale? Was everything that bad Before that she felt she had no choice? Hearing about people suffering, Physicals ravaging the population, with no access to medical care, just sounds too awful to be real – I can't imagine a society where health was not a priority, a right. But I'm a product of Florivale, a third Gen. Born and bred into my set of Conditions and monitored every day. Of course I'd think like that.

I knew I wouldn't get enough Quality sleep that night. I went to bed watching the tiny lights flicker on my BioBand and tried not to think about the IsoPod session that I'd be forced to endure for the infraction of being too stressed to sleep.

The next morning I woke to the usual squawks from Jack, swooping around the house looking for attention. Groggy and frustrated at my inability to control my sleep patterns, I shambled downstairs and had my NutriVisor pouch for breakfast, some sort of scrambled egg with mushrooms and peppers in. OK, like always. Nothing special. Medically precise, nutritionally balanced. Boring. Mum and Dad came in from the lounge as they heard the scrape of my chair legs coming up to the table.

'Vic-a-nic. I'm sorry I went off at you yesterday,' said Dad as he walked towards me, smiling cautiously. 'But you can't upset your mother like that. It's hard for all of us, but dragging up the past won't help. You look exhausted and I'll bet you get an alert this morning requiring you to have another IsoPod session today. It's not normal to need so much sleep support.' His tone softened further. 'We're worried about you. Please try to remember the good stuff about your grandparents, but forget the bad, the sad, difficult stuff. Be happy. It's what they would have wanted.' Dad's face looked worn, his skin looking like old leather in place of his usual sunny disposition. I figured he'd also be spending some time in the IsoPod today.

'I get it, Dad. But I want answers. I sometimes feel like I'm a character in a play. Living out something someone else has destined for me – and the shroud that covers everything about Before only makes it worse.' I had to breathe the way Clem taught me to calm myself before continuing. 'Haven't you ever wanted to know more about Outside? Or Before? Knowing about your wedding would have made me feel something of a connection to this place. I feel… adrift.'

'Vic, don't say that. You're not adrift. Florivale is your anchor. We are safe here. We don't need the details of the dangers Outside – they will only harm you. Why question a system which works so fluidly? Look at you - physically perfect, health at optimum levels, safe and surrounded by your friends. Look at Clem, and Josh. You have so much to love here. Why dwell on the things you can't change? We are all part of something beautiful. Salvation.'

'OK Dad. I'll drop it,' I said. But you saying things are fine doesn't simply make it so.' I kept the level of my voice flat, consistent. My calm breathing regulated my heart rate so a flash on my BioBand wouldn't give away my inner state. But I was furious. He was as blind of the rest of them.

'I need to go to the Community Centre,' I continued. 'I have to meet Clem and Josh today anyway. I guess maybe I need a distraction.'

'Thanks honey. Maybe you do. Remember, you are our treasure, and we love you. Nothing we do is with anything but your wellbeing in mind. You represent the future.' Dad patted me on the shoulder as he went to get a glass of water.

A future in a cage, I thought. Thanks Dad.

I headed over to the Community Centre, but I wasn't meeting anyone – at least, not if it went to plan. I wanted to go through the wedding archives, search for some links to that speech. Or through the general records for something that looked like the puppets on the stage I saw on the TeleCast. There were just too many threads unfurled, too few answers. And I was sick of it.

Arriving at the Community Centre, I swiped my Fit Band for access – which, in itself, is bizarre in a zero-crime, closed Community. When you think about it, which nobody else ever seems to do. Through the main entrance, with its typical white and chrome décor and over to the right, I took the corridor to the Records Office. We used to have to come here for EduCentre projects, to learn about the history of the Physicals, just enough snippets of information to scare us senseless. We also got some time in the Library for recreational learning, with the tiny kids reading books about kittens with furry tails and me reading anything I could get my hands on.

The Records Office is pretty standard-issue Florivale, as rooms go. A few white chairs dotted about and some overhead lighting to imitate natural daylight. A bank of CompStreams takes up the right hand wall, with a chair in front of each. There was nobody in here but me. I swiped my BioBand to log into the CompStream nearest the archive racks at the back of the room.

The racks take up the whole back wall, each about two feet wide, with two handles at the end of each rack. As you crank the handles round clockwise, the volumes inside rotate, so you can access years' worth of data without having to endlessly walk up and down the shelves. It's pretty cool, actually, especially in Florivale where data is king, where everything we can have available electronically is distributed through the millions of cables and airwaves that penetrate the Community. I like having something tangible in my hand, feeling a dossier of papers about something, even something insignificant. As insignificant as a transcript of a wedding speech, perhaps. For no Carer would have freestyled a speech. Not in Florivale.

I started my search with the CompStream,

tapping in WEDDING & FLORIVALE & STONE & HUNTER. The results started to scroll down my screen. Links to electronic scans and copies of everything you could imagine about my parents' wedding. The menu choices, the dress, the make-up. The name of the Carers involved in planning and overseeing the day, my parents' medical match data (high probability of childbearing: match approved). To the right of each link was an identifier you could use to find the right file from the racks. For most of them, I'd need to pull out dossier W-SH-354. But, scrolling through the list, a couple were greyed out, so you couldn't click into the link. To the right of those entries was simply 'N/A'.

Someone had recorded those documents, so they had existed. They had clearly once been available electronically. And then, just as easily, they'd been obscured. Access denied. These documents were 'Appraisal: Protector Ford' 'Success assessment: Stone Hunter Wedding' and 'Budget: Stone Hunter Wedding.' I must have clicked on each of those links thirty times. I tried to open them on the next CompStream, in another tab on my existing screen. But nothing worked. They were simply not there.

With a heavy heart, knowing I was not going to find what I wanted, I headed to the roller racking for section W (Weddings, I guessed). Cranking the handle until SH came up at the top of the small screen at the end of the rack, I switched to the bottom handle. Gently easing it from its starting point at 200, I ticked it round to 354 and walked along the rack to collect the dossier. Like all the others, it was a slim plastic wallet, with clear plastic covers and bound by an elasticated band around the middle. There were thousands of them, each containing data that someone might never read. Everyone uses the electronic versions because it's so much easier. But for me, even a print-out of something electronic feels more real than its original state on screen.

Dossier in hand, I headed back to my desk, so I could spread out the papers. Praying, wishing, that whoever had made the original electronic copies of those documents had omitted to take them out of the file.

But it was the same old story. Pages and pages of procurement information about the menu choices, timings. The level of planning that went into something which needed nothing more than the exchange of vows was unfathomable to me. Although, that said, the food did sound unbelievable. But again, that struck me as crazy. Why would they be so vigilant about our diet, exercise, sleep, vitamin intake, sunlight hours... everything... if only to ruin it all with a day of unparalleled luxury? This place makes no sense.

I checked again, page by page. Looked out for scraps of paper, annotations, anything that might lead me to another avenue to explore. But there was simply nothing there. A void.

I had to try another tack. I couldn't shake the image of that stage from my head, with the little puppets. I know I saw it, whatever my family says. They're probably too busy feeling smug about being the cure to think about anything wider than what meatless delight their next NutriVisor pouch will contain. I went back to the search function on the CompStream and punched in STAGE & PUPPET. I got thousands of results.

'Stage one trials' (Access Restricted). 'Jones Stephens Wedding: Bridal Stage' (W-JS-243). 'Stage in Community Centre: Booking Form' (Archived). This was going to take forever. But, as I ran through the endless lists of file names and locations, I knew something would stand out, something would stick. And there it was.

'Stone, Mike: Stage Request' (REC-MS-98).

Fingers trembling with excitement, I clicked on the link. Nothing happened. This entry wasn't greyed out; there appeared to be a file available. But the system had failed to link it. The systems here never fail. Never.

I glanced behind me, suspicious of being caught looking for this elusive file. Trying to calm myself down, I rationalised that there could be minor problems everywhere, that things break and people screw up. But they don't screw up in Florivale. Not when it comes to records and data. Precious data, leading us to the cure along a trail of breadcrumbs, through the Gens.

Gently easing my chair back, uncharacteristically avoiding making a scraping sound or slamming the feet down as I stood up, I went over to the roller racks for the REC section and started turning the top cog for MS. This must be my grandfather, Mike Stone – his personal section in this sea of information. Slipping my hand down to the lower cog, I rotated it round to 98 and it clicked home, telling me I'd found my folder. I moved down along the racking and found the file. Slimmer than the wedding file, the plastic binder felt hot in my hands, so desperate was I to open it.

Back at my desk, checking again that there was nobody else in there, I slid the elastic closure from the folder and took some deep breaths to calm my nerves. For I'd seen my grandfather's handwriting. I knew it was his, the cursive of his style mirroring mine perfectly. Nobody really writes in Florivale any more. Everything is digitised. But these were his markings on paper. His hand had held the very page that was beneath my fingertips.

The first document was a request form for the stage in the Community Centre. It's only really used for weddings now, or for when there is a formal announcement. But I do remember my Grandma telling me about how they used to put on amateur dramatic productions to fill the time, when the Pioneers arrived and missed their busy, stressful lives Outside. It was seen by the Carers as a valid distraction and welcomed by (most of) the Pioneers. Grandpa had arranged it all. A staging for the Community, over twenty years ago, of As You Like It, by William Shakespeare. Grandma has always loved that story, told me countless times about her role as the witty Rosalind. And there it was, in his careful handwriting, her name at the top of the cast list, next to his. How I wished I could have seen it. Which made me think, perhaps there was a video file somewhere. I'd have to check.

Absorbing every word, voraciously poring over the pages in the file for any clue, I spent an hour and a half looking at those pages. Forms. Approvals. Costume requests. Prop requests. Feedback forms from the audience. Of course, everyone loved it, save for Melanie's grandma Freya, who felt the lead female let the show down. Of course she did. I wondered, not for the first time, whether being a total bitch was a Condition for that family.

Everything I'd found so far was interesting, and I wondered wonder I could revive something like this with Clem and Josh one day, but it wasn't enough. I knew there had to be more. But there was nothing tangible, no more thread to follow.

Frustrated to have hit a wall, confused about the inaccessible files, I was just about ready to give up when my BioBand buzzed. As predicted, I needed a session in the IsoPod. 1.5 hours to be completed by the end of the day. I was making no progress here so, returning the file to the rack, I admitted defeat and headed over to the Health Centre to get this IsoPod session over with.

Following my well-beaten path and selecting an IsoPod room, I pulled off my clothes and stepped into the pyjamas. My mind a blur of Rosalind, Shakespeare, requisitions for props, velvet gowns for the costumes, I gritted my teeth, swung my legs round into the IsoPod, tapped my BioBand and awaited the IsoPod's customary nonsense greeting.

'Good afternoon, Victoria. We hope you're looking forward to 1.5 hours of restful Quality sleep. Did you know that the human mind processes more data asleep than it does when you're watching the CompStream?'

This woman was interminable. Mentally steeling myself to lose control of my body while my mind raged on through its maze of

Shakespeare and paperwork, I felt the golden glow take my toes and succumbed to the lavender fog.

My legs and arms grew heavy, and I willed myself to accept the weight, my inert body permitting the mist to take over where my mind raced on. Calming my breathing, I started a logical checklist of everything I'd seen in the Records Office. My grandfather had organised a play. Check. My Grandmother had played the lead female. So far, so average. Romantic, but nothing-earth shattering. They had worn brocade and velvet gowns, forms had been passed back and forth requesting and denying various equipment. The show had gone on. I realised I didn't know the story of the play, As You Like It. Only the one line. My Grandma's favourite quote, for whatever reason. 'All the world's a stage, and all the men and women merely players.'

It struck me. That was where I'd heard the line before. I had to get a copy of the play. For once, I let the IsoPod take me. I didn't fight this sleep. I had no dreams. Just the stage image from before, and perfect stillness. The words scorched across the CompScreen.

'Congratulations Victoria. One point five hours of Quality Sleep achieved. Enjoy your day, energised and healthy. Well done.' The voice came with the retraction of the fog, and the sickly lavender scent abated with it. My lungs re-filled with our usual conditioned, optimized air, and I was free. I scrambled from the IsoPod and back into my clothes, tossing the pyjamas into the bin on the way out.

Barely acknowledging Clem and Josh

outside the Health Centre – they had just finished up their daily exercise, by the dewy look of Clem's face - I jogged over to the Library, trying not to draw attention to myself, fighting my desperation to get straight there. The room would be inaccessible from dusk, so I only had twenty minutes to get in and find the book. I'd have to try to make a case for home reading, knowing they would want me to read an electronic copy which they could send to my CompStream instantly. But I wanted something tangible, something real. I needed to hold the truth in my hands.

I reached the door and swiped in, using Clem's calm breathing techniques to mask my urgency. I didn't want to draw any more attention to myself than would usually arise from a surly third Gen turning up and demanding to take home a copy of a musty old Shakespeare play. The Carer at the desk gave me a standard-issue Florivale smile and welcome and said she was glad I appreciated the importance of caring for the mind as well as the body. As she prattled on, I looked for an e-index so I could work out which section of the collection I needed. Brushing her aside with some bullshit about wanting to look into potentially staging a play, I moved away as I spoke. I didn't want her help. I was fine. I would have a good day, thank you.

The e-index safely in the palm of my hand, I made my way towards the fiction section, tapping in S-H-A-K-E-S-P-E-A-R-E as I went. There were hundreds of results, and I used a sub-search for A-S Y-O-U L-I-K-E I-T to find my row. Row F, level 5. There it was.

An unassuming EduCentre edition of the play, with the usual foreword and Dramatis Personae at the front. Rosalind's listing had a pencil annotation, tiny, saying 'SS' at the side. That had to have been my Grandma. My heart pounding, I went straight to the desk, looking for the overly-helpful Carer. I hoped she would be naïve enough to fall for my lines about wanting to take the book home.

'I'm afraid that's against protocol, Miss Stone-Hunter. I can arrange for an e-copy to be sent to your CompStream immediately, though? That way, you don't even have to worry about returning it,' she smiled. 'Much better all round.'

'Um, I just really want to read it in print,' I said. 'I need to really see the characters, which I find much easier when they are written physically in front of me. I need to feel them. Do you understand what I mean?' I realized I sounded crazy and I was clutching at straws. But I'd try anything.

'I'm afraid not, Miss. You can only read the hard copy in here and we will be shutting in a few minutes. Perhaps you could come back tomorrow if the hard copy is so important? These books aren't going anywhere!'

She was trying to be helpful. But I still wanted to kick her.

I looked at my shoes, and again at the book. I knew I couldn't take the book without permission. It would be micro-chipped like everything else in this damned place. Right down to its inhabitants.

'I guess I'll have to,' I sighed. 'I'll put the book back on the rack, don't worry.'

My mind racing, panicking about what to

do but accepting that I would be stuck with an electronic copy, I couldn't shift my desperation to have the original book in my hands. Anxiously flicking through it, as though that would quell my excitement, something caught my eye.

Pencil annotations, tiny, an asterisk at the side of a line. And that line was 'all the world's a stage, and all the men and women merely players'. Of course.

The Carer's voice came over the speakers. 'The Library will be shutting in five minutes. Please return your items and vacate the room.'

Bloody hell. I had five minutes to work out where the note was, what that asterisk would lead me to. Because I was certain I wouldn't find the book where I'd left it. Flicking through the pages, words leaping out at me as the sweat stuck my fingers to the porous paper, I eventually found it. About two thirds of the way down a random page of text, faintly slotted in between the lines of text.

'SLEEP LITTLE. TRUST THE ISOPOD. GET OUTSIDE.'

I was sure the Carer would be able to hear my heartbeat, booming around the Library. I nearly dropped the book, fumbling like an idiot in my attempt to slot it back onto the shelf, pushed slightly further back than the other volumes. Hoping nobody would see it. She announced that we were down to three minutes until closing. There was no time to work out any other plan, nowhere to stow it, nothing to be done. I wedged it as far back as I dared without taking so long as to draw attention to myself and slipped back down the aisle so I could emerge from the adjacent row of books.

'Thanks, I guess,' I said. 'Shame I left it so late in the day to come in.' I was trying to smile and keep it casual, light. 'I didn't manage to find the right version, so I'll come back. Maybe then we can sort a CompStream delivery?'

'Yes, Miss Stone-Hunter. That sounds very sensible. I do hope you have a good evening.'

At times like these, I wonder whether all of the Carers have to go through some brainwashing politeness programme. There is nothing exciting about them. How had she failed to pick up on the energy beaming off me, like electricity? It was all I could do to keep my feet on the ground.

I started my trip home, those seven words on repeat. 'Sleep little. Trust the IsoPod. Get Outside.' They were engraving themselves on the inside of my mind. With every step came another question, crowding me. Who would have written that? Could this be some crazy coincidence? What the fuck was going on? What did the IsoPod have to do with it?

It struck me. Had Grandma Sophie somehow known about any of this? Why else would she have always come back to quoting that play? That line?

25

The wedding speech is far from my mind today! Hard to think that was weeks ago. Rain is pouring down outside, almost milky and dingy grey with pollution. The Carers are talking about how to protect ourselves from the rain, but who knows how they'd even start to fix that problem. The window panes are awash with it, smearing our otherwise perfect view of our perfect slice of the world.

But who gives a damn about the rain? There is going to be a BABY!

It transpires that my advice on the withdrawal method was either useless or completely ignored. Annie and Toby are having a baby! A brand new, tiny, perfect little baby Stone-Hunter!

Annie broke the news to me this morning, when she came over for green tea (I do miss coffee). She is about eighteen weeks into her pregnancy – it's forbidden to speak of pregnancy in Florivale until after then, save to one's spouse or the medical team or your assigned Carer, in the interest of preserving morale and public confidence in conception. It's ridiculous that she couldn't tell me, her own mother In fact, I'm stunned that she didn't defy them and tell me anyway. But that's all irrelevant now.

With all the medical advances, they were able to tell immediately that my baby girl is expecting a baby girl of her own! She's known for ages, but I still can't believe it. But believe it I must. And it is wonderful.

Annie took up her usual place on the sofa and clasped her green tea in her hands (weak, the teabag left for only a moment in the hot water – the touches a mother knows instinctively), and gave me a nervous look. Like a child who had been caught smoking at school and had to confess to her parents. Or at least, that's the closest I can imagine to that feeling, from my own experiences. Twitchily, Annie reached to the table and put her mug down. Watching her face behind the steam rising from my own mug, I saw a shift. A glint. She reached down for her stomach, protectively nestling her lower abdomen in her hand. I knew instantly. Before I could even let her speak, tears sprang from my eyes, my heart bursting with excitement.

'Mum, don't cry! I haven't even told you yet!' Annie teased. 'I had it all mapped out, how I'd tell you, the way you'd react, and you're ruining it all!' She rolled her eyes. 'Toby knew you wouldn't let it pan out the way I had in mind!'

'I'm sorry honey,' I laughed. 'It's still the most perfect moment! You couldn't have made it better, no matter what you planned! Who needs a script, a screenplay, when you have news like this?'

I grabbed her and we sat locked in an awkward embrace on the sofa, neither of us wanting to break our pose and end the moment, both of us knowing that time would have to come. I just wanted to stare at her, to marvel at her biology, her brilliance. I knew Toby was a good choice. I knew their marriage was going to be a good one.

If only Mike were here to see this, to share this moment. How could he not know something like this?

Annie and I spent the day talking about medical appointments, dates, scans, names. She and Toby have pencilled in some dreadful ones, but I'm not going to write them down in case (i) I jinx it and something goes wrong or, more honestly, (ii) my granddaughter ever finds out I hate her name! I think in time they may come round and choose something better. Mike and I named ours impulsively on the days they were born, and we never regretted a single choice.

I have spent the whole day in a dream, picturing a tiny hand I my palm, a plump little foot, remembering that magical instant recognition of another being who shares your blood, the next member of the tribe. Instinctive, immediate, overwhelming. Innate.

This evening, I had a short bath (we aren't meant to spend much time in them, but if you claim you have muscular pain, you can weasel your way to an extra fifteen minutes in the warm water), dreaming of cuddling my little grandchild and smiling to myself like a mad woman. Perhaps a hint of madness is what makes us human.

On that note actually, I've heard a couple of concerning things about the Carpenters. Issy Carpenter has been spending far more time in the Health Centre than is usual. I heard at the Community Centre that she has been running over and over the speech from the wedding. That she is convinced of a conspiracy. One day, it's that the Lake isn't real, that it's some kind of hologram. The next, the Lake is full of poison, put there to keep us inside. She claims to have heard something from Outside, and then the next day denies anything and claims she made it up, that she was dreaming.

That speech stayed with all of us. But why would she continue so vehemently if she wasn't convinced of what she was saying? Why would she jeopardise what little freedom she has? Greg Carpenter is beside himself, wants to keep her at home and talk things through with her, but they won't let him. Apparently, she needs the attention of Carers with "expertise in these matters". But she comes back from the Community Centre ashen-faced and looking increasingly gaunt. No matter what efforts are made, her hair still refuses to be smoothed down, she looks like she doesn't quite fit inside her own skin. Uncomfortable. Jumpy. I wondered whether Jeannie might spend some time with her as a companion, although part of me thinks that might be unfair on Jeannie, who has enough sadness of her own. Is a problem shared a problem halved? Or does it just become two problems?

Anyway, I must try to get back to sleep. It's about three in the morning and my sodding sleep monitor is flashing and beeping at me like some sort of tiny dictator. A much less fun dictator than a tiny little baby. Oh, this is a wonderful day!

26

Despite her excitement about my arrival, things were clearly not right in Florivale when Grandma Sophie wrote that last note. Nor are they right now.

I've been avoiding Clem and Josh, ignoring their messages. Clem's read all the notes so far and wants to talk about everything. I see the pleading in her eyes. Josh is depressed because he has a transfusion coming up, and I can't handle the burden of reassuring him that everything will be OK, when we all know that he has pain and suffering ahead, made worse by his belief that something fundamental changes within him with every new batch of blood. I can't deal with him being like that, on top of working out what the hell is going on. What those the seven words mean.

I sat through another 'delightful' family meal, Jack babbling about the girls in his class being sissies, same old crap as usual. Mum and Dad manage to seem interested in all this, so I feigned ambivalence and nodded my way through a NutriVisor pouch meal of quinoa with roasted vegetables in tomato sauce. I made the right noises at the same time, avoided any confrontational topics with my parents and ran over the seven words in my mind.

Trusting the IsoPod: impossible. I could never trust the sensation of losing control, of being forced into a state I despise. As I mulled on it, the reality dawned on me. Being in an IsoPod was no different to being in Florivale, just on a smaller scale. In Florivale, the climate is controlled, the strength of the sun's rays are dampened before they reach my skin, my food is regulated, my toilet activities are monitored, my blood is tested, and my BioBand ensures everything ticks along in perfect biological harmony. This whole place is an IsoPod. And it seems to be only Clem (perhaps), and my grandparents, that get it. Got it, in the case of my grandparents.

After dinner, I made my customary ascent upstairs and took a shower. As the rain and steam (today I went for 'Onsen' steam, a salty, seaside smell which I find relaxing and clean) drenched my hair and ran down my tense muscles, I tried to start processing the information I had available to me.

Something strange had happened at my parents' wedding reception, a shift nobody would talk about since. My Grandma had clearly been stunned and concerned about it and then, as if by magic, my mum immediately got pregnant (despite not wanting to), and my arrival distracted everyone very nicely. More recently, there was the stage image on the screen, so clear to me, and so utterly ignored by everyone but Clem and Josh – and they were reluctant to even speak about it. There's also my memory of the phrase from As You Like It. The way those words led me to the Community Centre, full of unfinished records, incomplete links and missing endings. From there, on to the Library, to the original text my Grandpa had used. And his words. I simply they were his. 'SLEEP LITTLE. TRUST THE ISOPOD. GET OUTSIDE.' Not sleeping was not going to be a problem. My head was spinning.

Jack crashed about on the landing, demanding to be allowed in so he could brush his teeth. The noise bumped me out of my mental fog and out of the shower. Reaching for a soft grey towel, I dried myself and twisted my hair up into a towel turban, the way all girls seem to know innately, and pulled open the door, the cold air that rushed in behind Jack disturbing the clouds of steam.

'Sick Vic, get outta my way!' he screeched, bustling past me to the sink. Yes, the happy little moron still thinks 'sick' is a real insult in Florivale, preserve of the healthy.

I walked round to my room and pulled on my pyjamas, sending a message to Clem and Josh saying I'd see them tomorrow, because I had family stuff to do that evening. What I really had to do was go back through the notes, work my way back from the beginning and look for clues – any explanation. I knew I couldn't ask my parents, judging from their reaction to my question about their wedding. And Jack was simply useless.

I was going to have to figure this all out on my own.

27

Since I last wrote, I have not got any less excited about baby Stone-Hunter. The wodgy legs! The big eyes! Hopefully flecked, like Mike's. But I'll be delighted however she turns out, of course.

But that's not why I chose to write today. These are strange times in Florivale. Perhaps they are even stranger Outside. Who knows? We've been receiving unsettling updates on the TeleCast – it springs into life automatically when the powers that be decide a Bulletin is important enough. Every house has at least two TeleCast sets, so you can't escape by being on the first floor. I was putting my dinner plate into the utility room for sterilisation when it happened.

'Attention residents. Do not be alarmed.' Natural reaction: immediate alarm.

'It has come to our attention that certain residents have been receiving reports about matters Outside the perimeter. Things beyond the Lake are becoming unstable. You are safe. We repeat, you are safe. But you must all be strong and vigilant. Accept the protection we provide, and help us to protect you as effectively as possible.'

'There are those Outside who see your existence

as a threat. Radicalised, they see Florivale as a sign of the decline of humanit. They have no faith in the Community's commitment to improving human health and providing a cure to the Physicals which continue to ravage those Outside. The rebels beyond the Lake are making increased efforts to breach our perimeter.'

'Do not listen to their words of dissent, their lies. You are all the cure. You are essential. The way of life in Florivale is safe, healthy and productive. Whilst it is difficult to visualise matters beyond our Lake, hold in your minds this image.

'Cities crumbling, people trying to escape their overcrowded streets, using whatever means necessary. Physicals decimating families, leaving ghost towns in their wake. Consider the protective urge of a family under threat, and imagine the lengths parents would go to in order to protect their children. That is what we are up against. A brother will report his sister's cough to the authorities to have her screened and, if infectious, quarantined. Or worse.

'All this, to protect what little immune strength and health they still have. Mothers and fathers have transformed into violent machines, desperate to get their children out to the countryside, or worse, into Florivale. As you all know, we cannot accept anyone further from Outside into our Community, our bastion of health. With this in mind, intruders will be shot on sight.'

'My next statement is imperative. Under no circumstances is any resident to engage in contact with any Outsider. Their desperation may lead them to lie, steal and cheat. Be strong and remain a Community. Be resilient. Keep up your daily routines and this shall troubling time pass. Our Leadership is engaged in daily communication with the Government and it is a priority for all stakeholders that Florivale remains sterile, safe and free from Outside influence.'

'Any and all instances of contact from Outside, no matter how tenuous you feel they may be, no matter how much you may doubt whether they are true, each of you must join our efforts to protect Florivale by immediately reporting it to any Carer, the first Carer you come across. Respect the demands of the Carers and Protectors. Everything they do or say is a facet of their job. Their job is to protect and preserve you.'

'Until further notice, the Lake perimeter is strictly out of bounds. Leisure privileges will be suspended for anyone found to be within 50 metres of the perimeter. This is purely for your protection.'

Then came a united chant of voices, almost shouting – accompanied by subtitles to hammer the point home a little harder.

'WE ARE THE CURE. RESIST THE INFECTION OF OUTSIDE. STAND STRONG TOGETHER. 'FOR FLORIVALE, FOR LIFE.'

I'm reeling. What on earth is happening Outside? What about all the friends, family, even our acquaintances - what of London, which I love and despise equally? Is it now some derelict ghetto, some hideous modern twist on a Dickensian slum?

What if Issy Carpenter isn't mad? I haven't seen her in so long. Was it she who raised the alarm among the Carers? Perhaps the hollows of her cheeks were caused by the weight of some fearful knowledge.

This could be some kind of test of our commitment, of our resilience. With so many Conditions in here, it's impossible to know what any change actually means. But something feels sinister. A deep ripple is spreading on the placid surface of Florivale life. I question our decision again. But then, if it really is as bad Outside as they say, what would be left for us? When an opportunity presents itself to you, you just make the decision which makes sense at the time – that's all we did.

Mike would know what to do. He always had a take on these things. For now, I suppose we must wait and watch. And hope.

28

Life continues in Florivale. There are no trips to the Lake. No unwarranted social calls. People are closing in on themselves, families sealing off against others for fear of accusation, or to prevent themselves being watched. We all feel like criminals. And yet, there is no crime here.

I'm glad I still have Ella and Bertie living here – although they're stroppy teenagers, they are my stroppy teenagers. And there is so much of Mike in both of them, it feels like part of him is still here.

All the drama about Outside, the Bulletins, the encouragement to remain calm and continue life as normal (whilst simultaneously being told to remain ever vigilant, watching for anything new or any hint of a threat) is doing nothing to rally the Community. If anything, it's making the Gen below more curious about Before, about Outside. Ella and Bertie can barely remember anything of life in our damp, cripplingly expensive house. But they seem to remember something of the freedom. The odd Sunday morning in our pyjamas, watching trashy films on television all cuddled up, the kids with rumpled hair, Mike and I weary but happy - cocooned with our chattering children.

They want to know why we came here. Whether

it really is better in here. The hardest part is that I simply don't have the answers they want. I tell them in honesty about the daily struggles of life Before. Where we lived. The car journeys. Holidays, jobs, friends. The mortgage. Money!

Money is not a concept the children really understand, which astonishes me, but I suppose is one of the more charming outcomes of our move here – everyone has equal privileges within the Community. There is no hierarchy of wealth. There's no pressure to have a better house, car, or wardrobe than anyone else. Because we are all treated the same. Although, as is human nature, all things are not equal. Not for those who don't live up to expectations. Take Jeannie - or anyone in her position. Sure, she has the same treatment in terms of being given accommodation (although she'll stay with her parents, until they die), food and a place in the Community, but it is clear that she will never be as valuable as a procreating Florivite. It's sickening. But what can be done about it? The cure seems to be the only objective now.

Ella wants to know about the roads. The fact people could get in a car was hard to explain, in a Community where people get around by bicycle or on a two wheeled electric Zipper, speed restricted and ultra-efficient. And ultra-boring. She can't believe we could just get in a fast car and drive, anywhere we wanted. Whichever way we wanted.

For Bertie, the curiosity is mostly about swimming. It's hard for him to believe humans can actually swim – he remembers something of paddling in the sea on holiday when he was tiny. But anything more than that is, to him, a ridiculous risk. His view is that everyone knows water is one of the top inorganic causes of death amongst humans. That to even contemplate spending time in water any deeper than the prescribed depth of a Florivale bath would be madness. It saddens me. He has never swum out into the sea, felt the waves lap at his face as he comes up for breath, or had to make the difficult assessment of the point at which to turn and head back, estimating his capacity to continue. I wish I had given him that experience before he came in here. It would have made the Lake a thing of beauty, rather than the ominous border it now represents to him – as artificial as Florivale itself.

We haven't heard anything substantial on the Bulletins since I last wrote. More caution. Less freedom. The same old story. Stay Strong. You are the cure.

I'd never have thought this would be my life in Florivale. I don't think I really saw past the short-term escape from debt and the longer-term benefits of keeping my family healthy and safe. I think we'd have decided to take our chances on the Outside (for who knows what state it is really in), even if we had known more about what life would be like once we left the reality we knew and came into Florivale, the town we knew only from plans and pictures. Because, over-zealous as the measures taken by the Protectors and the Carers may seem, no stone lies unturned, no perimeter is unmanned, no Florivite is allowed to be at risk.

That is, not at risk from ill-health. Or attack from envious Outsiders. There are, of course, other risks. Perhaps risks within the Community. I have nothing to substantiate any of these ideas – just an unwillingness to comply and an unease at everyone's obedience. It's as though the whole of Florivale is complicit in the same deception, a façade I can scratch the surface of, but can't demolish.

This is not the time for such thoughts. There are preparations to be made. There is more excitement to be felt. With Annie and Toby's baby on the way, perhaps safety is the best thing for all concerned. Focus on the good.

29

How many Bulletins had there been? The Carers must have been pretty worried. We don't get anything like that now. Nothing on that scale. I guess maybe the threat went away. I'm sure that's what we're all meant to think, sitting here in our little bubble. But I don't buy it. Things like that, if they are true, don't just go away.

We get a Bulletin every now and again. Force-fed announcements, about engagements, babies being born, the occasional Pioneer death. Nothing about Outside. If we ask too much about Outside we just get shut down, no response. The only existence is this one, in here. I suppose, for some of us, that's true. Nothing but Florivale. That's enough for me. Nor for Clem. And, I think, not enough for Josh.

His T-day was looming and he was terrified, once again. Between that and the marriage hints from bitchface Melanie about the 'joining of the two hottest families in Florivale,' Josh is not having the easiest of times. I needed to get him and Clem together, away from everyone else, and talk all of this through, get some order to the myriad half-spun threads of my thoughts. But he wasn't ready. Perhaps Clem wouldn't be able to handle it either.

Maybe there's something different about discovering information for yourself that marks it as your own - sets it apart from being told, second-hand, the very same information. Mental proprietorship? Whatever the reason, this is my story. But there's another part of me which craved the acknowledgment that this was not just in my mind. It affected more than just me. It affects Clem and Josh. My family. Everyone. The Carers, Protectors, NutriVisors, Melanie and her cronies. Whatever this place is, we are all part of it and we are all bound to it. We define and perpetuate it. Florivale provides everything we need. Nobody seems to know where our food comes from, or our clothes. Nothing is made here, that's for certain. My questions about the provenance of the things we rely on receive no substantive response. Just the usual vague 'from the Ministry,' or 'the Minister arranges it'.

I needed Clem and Josh to be up to speed so we could talk about it. Going over everything in my head was going to drive me completely crazy. I knew I also needed to run, past the flashes on my BioBand and through the shocks, scream out loud - anything to shake off this feeling. I messaged Clem on my CompStream.

VSH01:   Hey Clem. Fancy yoga tomorrow? We could chat whilst I fall out of Tree Pose?

CP06:   Tree Pose my ass. You'd struggle with Corpse Pose. OK, OK, HMJ joke. A crap one. Yes to yoga, I fancy a laugh at your expense. 11?

VSH01:   Sure. See you by the FitHub? Going to try to sleep, can't stand another

IsoPod.

CP06:   You're kidding, another one? Man, I'm so jealous. Maybe I should be more stressed out and mental like you? My meditation tends to stop any danger of staying up all night. What I'd give for the bliss of the Pod!

VSH01:   You're the one who's mental. See you tomorrow yogaface.

CP06:   Roger. Who is Roger anyway? Thought for the day. x

Clem. How would I cope without her? I needed to keep it light, not to tell her how freaked out I am, not over CompStream. Given they measure the quality and quantity of my shits, I had no doubt they also review our CompStreams on a constant basis, if any of my suspicions were vaguely correct. If not, maybe I'm crazy - but at least it's an exciting diversion.

Sleep was not on my agenda. I needed that IsoPod session. I'd do whatever I could to keep myself up, watching my BioBand drooping down into the amber zone, then the red, until I was forced into another mandatory sleep session. I couldn't ignore that note. Especially not after what Grandma Sophie's next note revealed. The one that talked about me. And him.

30

I didn't want to write it before. But how on earth, in this medical municipality – swarming with Carers, screenings practically every ten minutes, tests, questions, assessments –did they miss the cancer that took Mike.

It was the arrival of Victoria that made me realise.

I received a FloriConnect call from Toby, from the Health Centre, telling me in gleeful tones (he sounded so ironically boyish, in his attempts to sound like a father) that their little lady had arrived. Victoria Frances Stone-Hunter. 8 pounds and 2 ounces, a perfect little package of life. I got the call around 10 am, although she was born at 5.43 that morning, allowing Annie and Toby some time with Victoria, getting to know the centre of their universe, without any interruptions from me, or anyone else.

Victoria Frances Stone-Hunter. What a strong name, a beautiful name. Victorious. And she shall be both of those things. Of that I am certain. Victoria has perfect, tiny, fat little fingers and toes (and an alarmingly strong grip!), a fine down of dark hair at the top of her head. Plump little thighs, no good for walking just yet. And the lungs of an opera singer! When she cries, everyone knows about it. Which is just as well, because it gives us another opportunity to rush over and see to her every desire. So indulgent.

She has Mike's eyes, with thick, dark lashes. Little flecks sparkling like spots of green and orange amber when the light hits them. So rare for a baby not to have blue eyes at first. Mike would have loved her so dearly, would have adored the opportunity to offer advice as she grows, watch her develop and spoil her rotten.

It was her eyes. Mike's eyes, looking back at me through the mirror of another generation. Unsettling and, at the same time, unsettling. Reaffirming. It's a confirmation that he was here, he was real, and he lives on through her. And a devastating reminder of what I have lost. Because now I have to return home, to a house that he no longer lives in, because he simply no longer lives.

I sit in the kitchen, alone at the counter. The enormous, wasted kitchen I had insisted on, long before I realised the 'country house, with home-cooked meals around the table' of my imagination was just that. A figment of my imagination. Not something I would ever have. So I'm here, at the counter. Writing on scraps of paper to someone who will probably never read them. And it's always the same thoughts that come creeping unbidden through the dark while I'm waiting to fall asleep, or which lurk above the surface of my bath water when all I want to do is stay submerged and out of their reach.

Thoughts about Mike. How could this have happened? I know cancer is hard to operate on, that the risks are enormous, but he was gone in weeks. How could he have deteriorated from perfect health, without any indication of a tumour, to dead and gone in so few days. I don't believe it. I don't accept it. I refuse it. Writing this is worse than when I wrote about the wedding, but I have to do it. My hands twitch if I stop. My heart pounds. If there are repercussions, so be it. This must be written, for me, for Mike.

The days immediately before he died, he was heavily sedated. Tranquilised might be a more appropriate term. So drowsy that he barely recognised me, he could scarcely lift his eyelids to acknowledge the outpourings of my heart. Being thrown into grief like that, experiencing bereavement while the other person is still alive, watching them fade away, it's unthinkable. Health was half the reason we needed to come here! It underpins why we need a cure. The Physicals are not just physical. They eat away at our minds, our families, our trust, our futures. Everything. What I'd give to have Mike back – for one conversation, an honest exchange.

Mike was never anything short of lucid. He was clear, brilliant, exciting. Even when he used to shuffle down the corridor in his socks in the early morning, ready to hit the road with a vat of coffee, he was never slow-witted, never dozy. But the very essence, the spirit, of him died when he entered the Health Centre. He wouldn't even squeeze my hand when I asked him to try.

And I know he would have tried everything. There has to be more to it. This man who claimed to be straight forward, simple uncomplicated – but who, inside, was a mass of emotions, clamouring priorities, contradictory stances. His character was never in question, his position as mediator always crucial in an argument. Mike was the one man I knew who could build a bridge of trust to get us through an impasse.

I don't accept that such a person could just be gone, of his body's own design. Had he asked to be allowed to die? I can't see how it could have all happened in any other way. That he would have wanted to leave me is almost as heart-breaking as the daily reminders that he truly is gone.

I want to cause a riot. I want to run toward the Lake and jump in, in full view of all of the Protectors. Get some attention, shake things up. Ask questions. Get some answers.

But I can't. I have to stay, hold the status quo, and provide support to Annie and Toby. What would happen if I did something crazy? Would I be followed or ignored, written off as an old bat who couldn't adjust to Florivale? Or would I be sedated and left to see out my days in a bed in the Health Centre?

What if all they say about Outside is true? The Physicals. The violence. Surely safety and health have to be the most important things, for now. Now that there is another person in this world who needs my protection. A person whose life is more precious than mine. A person for whom I will do anything in my power. Victoria Stone-Hunter.

I realise I sound utterly deranged. But this note will go with the rest, sequestered and waiting for you, whoever you are.

31

I wanted to turn and scream, but all I could do was whisper into the air, 'I hear you,' as I fought the urge to slip into beautiful, welcoming sleep.

Did she ever know I'd find these notes? These keys to her mind? Did she hope for it, like I hoped for every new note I found? And her pain. Her loss. What had happened to Grandpa Mike, stager of plays, maker of jokes, bringer of joy? How could he have just slipped away, here, in this cornucopia of medicines and Carers?

He was no threat to public safety or health, he was part of the Community. Was he somehow medically flawed? Some of the Pioneers were – take Grandma Sophie for example. She'd led a healthy life in here for decades and suddenly, by some monstrous twist of fate, she became riddled with tumours. Nothing they could do. Just like Mike. How could that happen in here? With the scans, the tests, the constant checking and updating, measurement after measurement. We're told the Pioneers were still affected by Before, the roots of disease plated and developing within some of them, emerging only as they aged. We're told it's natural, that the reason we're here to reduce those instances, those fatalities. We're told a lot of things.

Clem is told the best way to be healthy is to go through all the meditation, green tea, HMJ nonsense. I'm told - although whether I listen or not is another matter - that vegetarianism is the key and meat and fish contain compounds which humans no longer need and which are harmful to us. Josh is told he needs transfusions to keep his cells developing, adapting, to be the best he can be. But he hates it every time. Every single one of us is told something about our Condition that makes us unique, special, better. There's no secrecy to it. The Carers are always at pains to get us to take pride in our Conditions. Well, screw the Carers. I don't even know where they live. Isn't that odd? This whole town, teeming with Carers, Protectors, NutriVisors, the people who replace our clothes once they've been sterilised, the people who make our little NutriVisor pouches. The people who clean the IsoPods. For no Florivite does any of these jobs. No Florivite knows anything about the providers, the people who do everything for us and on whom we entirely rely. I know the carrots I eat grow in the ground somewhere and that someone or something picks them and prepares them, because I saw it on a CompStream. But I also saw talking animals eating talking carrots on a CompStream kids' show - not as upsetting as it sounds, they were all very jolly and the carrots were happy to be munched - and that wasn't real. So what am I meant to believe about anything? It's a lly example, but you see the point.

Jack watches those shows. He doesn't question them, just accepts them. He is kind. He is accepting. He is happy - I'd be happier if I were more like him. Staying awake running over everything is exhausting, and I can't overdo it and draw attention to myself. Which is why I need some sleep tonight, but not tomorrow night. Tomorrow is the day to chat to Clem. Clear my mind by sharing it. She's read the sodding things – and I can't fathom how she can be so calm? Tonight I'll sleep. Tomorrow I'll stay awake. Get my sorry self back in the IsoPod suite in the next day or two. My stomach lurched at the thought of it.

And then again, I can't sleep. How could I possibly do that, with all of this on my mind? How on earth did my Grandma cope? I bet she never even told my mother about her doubts, her thoughts. And if she had, would mum have listened? Would she have dismissed it all as the meandering mind of a bereaved and lonely old Pioneer? I hope not. I wonder how many people have stories like this in Florivale. How much complexity there is behind our picture-perfect, healthy (always healthy) façade? And how much of that is façade is built on a foundation of utter bullshit. The words haunt me. So few of them – so many possible purposes.

SLEEP LITTLE. TRUST THE ISOPOD. GET OUTSIDE.

I'm lost.

32

My body is betraying me. Constantly exhausted, I flit between wondering whether it's all in my head on a good day, and being brought slamming back to earth on the bad days. I feel like I'm going crazy and I find myself lying to the Carers about how I feel, saying I'm fine when I'm not, trying to trick the system. God knows why, or what I'm trying to achieve –I think I just have a child's wanton urge to defy, to destroy.

I'd put the tiredness down to being a grandmother, running around all day. Not that I mind doing that – it's the best part of my routine. I was sure I'd feel better soon. Victoria is four now, charging about Florivale like a tiny queen. So strong and so spirited, a stubborn streak that can only be from the Stone side of the family, with Mike's eyes flashing up at everyone she speaks to. She has charmed the whole Community. Annie's friends have all started to marry, plan and children – the human cycle of life in Florivale echoing what I remember of Before. You don't think you want children until someone else has one. And then you need one.

So I thought, perhaps it's just that. Adjusting to grandmotherhood, rushing about for Victoria, spending so much more time with Annie, Ella and Bertie as a result of this wonderful new little person we share.

I figured I'd find out soon enough if it was anything more than that. The endless tests would have flagged up any anomaly. Perhaps there was nothing for them to find out. But my symptoms haven't faded.

Something was wrong. I now know that within me lies a cancer, growing and gnawing away at the good parts of me like some awful rat. And, like a rat, it seems most active at night, lurking in the shadows when I'm alone in bed, wishing more than ever that Mike were here. But cancer has already taken him, my ultimate comfort.

The call for additional tests came so quickly after I last wrote. They must have been monitoring me closer than usual. Of course, there were the usual tests – urine, stool, blood, hair sample, weight, height – we are all used to that weekly delight. Lab coats and sterile containers, staring at the panelled ceiling while they draw a blood sample. I still can't look at the needle as they use it. Pathetic I know, but that's just me. I have literally no idea how the McLaines cope with their transfusions. That is a Condition I could not handle.

It was the second round of tests that marked the shift. My usual Carer, Ellie, wouldn't meet my eye when she started packing everything away after carrying out her usual suite of prods and samples. She stuttered when she said a colleague wanted to speak to me. Her walk had an odd, shuffling quality. It was clear to me then that she knew the gravity of my situation, though I did not have any specifics. She left hastily, and my gaze reverted to the ceiling tiles. They reminded me of the old spy movies Mike used to love, lithe men dressed head-to-toe in black, shuffling along the air vents concealed behind tiles like those, to their unlikely and adrenaline-fuelled escape from imminent doom. Another Carer came in.

'Mrs. Stone. I'm Doctor West. I'm here to talk to you about some of your test results, and to discuss some further tests we are obliged to carry out together.'

No Hollywood spy-style escape for me.

Doctor West had a kind manner (for a Carer), a soft intonation rather than the usual walking, talking medical textbooks we tend to face. This was immediately disconcerting. Why were they sending someone who acted like a fellow human, when everything about the Health Centre is disembodied and remote? It's always been clear that the Community Centre is for emotional issues and the Health Centre is for Physicals. The Community Centre is for us; the Health Centre is for them. Their data. Their cure.

As she pulled up her seat and settled her papers on the desk, a strand of her dark blonde hair came loose from its band. She tucked it back in and her slightly wavering hand betrayed her calm exterior – I knew this was going to be a serious discussion.

'Mrs. Stone,' she started.

'Sophie. Call me Sophie, please. Mrs. Stone makes me sound ancient.'

'Sure. Sophie, then. As I said, I'm Doctor West. I've come to discuss some tests with you. If you've got any questions, at any point, just let me know and we can see if I can cover them off for you today,' she said.

'Your standard tests have revealed some unusual activity in your blood count – we are seeing changes in the amount of certain types of blood cells that we would like to look into. We've also noticed you've been consistently losing some weight, although your NutriVisor pouches have remained balanced as they should – so unless you have not been eating them, and every record suggests you have, something has changed. We have started the process for some further analysis at the HQ lab, Outside.' She crossed her legs, tapping her CompStream screen for more information.

'We need to take some more samples for testing, and run some full body scans. If you agree to this being carried out today, all the better. Otherwise, under your Entrance Contract, you're obliged to consent to the additional tests being completed within the week, so I would recommend going ahead today to save some time. Of course, if there is someone you want to call in, to sit with you, we can arrange that.'

'No,' I cut in. 'Let's just do it. You don't need to handle me so softly. I want to know just as much as you do.'

'Okay Sophie. Follow me.'

Autopilot kicked in and I followed her lab coat

through the door into room, mesmerised by the strand of hair she had tried to tuck in, which was infuriatingly looped around the band. I wanted to pull it out, smoothen the pony tail, and go home. No more tests.

We reached the medical bed in the next room and I lay on the crumpled tissue paper that covers the plastic-coated mattress, my hands patiently folded on my chest. Doctor West logged into a CompStream by the bed and pulled up my previous 'standard' test results. As she ran through the list of additional tests to be carried out, my mind wandered back to the times I lay on beds like this, having my pregnancies confirmed, such different circumstances. Now it's 'biopsy'. 'Markers'. 'Bone marrow'. 'MRI'.

It's so surreal. I can't quite believe the path my day has taken. I knew I wasn't feeling right but I ignored it. I outsourced my worry to the Carers of Florivale, knowing they would be watching and pick up anything. I'm angry at how selfish I am for feeling hard done by about my prognosis when so many Outside - if what they say is true - have no access to healthcare like this. There is nobody checking, on their health, no means to evade the Physicals.

It will be a few days until my results are back. A few days to simply enjoy my family, choosing ignorance over knowledge. Although I know in my heart that something is wrong. Very wrong. Something inside me.

33

It must have been months since I last wrote, although I've stopped tracking the days, because I have so few of them left. Instead, I trace the passage of time by tracking my memories, reflections, and introspections.

The night after I last wrote, I slept in the kids' old room, beneath the ferocious tiger and sheltered by her protection, like the watchful, wary sheep gazing by.

I woke and knew this was it. I didn't need the latest results. There have been so many, and it was inevitable now. I simply know that my body isn't right any more.

So this is my decision. The notes are going to all be stashed, stowed, for someone, one day. If I have to leave this world without seeing everything I want to see, without leaving Florivale and finding out whether Outside really is as terrible as they say, I want to leave something of me behind. I don't want to disappear or evaporate, leaving no trace. I want there to be a record, a remembering of things, the way life was. Even if nobody ever reads a word I wrote, just knowing I wrote it will be enough.

I'm going to give the house to Annie and Toby.

Their place is smaller, being one of the next Gen's starter homes, built when the town was already becoming limited on space. No doubt because of those ludicrous enticements we were given where we were allowed to design our own homes. I can remember the foolish excitement about having all that space. That kitchen. Used a handful of times, having had no time to establish the traditions I'd planned. The kitchen that is nothing more than a repository for NutriVisor pouches and the various machines we have to heat this, cool that, freeze the other.

I don't need all this space. I'll make a request to swap homes with Annie and Toby. They can re-paint this one, or keep it as it is, I don't mind.

I lie – there's a caveat. I would mind if the tiger and sheep were to go. But you can't give a gift with conditions. The house will be theirs to treat as they wish, and if those wishes include keeping my painting, I'll be a happy little ghost.

Truth be told, I want something of me in their lives, and sharing the walls we have lived and breathed in seems like the perfect place to start. Plus, they're going to need the bedrooms much more than I do, rattling about on my own. Victoria's thundering around now she has found her feet, quite the inquisitive little thing, and little Stone-Hunter number two won't be far behind, I'm sure. I'll go and speak to the Carers about a house swap tomorrow.

They said I might take a few years for me to die. That I'll be comfortable here. If I can stay around long enough, I'll get to see Victoria flourish. I can tell her, and any siblings or cousins she might have, them about my life, about their Grandfather. That's my goal now. I don't think I'll write again. I'll live instead – write my own memories instead of these silly notes.

34

That was the last note.

I'd slept deeply, way longer than I'd intended. I needed to get through my breakfast pouch, into my sportswear and out to meet Clem. I could kick myself for sleeping in. I'd never get into the IsoPod at this rate. The irony wasn't lost on me, that I was so anxious to get into the worst place in Florivale, so exhausted that I'd overslept, and yet resisting sleep was the only way to get myself there.

My high-protein yoghurt and granola stuck to my tongue like glue. No amount of water would get rid of the cloying, sickening feeling. I couldn't stop running over the notes in my mind, which was becoming a daily habit. How could someone as enigmatic as my Grandma just disappear? This woman I barely knew, yet who seems so much like me. I want to know her, to talk about the world and Before and Outside, my mother as a child, all of it. But I can't ever know any of these things. I'm on my own.

Chucking my dish in the sterilising unit and scrambling past Jack (noisily playing with his dinosaur toys) and back into my bedroom without having to say a word to anyone, I pulled out my sportswear drawer and selected some leggings and a shell top to throw on over my sports bra. Clem always wanted to do yoga outdoors and I freeze my ass off every time I forget a jacket. Don't say I don't learn. I slammed the door and jogged over to meet Clem.

'Hey Vic,' she called from outside the FitHub. 'How do you feel about strolling over the way towards my place, where we can stretch to our hearts' content in the garden, without any of the usual idiots throwing us off our centre?'

She wasn't even joking. Her 'centre' was of utmost importance. I'm not sure I have one. Unless we're talking about being self-centred. Yeah, crap joke.

'Love to,' I laughed, already feeling the lightness of being around Clem. She's just so, well, Clem.

'Shut up veg-face. Get your ass over here and jog with me'.

Over at the Petersens', we passed through the side gate and straight into the garden, so we didn't have to waste any time with parental pleasantries or execute the awkward attempt to escape. We could just get on with what we really wanted to do. We could discuss the notes. With nobody listening.

'So, Clem,' I faltered once we'd reached the garden. 'You finished the notes, right?' I could see her itching to interject. 'Before you speak, I just have to say this. If you don't want to go through it, if you want to just chill doing

Downward Dog or Sun Salutation, that's fine. But I have to do something about all this. It's not just the notes any more. I just know it – there's more.'

'More? What do you mean? That stupid stage image thing?' she asked.

'Yes, the stage thing. And it's not stupid. It's a code. I instantly knew there was more to it, and nobody else gives a toss. It's like I'm the only one who sees what's happening, while you all just stare into the sun, blinded by its light but undeterred. When I saw the image on the screen, the words 'all the world's a stage' stamped across it, the realisation that there was more to know just walked straight into my head. It came through as clearly as you speaking to me now.' I paused. She stared. 'Don't look at me like that!'

I explained that awful conversation with my parents, my time researching the play, the wedding plans I'd checked, everything. Clem's face repeatedly went from awestruck to disbelief and back again the whole time I was talking. I knew I sounded crazy. Maybe I was, but I needed her to stay with me, to hear this out.

As we shifted from position to position, her well-practised body artfully bending into each pose she announced, I awkwardly huffed and puffed my way into the closest approximation I could muster of the pose. I tried to keep my breathing steady and explain everything to her in as chronological and methodical a manner as I could muster, but it's pretty hard to concentrate on explaining the biggest thing you've learned your whole life, which you don't understand, whilst half upside-down, to someone who blusters between laughing at you and visibly blanching as she decides you have utterly lost the plot. So I may have missed out a few bits.

Maybe, just possibly, I didn't tell her about the latest piece of the puzzle. The note in the copy of the play about getting outside, and trusting the IsoPod. The seven words that were burned into my every thought. So, omitting to tell her may have been more of a conscious decision than I'd possibly have had you think. But it was my information. Mine alone. I was the clever one who'd found it out. All I told her was that the line on the screen was from that play. No harm done. She could always go and find the book if she wanted to work things out for herself.

'So. You're telling me that this is some crazy conspiracy,' she said. 'The whole town is duped and the Gen above us were so terrified by some stupid wedding speech and a bunch of Bulletins that everyone just shut down and refused to acknowledge reality?' She raised an eyebrow and tucked her escaping fronds of red hair back. 'It's quite a stretch Vic. And, when you think about it, why would they pay any attention? The Pioneers chose to come here, which means it must have presented a better option than Outside. They probably told our parents' Gen all about how miserable it was Out there and everyone has realised that life in Florivale can be pretty great. Look how healthy we are. How much we can learn in the EduCentre. Maybe this is all just blown out of proportion, maybe your Grandma was -'

'Nothing,' I snapped. I fell out of my poor attempt at whatever pose we'd forced our bodies into. 'Say nothing about my Grandma. She was not mad. She would not have made that up. She might have been... confused. Misled. But she would not lie. She would not deceive.'

'Jeez, Vic,' she said, as she looked me in the eye. 'That's not where I was going with this. You know I loved her too. I was just going to say – well, I'm not sure. I don't know what answer you want. Do you want it to be awful Outside, like the picture alluded to in your Grandma's notes? Or do you want it to be the other way round, us trapped in here and lost in our ignorance? Which reality would make you happy? What if it's neither? If everything is so bad out there, why would they, whoever they are, the Ministry or the Carers or whoever, continue to keep us in this comfort, with this level of attention to our needs while they remained Outside? Has it ever struck you that you've never seen where a Carer lives? Where a Protector's family is? Who collects your clothes for sterilisation? There is nobody living in Florivale but us Florivites. Why would anyone support this microcosm if it wasn't for something good? Can't you just accept that maybe we are 'the cure' and maybe that's not a bad thing? If everyone's dying and rioting Outside, I'd rather be here. With my family, my friends, my health and my life. Why do you want to push your way out of this existence?'

'I don't. I don't know what I want the truth to be.' As I spoke, I realised that what I was saying was true.

'But I know that I do want the truth. I'm not sure a healthy, safe life in here is what I was meant to live. I'm not like Jack, or my parents. I love them, but they don't exactly push the boundaries. I want to find out more and I want to do it with you, Clem.' I looked back up at her. 'Will you help me? Or at least listen to me, so I don't feel like I'm just slowly going crazy on some sort of mental treadmill?'

'Sure,' Clem replied. 'But Vic, take a step back. Step out of your mind and into your body – breathe the air, walk the paths, just slow down. You look pretty awful.'

Thanks Clem. Measured, reliable, annoyingly honest. Without time to respond, I felt a buzz and looked at my FloriConnect Messenger.

ASH01:   Vic, I think you might want to go to see Josh. He's not doing well. T-Day? Poor thing. Be back by 8. Mum x

Clem had a message too. For our parents to actually give a toss about Josh's regular T-Day meltdown, something had to be up. Without a word, we rolled up our yoga mats and sprinted out of the garden in perfect unison.

35

We got to the McLaine house in under eight minutes. Eight sweaty, panicked minutes. Our BioBands had shocked both of us, in case our beads of perspiration hadn't been enough of an indication. Sure, Josh had been weird prior to a T-Day before, morose, angry. But the parents had never got involved. It was always attributed to teenage adjustments, hormones, melodrama. This was something new, something worse.

His mum came to the door, immaculately turned out as always, but completely prepared to greet us with her mask of disdain. Mrs. McLaine did not like Josh spending time with me or Clem. The fact we turned up drenched in sweat, out of breath and utterly dishevelled will not have improved her opinion of his choice of friends.

'You two. I suppose you'd better come in,' she snapped. 'I'd hoped he would be acting normal by now. But. Well. You just go up. You'll see for yourselves.'

The McLaine house is like all the rest in Florivale – all of them are similar - but each has something customised for the Pioneers who'd had it built. Different configuration but basically the same format, no space without some use, no alcove unfilled. Unlike ours, the colours here are all completely muted. No mural. No splash of brightness here or there. Dove grey, cream, neutral. Pacing along the hall and up the stairs, we reached Josh's room. Like all the McLaines' bedrooms, and unlike mine or Clem's, his room contained an array of medical equipment. Tubes, needles, monitors. Josh was in bed, hooked up to a monitor which beeped at us in the dim light. Thin voile curtains billowed softly inwards in the evening breeze. Eyes half open, staring aimlessly at those windows, Josh lay quietly. Faint music played in the background, something which reminded me of the old ballets I'd seen in videos from Before. Tchaikovsky perhaps. He seemed lost in the music, entranced.

'Hey, Josh. We got a message to come see you,' I said, trying to inject some levity into my voice. 'What's up? What's different?'

'Yeah, Josh, it's Clem too,' she chipped in. 'We came as soon as we got a message. What's going on?'

'Nothing,' came the response.

'It can't be nothing,' I said.

'Everything is the same as nothing. I realise that now,' he said. 'I'm nothing. Just a vessel. Every few months they take part of me away, put something new in. I always feel exhausted, jaded. But this time, nothing. There's nothing left of me inside.'

'Josh! Don't say things like that. You're everything! You're, well, you're you,' said Clem, edging towards him. As she stepped closer, he closed his eyes. Gently, without urgency. But with the utmost sadness, like closing a door to shut out someone you love.

'You don't know, Clem. You have no idea what it's like,' he replied, his eyes still shut. 'I lie in a bed, here or in the Health centre. A Carer soothes me into a chair, does everything except for stroking my hair. Placates me like a scared kitten. I sit, pretending I'm OK. Pretending I can cope. I can't.' His breath caught in his throat. 'The first tube goes into my inner elbow and I know my fight is over, that I have to sit there. Captive to the tubes, the beeping, the monitors. I feel them drawing my blood, and with it, my soul. Then comes the replacement blood. Sometimes it's red. Sometimes it's white – they call the white stuff plasmoid. That's not even a word. I literally have no idea what they're putting into me. But I know it changes things. I feel the old me, trickling away. I can't do it any more.'

He was fighting tears, speaking through gritted teeth. His eyes were still shut, keeping us out.

'Josh, you're right,' said Clem. We don't understand. Which is why we need you to tell us. Tell us what you're going through, what you need. What we can do. We can't spend a day in your shoes, so you're going to have to tell us what it feels to walk in them,' said Clem, perfectly soft in her tone, measured in her delivery.

I wanted to kick the medical stand from his bed, pull out the tubes and throw them out of the window. But, then again, I've never been the logical one. Clem's a much better planner. Josh stirred a little, but kept his eyes closed. 'Come here. Take my hand,' he said.

We did. One hand each, to be precise. He squeezed mine hard, and from Clem's jump of surprise, I think he must have done the same to her. His eyes flew open.

'I have to get out of here. They'll kill me with this stuff,' he blurted.

Clem and I stood there with our mouths agape. We were unable to move, as Josh's BioBand lit up red and he pressed his call-alarm. A Carer came bustling in, telling us not to exhaust Mr. McLaine and to leave. Perhaps to call back in a few days if we wanted to see how he was doing.

We called out to Josh, asked him to let us stay, and if not, to message us, tell us how he was feeling. He said nothing. His eyes were shut again. We found Mrs. McLaine in the hall.

'Dreadful, isn't it?' she said, and I thought for one ill-informed moment she was referring to her son's suffering. 'Such weakness. Why he can't just pull it together like the rest of us is beyond me. Jesus wept.'

Like I said, she's not the warmest person. We said our perfunctory goodbyes and set off. As we walked from the threshold of their property and onto the path, I selfishly felt relieved to be free of that house, with its shroud of melancholy. And that woman.

'Clem,' I asked as we gained some distance. 'Just, hear me out. I know you think I'm overthinking it all, building everything into something it isn't. But doesn't it strike you as odd?'

'Doesn't what? It's not odd, Vic. It's a total nightmare.'

'Odd that the only one who gets ill like this is Josh. Nobody else ever suffers like that. They have family T-Days across the same week. Even if his mum's was days ago, how come she's back to her usual charming self. What's so much better about the blood she gets? Does she get this plasmoid stuff? And why do they have to have it. You have to agree, it's the worst Condition.'

'I don't know, Vic. I don't know about anything any more. I'm getting a headache - and I'm getting upset. I have to go now. Home. I need some head space. Got to think things through.'

'You are kidding, right?' I snapped. 'How can you stop and think and do nothing while all this goes on? Our whole lives have been spent in this nowhereland, and I can't ignore the signs any more. Things are changing. People are changing. Josh looks half-dead. And you want to go, drink a green tea, meditate and think things through? What's wrong with you!? We should be talking about it. Figuring this all out. Doing things to change it. Bloody hell, Clem.'

'Drop it Vic. Not everyone wants to smash everything to hell and then figure out what the broken pieces mean afterwards. We're not the same – that's fine, but don't take your frustration out on me. It upsets me too.'

'Great. Just great. See you whenever you decide to pull your head out of the clouds and accept that things are bad. Things can't go on as they are.'

I stalked further down the path, cold with rage and furious at being left without anyone to talk to, nobody there to validate my theories, to confirm that I wasn't just going crazy. Maybe I was crazy. But even if that was the case, I still needed to talk about it. Pushing a wave of nausea down, I went towards the house. I needed to make some kind of a plan, on my own. With the notes as a starting point.

36

I scrunched the notes back together and put them in a new stashing-place. Peeling back the carpet in the corner of my room, beneath my bed, I'd managed to wedge them under a carefully-loosened floorboard.

My rage was dissipating and, in its void, thoughts ran through my head. Each one linked to another idea, every question met with another and found no answer. Every road I thought my way along ended up blocked in at the end of a tunnel, and I had to clamber back to where I'd started - only to set out on another fruitless mental journey.

I paced the floor. My BioBand was glowing with various alerts. Too much exercise earnt me a green light. Too high a heart rate brought a red flicker. High cortisol meant the asterisk in the top right hand corner lit up every few minutes, to remind me I was stressed. How utterly ridiculous. I imagined Clem meditating her way through this, calm as could be, and hated her, just a little, for a few minutes. Before I knew it, I was watching the (very few, for this was Florivale) dust motes dancing in the rays of sunshine peering through the window. Morning was breaking and I was no closer to any closure. Exhausted. I decided to get into bed and tried to seek some comfort in sleep. But none came. I could hear Jack scuttling around in his room, no doubt spilling his toys all over the floor and planning another day of being unbearable. Mum and Dad came next, slipping into their dressing gowns and heading downstairs to the kitchen. There'd be no sleeping now.

Sure enough, came the daily call up the stairs. 'Vic! Breakfast time, come on down!'

Isn't it funny, how you can be wide awake all night, and as soon as you have to do something 'normal', some menial daily task, your eyes start to droop, your head goes foggy and you lose any ability to function as a human. I'm not a morning person at the best of times, but this was clearly not going to be a good day. Down the stairs I went.

We had the usual NutriVisor pouch breakfasts. I grunted my monosyllabic responses at the right times and got myself through the meal. And, more importantly, upstairs again and into the shower. My little piece of privacy, more rejuvenating than a night's sleep – making me a damn sight more fragrant in the process. I breathed in the steam and tried to breathe out my frustration.

Unable to prolong my shower as Jack banged incessantly on the door, I admitted defeat and left my sanctuary. I pulled a sterilised towel from the rack and wrapped myself in it, taking my time to enjoy the way the steam drifted around in the room, pouring off my skin and leaving trails in the air. I unlocked the door and went back into my bedroom. I checked where I'd tucked the notes from Grandma Sophie. Still safe. Still stashed.

I figured I'd head to the Community Centre and see what books there were to read. I wondered whether I could go through the copy of As You Like It for any other clues. Or anything else to take my mind out away from its cryptic maze. Anything to stop the litany of questions scrolling through my head. My BioBand was bleeping and flashing at me again. It wanted me to sleep. I could empathise - I wanted me to sleep too. I knew I'd have to go back into the IsoPod. No matter what that note said about trusting it, or how determined I was to go back in and work it all out, there was no trust. I decided I'd put off fulfilling the sleep orders for as long as I could, nose in a book. Total rebel, right? Sitting in the library as my petty act of self-important rebellion.

I checked out some old book about wives and husbands cheating on each other, glamorous cartoon women on the back cover. Utter drivel. It was so bad that I could only stand it for so long before the IsoPod actually seemed like a better idea, which is saying something. And at least the IsoPod would stop the damn BioBand vibrating and flashing at me.

Steeling myself for the experience, I headed into the IsoPod corridor and tried to breathe normally. It was all very well for the mysterious message to tell me to 'trust the IsoPod', but a few coded words in a dusty old book hardly filled me with confidence. I'd spent my whole life in and out of those egg-shaped chambers, enough times to know I utterly hated it. I wondered whether it genuinely was a different experience for me than, say, Clem, who loved them but (Sod's law being what it is) rarely got to go into them. Maybe she meditated through it. Anyway, her brain and mine do not seem to work in the same way. So she loves it, but can't get sufficiently sleep-deprived to experience it as much as she'd like. I can't bear it and yet find myself having a session more than once a week at the moment. The weight. The inertia. Maybe that's what sets me apart from Clem – I can't stand being unable to anything but think, being trapped in my own mind. My worst prison. Once I'm inside, all I can think about is escaping the pod and getting back out into the real, tangible, breakable world.

I picked the fifth IsoPod chamber from the central atrium. I select a different one each time. Just to check that the last one wasn't faulty, or that it didn't sync properly with my BioBand. I'd accept any reason to hope this time would be different. But I knew deep down that they were all the same. Carbon copy eggs of white plastic, dotted around at perfectly-placed intervals. I walked through the door and tapped my BioBand, which had escalated to buzzing every ten minutes, against the reader on the inside of the door frame to seal the door to anyone but me or a Carer. Removing my clothes and pulling on the grim pyjamas with their cloying lavender scent, I climbed into the capsule.

'Welcome back, Victoria. I can see this is

an urgent visit. You need seven hours of sleep assistance. Your records indicate this is the first time you've needed to make up for a whole night's sleep. You must check in with a Carer afterwards so your biometrical readings can be verified. You must not allow yourself to lack this much sleep again. You are relying too heavily on the IsoPod.' The disembodied voice, barking orders, as usual. Great.

'Now, please lie back and ensure you are comfortable, ready for the process to commence momentarily. Enjoy your Quality Sleep.'

There was a pause. Things were taking a little longer than usual, presumably due to the fact I'd need more than a double dose of SleepSteam. I guess the machine was calibrating or something as I felt the tiniest knocking and tapping noises from within it. I'd never noticed those before, but I guess I'd been focusing on not freaking out. I'd always had bigger issues to focus on. That message about trusting the IsoPod was obviously a load of crap. Maybe it was Josh or Clem taking the piss after I first started telling them about the notes, talking about the image of the stage. I was considering this very possibility as the SleepSteam started to pour in.

Everything went silent, the IsoPod's noise filters doing their job brilliantly. The lights had faded to their usual blackness and the steam began to rise through the IsoPod, from my feet up towards my face. But there was no acidity this time. No lavender. Instead, a medicinal, ammonia tang danced at the edge of each cloud.

Nothing burned my throat, although it tasted like it should. A wave of nausea shook me, as the panic set in earlier than usual. This wasn't right. Was this a seven-hour dose? If so, I wanted out. I wanted to go right back to my three-hour horrible lavender. I'd take the suffocating heaviness of that scent over this new, stripped back, medical fog, any day. I went to bang the door of the IsoPod, hoping the monitor would register my movement and alert a Carer, but my useless arms remained pinned to the bed. My heart rate must have been going wild, but my BioBand wasn't flashing. Nothing had lit up. It was as though it had powered off. Not possible. For as long as we're alive, the chips process data. Which brought the next horrible realisation. Was I dying?

I wanted to vomit, retching to get this new kind of steam out of my body, but nothing worked. My body was utterly immobile. None of the heaviness of the lavender, nothing seeping upwards and into me, starting from my toes. Just completely numb. It was more terrifying than anything I've ever experienced. No warning. No chance to fight. I prayed a Carer would be on their way. My retching came to nothing, no matter how hard I urged the bile from my body. This was a case of matter over mind.

I calmed my breathing as best I could, although my body seemed to be on autopilot in the darkness. It felt as though the IsoPod was tilting, shifting every few moments, but surrounded by sheer blackness, it was impossible to tell. Fearing that the sensation was the manifestation of my nausea, I tried to still my mind, to calm myself. But there was nothing to be done. I was utterly trapped, within my own body and within the IsoPod. I pleaded in my mind with anyone who'd listen. I'd never miss another night's sleep again; I'd never question Florivale again. I just wanted out. I wanted air. Freedom.

Just as quickly as it had come over me, the sedation disappeared. I reached out with my arms, kicked my legs, and touched my face - to check I was still there, that I wasn't going mad. And then came the result of my fruitless retching. I vomited all over myself, inside the IsoPod, the burning acid scent mingling with the remnants of the medical steam. My head was pounding, but my stomach was finally rid of its foul contents. I realised I had no idea how long I'd been in the IsoPod. It could have been hours, or equally, minutes. 'Trust the IsoPod,' my ass.

I hurled again. I had to get out of this shell – I was going to asphyxiate in the fumes of my own stomach juices at this rate. The thought made me panic once again, and yet again, my BioBand showed nothing. Dead as a doornail. Was it defective? Had I been dosed the wrong kind of steam because my metrics were wrong when I got in?

I felt a dull thud and everything stopped. It was like someone had switched my brain off. Perhaps they had, I thought, as the world faded away.

-PART TWO-

37

'We have to get her out. If nothing else, that smell will kill her.'

'No, Alex. You know we can't do that yet. You know he has to be here. He has to check her stats and metrics. He has to be the one to open the pod.'

'It's absolute bollocks, Ad. Bollocks. She'd better be glad she's knocked out in there. She'd go full-scale crazy otherwise. What the fuck is he going to tell her?'

'I don't know, mate. That, I don't know. Never had to extract a Flori-born before. Not sure if they can take it, the shift.'

'Forget her mental state. What about the pouches? How do we know they had enough antibodies to give her a fighting chance, to give her immune system enough preparation to cope? And what's she going to do in the rain out here? And the sun? The water? Every little detail of our lives will be a daily threat to her. And then there's the added danger for everyone in there who helped us bust her out. I worry for them, and for us all.' He paused. 'We didn't have enough time to prepare. This is not going to go down as a minor infraction. We need to get them all out, and soon.'

'You're right, Alex. We didn't have enough time. But you saw how the programme was accelerating. We had no choice.' He let out a sigh. 'Let's leave our little chick to incubate. She needs more time and I can't stand watching the pod and being unable to get her out. I really hope to God we picked a strong one. I know he insisted. But she's so young. Barely even a woman.' He tapped the casing of the IsoPod, his fingers clicking on its shell to a steady rhythm. 'Let's go. The others will need our help soon enough.'

38

I heard muffled voices. It was still dark and the smell was dreadful. Acrid vomit and stale air. It was all I could do not to be sick again. I felt so weak, but the inertia had gone – I was free to move my limbs and head – but what good was that, when I was still trapped?

I couldn't make out what was being said by the voices outside. Their tones were low and gruff. Not perky or chirpy, like the Carers usually sounded. Maybe it was a pair of technicians, fixing the IsoPod, working to release me from my plastic shell? I banged on the wall, but nothing happened. I was stuck inside the sound-proof walls.

My BioBand was still acting up. Considering how annoying I found it, I really didn't like the fact it was dead, no longer telling me that I was A-OK, healthy, burning and eating enough calories, sleeping insufficiently, exercising enough. It was now just a ridge under the skin on my wrist and a floating bracelet above the surface. No vibrations. No lights. No shocks. I wondered, not for the first time, when they put the chip in, because I sure as hell didn't think that babies were born with BioBands. Was it one of the many crazy rules of Florivale that you had to do this immediately to any child born there?

Exhaustion and frustration vied for the remnants of my strength. I checked off my list of confusions. I still didn't know how long I'd been in there, why the steam was so different, or why it felt like the pod had been tilting. I tried to calm myself, which was significantly harder without the reassuring feedback of the heart rate monitor on my BioBand. The muffled voices came back, and again I felt a shift in motion. Hopefully the technicians were getting things sorted. I knew I couldn't stay in here much longer. I gave up, let my head fall back and gave in to restless sleep, having succumbed to my fate. Whatever it was.

I woke as bright lights blazed in at me as a pair of tough, gnarled hands put a mask over my face. It was connected to some sort of tube, which was in turn connected to something else. Now I was beginning to understand how Josh must feel every time T-Day comes around. That powerlessness, the weakness. I fought against it, tried to sit, or to lift my arms to take the mask off, but to no avail. The mask was staying on. My arms were bound, loosely, to the side of what looked like a medical bed. I was out of the IsoPod. How did I end up in the Health Centre?

Blinking furiously as my eyes adjusted slowly to the dazzling light, shapes began to come into focus, moving in and out of the light source. I wished I could turn it off. I went to speak, but my lips were wrapped around an inner tube within the mask. There was no space for me to move my lips or my tongue – I couldn't utter a word. The tube was providing some sort of sterile-tasting air. Maybe it was medicinal. It was certainly nothing like the air in either the IsoPod, or the crisp air of the outdoors. I tried once more to calm my heart rate, but I wasn't doing a great job. A woman began to speak, from somewhere I couldn't see. I strained to move my head, the tube jarring against the back of my mouth as I misaligned it in my attempt to see the woman – a Carer, I presumed.

'She's trying not to panic. Let her work it through. Let her breathe it in,' she said.

'I want that mask off. I want her to feel safe,' came a male voice, deep and calming.' I liked this guy. 'She'll be fine. She can be trusted. Look at her arms, she's tied to the bed for God's sake. Where exactly is she going to go?'

'You know we can't accelerate this process,' said the other voice. The snotty sounding woman. Definitely a Carer.

'Elle, I can't watch this and do nothing. She isn't an animal. She's got no reason to harm anyone. Look at her.'

'That's not an option. Be patient,' she said. 'Pass me the syringe please. And don't look at me like that. You know as well as I do that she'll be all the better for the infusion. We just need to pump her full of vitamins and a decent sedative, let her mind and body adjust. You know it's true.'

I definitely didn't like this woman. At the word 'syringe', I tried to wrench my hands free of my restraints. I started to push the tube away with my tongue, but ended up with it just jutting painfully against the back of my mouth. Then came the swift sting of a jab in the inner wrist.

'Calm down, honey. This will make you relax. You'll sleep, and everything will seem better when you wake. I know you're scared, but you're safe. Trust us.'

I'd been hearing a lot about trust recently, and in my opinion, it's not all it's cracked up to be. My head began to spin and my eyes drooped, I felt my tongue go flat in my mouth as the words of the strangers by my bedside retreated into gentle mutterings.

So much for resistance.

39

A warm hand was holding mine, as another gently stroked around my eyes in a soothing figure-of-eight pattern. In low tones, a man's voice was gently making the sort of noises you would to a frightened animal. Calm sounds, no any real words behind them. I caught a scent - slightly musky, the salted aroma of sweat. Opening my eyes, I was instantly confused again. The lights were dimmer than before, but something still wasn't right. This simply couldn't be right. I was looking into my own eyes.

Flecked. Green and hazel, glinting as the light beamed in gently from the side. But surrounded with tan skin, wrinkled like old leather. I wondered for a second, had I been in here for that long? Was I looking into some kind of mirror? But I knew in my heart that couldn't be true. If nothing else, the marks around my wrists from the restraints were enough to prove that. Perhaps I had officially lost my mind.

'Welcome, Vic,' that soothing, low voice again. 'My little Stone-Hunter. You made it. I'm so proud of you.'

I felt my heart falter again. I opened my

mouth to speak but the tube blocked every attempt, and the mask still covered my lower face.

So, I was here, with Grandpa Mike. My dead Grandpa Mike. Insanity it was, then.

I wrested my hands once more, until he helped me untie my restraints to let me touched my hands to my face.

'Whoa, whoa, little Vic. Not that you're so little now, of course,' he said, slowly gathering his thoughts. 'You need to take it easy. I've always watched you, since they got me out. I knew you were something special. Resilient. You didn't just accept everything they told you. Your grandma Sophie, bless her soul, she knew that. The tiger on the wall, the sheep. All of it. It led us to you being the first one we chose to extract. The first Flori-born to make it out here, with us. You're the catalyst. The beginning of the Liberation.' His pitch was rising, his fervent excitement filling the room. He took a breath. 'But less of that now. There's so much we have to tell you.'

As he spoke, he carried on with the eye-stroking thing, instantly taking my mind back to being four or five, comforted after a nightmare.

'I'm sorry, honey,' he continued. 'We can't take that mask off you yet. That's why you had those restraints – we knew you wouldn't be able to resist pulling the mask off. Interfering. You need this air, these antibodies, the drugs. Otherwise this will all have been for nothing and your first experience of Outside would be to die of a common cold.'

I gasped, a gasp being the only sound I could make and which rewarded me with the pain of a sharp jab to the back of the throat from my tube.

'Yes, Vic. We busted you out. Welcome to the world. You're safe now. With me, your grandfather.'

This was a dream. A malfunctioning IsoPod. It simply couldn't be true, and that was it.

And yet, I knew I was lying to myself. I knew it was real - from the pain in my wrists, the acid emptiness of my stomach, the grim taste in my mouth. The tubes. The beeping. I was like Josh on one of his bloody T-Days. Although less prepared, more afraid. Because I wasn't in the Health Centre, or at home. I was in some weird room. Coloured drapes hung about the walls, faded in places, threadbare in others, deeply beaded in the odd forgotten corner here and there. Dim light came from side lamps, nothing like the uniform and straightforward no-nonsense overhead lights I was used to. My clothes were strange. I was in some sort of tight, yet stretchy, trousers, with an elasticated waistband. My top was similar – high necked and long sleeved, close fitting. But not restrictive; it was an exoskeleton that moved with my skin. And not a regimented Florivale colour scheme. No, these were a deep cyan blue, with a flash of neon orange down the sides. The stripe seemed somehow to capture the light and send it back out again, reminding me of my movements. Or alerting others to any attempt I made to move. Cynicism dies hard, when your world is shattered by the work of a moment.

And the old man. Grandpa Mike. I wanted so desperately to trust him, but what I needed was answers, not a bunch more questions. Was this an enclave of Outsiders, as they'd have me believe? Or was I enduring another Condition, a test of some kind. They've been increasing the pressure of lots of Conditions recently – so why not mine too? But again, something kept me from subscribing too heavily to that idea. This was too real. And there was the Shakespeare code. That had definitely been real, unless I'd been hallucinating for weeks. So why not this? My head spun.

For a moment, I was glad I couldn't move. I couldn't figure out reality from dreams, so I guess walking was going to be a while away. The door opened and I heard people cross the room. Perhaps two or three of them, joining Grandpa Mike. He leaned in to whisper to me as they approached.

'Hey, Vic. You're going to have to be pretty calm now, and work with us, or we will have to bind you again, for everyone's safety. Do you think you can do that?' He paused, waiting for a reaction and realised I couldn't speak yet.

'Nod - if you think you can.'

I nodded.

With that, a pair of gentle hands eased the mask strap from the back of my head and gently lifted it up. With a count of one to three as a gentle warning, the mask, and the tube with it, came off my mouth and out of my throat. I fought the urge to cough, knowing how much it would hurt, but to no avail. It was pretty disgusting.

'That's better isn't it,' asked the woman, as she set about cleaning up the phlegm and vomit from all around me. So far, I wasn't convinced.

'Maybe you should try it,' I wheezed. 'Then you wouldn't have to ask such a stupid question.' I hunched over, coughing although there was nothing left in my throat. 'Any chance of some water?'

Someone handed me a NutriVisor pouch without any labels. It looked reused, battered and worn. Still, with no alternative, I drank. But this wasn't water as I knew it. It had a metallic, slightly saccharine taste. The kind of aftertaste that makes you absolutely sure it's concealing the flavour of something much worse. Some medicine, I figured.

'Hello Vic,' came the same female voice I'd heard, before. 'Don't worry about the taste, you'll get used to it. That's down to how we have to treat the water out here. I'm afraid it's not as good as your multi-filtered Florivale water. What I wouldn't give to swap just our water for yours. I could forgo the food. But that crisp, clean water – I still dream about it. One of our Medics smuggled a pouch out once. She could never go back after that, of course, though she tried.'

I drank. And worried. If the water was this bad, what was everything else going to be like? This woman was wearing similar clothes to me, although hers were black with a pink stripe. As I drank, questions began to formulate in my mind. But I wasn't going to be the one asking questions for a while – that much was clear from the eager looks on my visitors' faces.

'You're amazing Vic. We've watched you. We logged your IsoPod visits. Your fitness. Your education. We saw you react to the image on the screen and when you broke the Shakespeare code, well, that just confirmed it. You were instantly clear to us as the one we needed to break out. Enough cynicism to kill a man, enough wit and intellect to evade one.' She broke her monologue and touched my shoulder protectively. 'We're so glad you're here. But that's why you have to stay, in this bed for now, and trust us. Your body won't be able to cope out here without our help.'

'She's right,' said Mike. 'There's so much I want to tell you, to show you. But I have to be as patient as you do. I know it won't feel like that right now. How could it? You're trapped, exhausted and confused' He paused. 'But it's all for the best, I can promise you that. All the world may be a stage, Vic. But the production being played in Florivale has to stop. They've gone too far.'

'Who?' I croaked. 'What are you talking about?' This was ridiculous. Every word they uttered just brought with it more confusion, more questions.

'All in good time, Vic,' came a third voice. A man, younger. He was out of sight, and I figured he was sitting behind my bed. I was too stiff to turn my head to acknowledge him, but he carried on.

'Do you mind me calling you Vic? We can call you whatever you want. But you have to understand, we had no choice but to get you out sooner than we had planned. Josh was right to be scared. You were right to be cautious. And we were right to take drastic action.'

Before I could try again to turn and see him, even before a word could leave my parched lips, I heard his steps, followed by the finality of a closing door. I heard frantic beeps and realised it the sound was emanating from the machine I was hooked up to.

'Great, Mike. That's just great. Now that Alex has gone and freaked her out, she'll get zero sleep – which will only set her back longer. Jesus, I never thought I'd wish we had a functioning IsoPod.'

'Don't worry about it Elle,' said Mike. 'He was always going to react like that. You know better than most how involved he's been in the Liberation plans. You know he can't just sit and watch these things pan out.' Mike turned to me. 'And Vic, he's right. I don't want to sugar-coat it, but we've also got to ease you in to this lifestyle, to drip-feed you the truth. A lifetime in Florivale is a lifetime of lies. You just have to let us in. Slowly. We need to paint over your picture of the world. The colour we'll add will be the truth.'

It didn't feel like I had much choice. I felt another sharp prick in my arm and any fight I had left in me disappeared. I felt the room start to tilt, my mind sliding away from me. My body lay still as I succumbed to the warm drowsiness which enveloped me.

'Don't worry, Vic. By the time you wake up, we'll have gotten some nutrition into you. You'll feel much better. And believe me, we'll tell you everything you need to know. It will just take some time. There's simply too much to say.'

40

I stirred, feeling the shift of my blanket as I rolled towards the side of the bed. I ran my hands down the side of the sheets and realised my restraints were gone. Elated, I lifted my hands to my face, which confirmed that the mask and the tube were also history. I still felt heavy, and my BioBand still wasn't lighting up. In fact, it hadn't activated.

I lay with my hand resting on my chest, soothed by the metronome of my heartbeat. I was bathed in the same muted light as before, but now a filmy layer fell between me and the walls of the room. It was some sort of tent, made of clear plastic. There was a curved zip for a door and room for about two people to come inside and stand by the bed I lay in.

A bashed-up medical monitor stood next to me, nothing like the ones on the side of the IsoPods or in Josh's house. Instead of a smooth, simple touch screen, this was all faded cream plastic, with buttons and lights all over the place. If you can believe this, the screen was actually held together with silver plastic tape. Like a discarded old toy. A fossil. Anyway, this thing was happily beeping and chirping away, and was kind of cute in its antiquity.

A plastic tube pierced the back of my left

hand. There was some clear liquid flowing through it and into me. This didn't make me feel anxious, and couldn't fathom why that was. I was just... mellow. Tired. Anyway, I sat with my beeping companion and my drip, processing the bits I could remember from my last conversation. It was fuzzy, but I was pretty certain I had met my Grandpa Mike, who wasn't dead and who, in fact, along with some strangers, seemed to have busted me out of Florivale. Sure. Why not?

It's true isn't it, that you should be careful what you wish for? Here, I have absolutely no idea what's going on. But in Florivale, although I knew things weren't right, at least I knew what they were. I had my own system of understanding, in there. Whereas here I was in a tent, feeling inappropriately calm, hooked up some ancient medical equipment and with nobody around to ask any questions. This was somewhat out of character, to say the least.

I got to looking about the room, through the translucent plastic. I could make out the fabrics I'd seen when I first woke, which covered the walls. This must have been the same room, but I figured they'd brought in this tent while I was sleeping, for whatever reason. I wondered why anyone would go to the trouble of layering multi-coloured fabric all over the walls, when they could just paint them, paper them, whatever. But maybe the décor out here is a bit more 'Clem'. There were no windows, there was no breeze. But, unbelievable as it seemed, I simply knew I was Outside.

But that meant my family, and Clem and

Josh, were still in Florivale, and I wasn't there with them. I wasn't there to prove a point, or to make a scene. To tell them I was right! Or to explain my adventure, the Shakespeare code, the notes, all of it! But most importantly, I wasn't there to tell them there was danger. How long would it have taken them to notice my disappearance? Would they be subjected to questioning? And what might they have to say, if they were?

I didn't have much time to mull on this, because I heard steps coming towards the room and, sure enough, in strolled Grandpa Mike - for there was now no doubt in my mind that it was him - and the female Carer-type from before. They unzipped the 'door' into my tent and proved me right. There was just enough room for them around my bedside.

'How's it going?' asked Grandpa Mike. 'You slept for a very long time.'

I had no idea how long I'd been asleep, or how long it was since I went into the IsoPod. I was so sleep-deprived when I went in, and so messed up by all the SleepSteam and the sedatives that it could have been five minutes, or equally, five weeks. Turns out neither was correct.

'Yes, Victoria,' said the woman. Elle, I thought. 'You've been out for just under a day and a half now. Your body must be adjusting to everything. You must be exhausted. You didn't even stir while we erected the tent and took away your mask. We hope you feel more comfortable. That was Mike's idea.'

'Well, call me soft, but I just couldn't stand my little granddaughter tied up like an escaped animal, hooked up to a mask so tight she couldn't speak. God knows how many questions you must have.'

'Yeah,' I said, pleasantly surprised that it hurt much less to speak now that the tube was gone. 'Right now, every thought that marches into my head is a question. Like, why don't I want to escape, fight, shout? What's in this drip? Why me? What's happening to the others, to everyone in Florivale?' I raised my head, dizzy at the effort as I glared at Mike. 'And how the hell are you alive? I heard about your funeral!'

'Whoa, whoa, Vic. I get it. You've got all the questions in the world. But you're simply not ready for all the answers just yet. We need to start with the basics. Smaller pieces – little strands for you to wrap the bigger answers around once they start coming through.' He gestured to Elle, in the direction of the door. 'Can you leave us for a minute?'

She was pissed off at having been dismissed, and although it was politely phrased, Mike's meaning had been clear. As clear as her huffy response. A twitch of the nose. The eyebrows arcing slightly. Infinitely small gestures, but there if you knew where to look.

'I don't want you overloading her,' she muttered. 'And I need to check this godawful monitor first. I'm sorry Victoria, I know it's nothing like the sophisticated medical equipment you were used to in Florivale.' She fussed with my charts, adjusting the odd screen with a swift stroke from her finger. 'But if I'm honest with you, it's much more difficult for me to adjust everything to suit your needs. Whatever was wrong with that place, they had medical provision just right.' She caught Mike's stare and silenced his anticipated outcry. 'Yes, OK Mike. I agree it's a shame that such clinical excellence comes at such a cost.'

I stared as she flustered about the monitor, poking buttons, writing things down, twisting a knob here, looking at a screen there. Grandpa Mike rolled his eyes. In Florivale the data would have just automatically synced through my BioBand and the CompStream system and updated my meal, exercise and sleep plans in a moment. But more amazing, and harder to believe, was that this woman had been inside Florivale. And it sounded like she had been a Carer. Which meant that people did come and go from Florivale, if not the residents. Just as Clem and I had talked about. But how had that worked? How was infection control handled? Unless... had she been busted out like I had? My thoughts were interrupted by my fellow escapee.

'OK, Mike. She's all yours. But don't overdo it. We talked about this. She is strong. But she is human. Goodbye, Victoria. I'll be back to check on you later.'

She left the tent, zipped it back up on the

other side and hesitated a moment, looking at me, before she turned and walked, in the usual clipped 'Carer' way, out of the room. I wondered what things looked like on the other side of the door.

Grandpa Mike winked at me conspiratorially as she left. Formality thrown aside, he came closer, sat on the end of my bed, adjusted himself into a more comfortable position and took the hand which wasn't connected to the drip. He held my gaze, a second longer than would have felt comfortable with a stranger. I was looking into my own eyes, into my past. And I realised – my future lay in the palm of this man's hand.

'First off, I'm going to need you to try something important for me,' he said. I nodded. 'It's a small thing, don't worry. But I need you to stop calling me Grandpa Mike. It only reminds me of your grandma, my wonderful Sophie. And, what's more, in the Collective, out here, there are some who think we selected you to be our first Flori-born breakout because I wanted you out. And I sure did, they're damn right.' He smiled. 'But it's not just that, chickadee. I knew, we knew, that you had the tenacity, curiosity and the sheer strength of will you'd need to get Outside. And to survive out here.' He took his hand and ran it through his pewter-grey hair as he spoke.

'I can try. I can try really hard. But are you saying there are people out here who wish I hadn't made it out? That someone else could have been picked? How am I meant to do it all - learn everything you want me to, process all this new information you keep promising, and fend off any malice from anyone who wishes it had been someone else out here instead of me?'

'It will be tough sometimes, sweet pea. But you have to just try. Be yourself. Your determined, intriguing, pugnacious little self. That's how you'll prove you were the right one. And I know you were – we've watched you for years.'

I shuddered. He paused as he clocked my discomfort at the idea of being watched, reassessing his words before continuing.

'But I think I'd better start with something more tangible. Like the tent. You're in here because you just couldn't cope out there yet, in our air. In Florivale, nothing was real. Your air was filtered. Oxygen was added to it and the harmful pollution we have out here was siphoned out. Hell, even the water in your showers contained sun protection, so that you couldn't get burned by the strength of the sun, now that the ozone layer is so thin. Then again, I guess you don't know much about the risks Outside. That the ozone is now just a flimsy skin, flapping in the atmosphere, the protection it used to offer dissipated to near-uselessness by the side effects of human greed. We're talking back to basics here, sweetie. This is why you need time.'

'But what does the ozone have to do with

the tent?' I asked. I still didn't fully follow what he was talking about, but I figured he needed to keep talking for me to get a handle on the message he was working to convey.

'The tent is your protection. We've managed to blend some smuggled Florivale air in with ours, and we're gradually adjusting the proportions. That's another reason only up to two other people can come in here. Everyone wants to breathe your filtered air, even when there's only a trace amount left. And it was too costly to obtain, too difficult, for us to let it be frittered away in the hope of an oxygen fix for a couple of people across our team.' He looked across at the fluid pouch and smiled wryly at me. 'I think you will recall the taste of the water.' I grimaced. Life Outside was sounding pretty crap.

'But what about the reports we had in Florivale. The violence. The disease. Isn't everyone out here dead or dying, fighting to survive? How exactly are you guys all just ticking along, in this place? Speaking of which, where are we?'

Almost in answer to my question, a siren of some kind started to sound. This was metallic, not like the clean, electronic sirens in Florivale, like they use when there is a CompStream Bulletin we need to listen to, or a precautionary drill to carry out. It struck me, maybe I wouldn't hear that clean electronic sound again. With no sign of panic, and clearly not inclined to acquiesce to whatever the sound demanded, Mike waved his hands in the air, shooing the noise away.

'Sounds like question time is over. What a bloody racket.' He waited for the bells to end. 'That means dinner. You've slept through the other meal bells, and we're controlling your diet at the moment anyway, so it's not like it mattered. But don't worry. We get bell rings for dinner and meetings. You'll get used to them. But this means it's time for me to go and eat, chat, tell everyone all about you.' He winked and went to stand up.

'I hate leaving you. But in leaving, I know there's the reward that I'll get to see you again. You have so much of Sophie in you. I want your adjustment period to finish as quickly as possible, so I can show you off. And don't worry too much about your safety – we'll do everything in our power to protect you. But you have to help us. That starts by trusting us. You're something of a prized possession.' He ruffled my hair, which was by now a hideous greasy mess. I don't know how he could stand to touch it.

'Grandpa. No - Mike. Sorry. I'm still not used to any of this - I'll start again. Mike. Can you find out how long my adjustment will be? And when I can take a shower?'

He laughed, walking away with his back turned.

'Shower? Sure. Just don't expect any of your steamy nonsense from Florivale. We don't, can't, do things that way in here. But I'll see if we can't get you cleaned up a bit.'

He left the door, turned as he closed it, and smiled as he left, the ghost of a laugh clearly hiding in the back of his mind. I was not looking forward to whatever alternative to a shower I was going to have the pleasure of experiencing.

I guessed I had some time to kill while everyone had their meal and dissected the details of my arrival. That I was here wouldn't remain secret for long, buy the sounds of it. They probably all knew by now - everyone would have known immediately in Florivale. Imagine if an Outsider had come in to us, with different ways of speaking, meals, even different water... It would have been the most fascinating thing that had ever happened in the Community. Clem would have had so many questions. Josh would have grilled them for ideas of how to escape his T-Days. I worried for both of them, wondering what they made of my absence. Whether Josh even knew I'd gone, or whether he was still shutting everything from his solitary bedroom. My mind turned to my parents. Did they believe I had died? Would they be grieving, while I was coming to terms with my new-found freedom, and learning what it had cost? It was too painful to dwell on. I thought of Grandma Sophie, who ended her days without knowing her beloved Mike had lived. I thought of Mum, and hoped she wasn't crying, although I knew she would be.

Assuming the town of Florivale thought I was dead - which I imagined to be likely considering that's how they explained the disappearance of Grandpa Mike - there would be a Carer visit to my parents. A rolling out of the facts they knew, a careful sweeping aside of the aspects they didn't. Maybe they'd say they thought I was in the Lake (headstrong girl, pity), or that I'd contracted a rare fever (a quick fix, if they wanted to cover things up, although tarnishing Florivale's objective of protecting health at any cost). I didn't think they would say I'd escaped or been removed; control was key and anything undermining the authority's absolute control would simply not be tolerated. Once my family had been told, and maybe Clem and Josh, they would issue a sombre CompStream announcement. One of the Community had perished, drowned, whatever. The Community would be called upon to use this as a catalyst to strengthen their resolve to find the cure. To work together, to be the best Florivites they could be. There would be tears. A memorial service, perhaps, given they'd have no body to bury. Jack would probably cry and say something sweet, tugging a teddy along behind him. Mum and Dad would be devastated, and no doubt they'd cling to Jack all the more for my loss. The mollycoddling would never stop.

I'd wondered in the past what would happen if I had died. The vain musings of a bored adolescent, indulging in the idea of people missing me, feeling sorry for any ways they had wronged me. It was usually instigated by a rare CompStream announcement about a death. They were few and far between but, for a few days, the person who had died became a sort of hero. Idolised and praised for their good qualities, many of which had been either secret (benefit of the doubt) or non-existent (cynic) prior to their demise. Deaths were swift in Florivale and the sick were not left long to flounder. Perhaps it was damage limitation and things weren't done to slow their passing. If Florivale thought I was dead, I was sure they'd all be talking about how sweet and intelligent I was, devoted to my friends and family, rather than how they had actually perceived me while I was around. No doubt Melanie would keep her taunts to herself and make out to anyone who'd listen that we'd been close, anything for a little more attention.

Whereas, for me, contemplating Florivale from my remote tent on the Outside, I had begun to peel back the layers of fiction that made up our daily lives in there.

Funny thing about a fake death, it doesn't half give you some perspective.

The minutes ticked by and finally something broke a link in the chain of my thoughts. There was muttering outside the door, chattering sounds like the bickering monkeys from the Community Centre's wildlife videos. I hadn't even imagined there might be children Outside. But of course there could be. Everything else was a lie, so why not this? With all the stories of illness and disease, violence and danger, I had assumed fertility would be at an all-time low Outside, hence the pressure to procreate with as perfect a genetic match as possible within Florivale. But sure enough, three children came peering round the door. The first thing I saw was a slightly grubby hand reaching around the door frame, controlling the creaks as the door opened. Then came a couple of feet in filthy socks, followed by the emergence of the first of my juvenile visitors into the room. Probably about eleven years old, this little guy had a pouting lower lip, which I suspected was his attempt at defiance - whilst still being fairly terrified of what lay inside. Of me.

Behind him trailed a girl, slightly younger, and a boy, of about eight or nine years old. The girl was trying to look brave, to similarly abysmal effect. The younger boy had a vague resemblance to Jack, and a similar lackadaisical approach to dressing and personal hygiene, for his hands were even grubbier than those of the first visitor.

'Is it just you in here,' asked the first boy. 'A bloody girl?' He was incredulous. 'All that bother for a girl! And she gets the fancy water. The special food. The little tent that we're not even allowed inside. That's just stupid. It could have at least been a boy.'

Well, that put me in my place, didn't it?

'You're quite correct,' I said, smirking as he jumped at the sound of my voice. 'I am a girl. I'm sorry about that. What's your name? I can see you're obviously quite important in here, so I apologise for not knowing immediately who you are.' Years of dealing with a stroppy Jack had taught me that flattery would get me, if not quite everywhere, certainly most of the way.

The boy paused and considered my words for a moment, looking back at his confused companions for guidance which was not forthcoming.

'Yes. I'm a boy. Which means I am better than you. And her!' He pointed at the little girl, who went from nervous to pouty immediately and looked like she wanted to kick him. 'But as you asked, and considering you're new here, I'll let you off. I'm Dom. This is Heath. And the girl, her name is Lexi. But I told her not to come and she shouldn't be here so she isn't meant to say anything.'

Lexi took umbrage at this and the anticipated kick materialised. She got him square in the back of the legs and deftly dodged back as soon as she had done it, cleverly anticipating the lash she'd receive from him once he had recovered from the shock. From a few safe paces behind him, she piped up.

'I am a girl, but girls are better than boys.' She pointed at me. 'She knows I'm right. And it must be true. Otherwise, why would they have broken her out instead of a boy?'

She made a good point. I liked Lexi a lot. With a defiant little sneer, and her hands on her hips, she looked like an olden-days housewife, from Before. But she was only a little kid. Crazy how some things endure through the ages. All she needed was a rolling pin to wave about and she could have stepped from the pages of a dusty old comic book.

Not to be upstaged, Heath took a couple of steps forward and stood next to Dom, where it was safer. Lexi's legs couldn't reach him there.

'I'm Heath. And one day I'm going to be the leader of the Collective. That's us. We don't have the same rules, like the other people. We have our own rules. And we don't live in la-la dreamland like you idiots in Florivale. Even if you get all the good stuff in there, we know it's all fake. My mum said so and she should know. She used to be an undercover Carer. She nearly died for idiots like you.'

I was struck by the idea of there being other groups, factions of people with their own rules. Without every breath, meal and movement planned out for them like we'd had in Florivale. The idea of undercover Carers made me feel very sick. The very people I'd resented my whole life could have been risking their lives to get me out! But what for? What world had I found myself in?

'Hold on,' I said. 'Undercover Carer? Tell me more about that. I bet you know loads of interesting stuff about the – Collective, was it?' I was met with a stern face and a shaking head. He was not going to play along. But of course, that didn't stop me trying. 'Is your Mum here? Can I speak to her? She sounds so brave. Well, she must have been brave to have a strong son like you. I bet she is very proud of you.'

'I'm not telling you anything. We don't

know anything about you. You might go back to Florivale somehow and tell everyone about us. We escaped them once and we're not going back.'

'You were in Florivale? All of you? How come I can't remember you then?' My mind was racing. Could they have been what were referred to as still-borns while I was still too young to question anything, but perhaps they'd been perfectly healthy, and somehow stolen away from Florivale? 'How many children are there out here?' I asked. I was panicking, my breath catching in my throat as I spoke.

'No, stupid. None of us were born in there, or you couldn't be the first Flori-born to break out, could you?' Smart cookies, these kids. I clearly needed to think carefully, or they'd be running rings around me in no time. Dom, the wise cracker, was back in action. I was put back in my place. The only ones who escaped were the ones who weren't Flori-borns. 'We're all natural, no health support, no government nonsense and no stupid Conditions. We're resilient. We're the Collective'

Lexi was next to pipe up. 'But I like you. I want you to stay. You don't look angry.'

'Shut up, Lexi,' said Dom. 'We're leaving. We don't know if we like you yet. Just don't do anything bad. And stay in your tent like you're supposed to.'

With that, he turned impetuously on his heels and marched out of the door, leaving a slightly bewildered Heath and Lexi behind him. They turned and stared at the space Dom left behind him, and then back at me. Just then, Dom poked his head back around the door frame.

'Come on, you idiots. I said we're leaving!'

And with that, they trotted out, Lexi turning and giving me a fleeting smile as she shut the door behind her.

41

I had my first experience of food on the Outside today – well, in terms of food you actually have to chew. Beforehand, they were getting nutrition into me through my intravenous drip, along with all these antibodies and chemicals they keep taking about. They're trying to adjust my body ready for life out here. I can't say I felt hungry, so whatever they were doing clearly worked. But I was definitely ready for the feeling of food in my mouth, all those textures. I was even missing my scrambled tofu NutriVisor pouches, and that's saying something.

Someone new brought it to me, this afternoon. She knocked gently and asked if she could come in. I was getting sick of being hemmed in here, but I was also terrified of leaving it and not being able to breathe. The taste of the 'water' was enough to see to that. In came this lady, probably mid-thirties. Her clothes were like everyone else's, same dark stretchy base, stripes down the sides in bright colours. She was slim but looked pretty healthy, with hair lighter than mine, a sort of mouse-colour. Wisps of it framed her face, which seemed all the sweeter for its soft lines and crinkles. She placed a covered plate on a chair near the door and came nearer to the tent.

'Hi, Victoria. Gosh.' Her hands were

trembling slightly. 'I can't believe you're really here. I mean, I knew you were, you would be, but here you are. And you're doing so well! Responding so well! I couldn't believe it when they asked me to make you a meal! It made the rumours true.' She fidgeted constantly, her fingers endlessly interlacing and coming apart again.

'Sorry, I'm running away with myself. I'm Lizzie. Do you mind if I come in?'

I nodded and beckoned her into the tent. I could feel her wanting to ask questions just as much as I did, and invited her in immediately. She carefully eased the zipper up and stepped in, coming into better focus. She was prettier than I'd first thought. Younger.

'Hi, Lizzie. Welcome to my humble abode,' I said, as I gestured around the bed. She smiled.

'Oh Victoria, I'm so sorry you're stuck in here. But, you see, it really is for the best. We need you to keep getting stronger. But just look at you. Twenty-odd years of perfect health and nutrition, all there. Amazing.' She barely paused for breath. 'I came in while you were out of it, at first, and they've brought the air quality so much closer to ours. Sorry about that, it must taste horrible for you. Hopefully it still feels like you're getting enough oxygen? But here I am rabbiting on! The good news is that with the air adjustments coming on and the request for real food, I think you'll be out in... well. A couple of days? Maybe four or five? Everyone is dying to meet you.'

I wasn't sure which of her comments to respond to first, so I went generic.

'Yeah, it sucks to be stuck in here. But I'm more scared of what's outside the tent than in, so maybe a few more days would be good. Plus, I have zero energy. I don't even have the air I'm used to. Or, for that matter, any actual food in my stomach, just a bunch of nutritional gunk through one of these tubes'.

Suddenly, I was hungrier than I'd ever been. I imagine that sensation wasn't helped by the wisps of steam I could see rising from the tray on the chair. Or the aromas swirling towards me.

'I'm sorry, I have to ask. What's on the plate!? And can I actually eat it? Now?'

An embarrassed flush ran across her face and Lizzie jumped up.

'Oh god, of course. I'm so sorry. I got totally side-tracked by taking in the fact that you're real, that you're here. Let me grab your food.'

She crossed the room and picked off the cover, releasing another billowing cloud of steam. Now, I wanted to get out of the bed. I could have clawed the tray from her hands, saliva welling up in my mouth. I sat up in my bed and smoothed out the covers for the tray, which held a bowl of tomato soup, and a roll of bread, with a small pat of butter on the side. I hadn't had bread and butter since the last Florivale wedding, given that it contained 'inefficient' calories and fat without much nutritional benefit. But that didn't stop me remembering how delicious it was.

The soup, with its glossy sheen, was as inviting as any meal I had ever seen. Almost feral in my haste, I ripped open the bread, which was denser than the white roll I remembered. This was dark brown, flecked with seeds and grains, crusty on the outside and pillow-soft within. I spread the butter over it, awkwardly ripping the soft inside of the bread as I went, as it was too cold to be malleable. And, with a moment's hesitation to fully enjoy the anticipation, I dunked a piece of the roll into the soup and brought it to my mouth.

Nothing I ever eat will taste as good as that meal tasted. I am sure of it. Rich, creamy butter with hot, tangy, almost peppery tomato soup, semi-sweet. The dense bread brought texture to my mouth, which I hadn't realised I'd missed, until today. And this wasn't from a pouch. It contained excess salt and fat. And inefficient calories. It was marvellous.

I had a feeling I'd be making sure Lizzie became a close friend. My exalted Bringer of Soup! Everybody would rush to escape Florivale if they knew there was food like this on the Outside. Screw the rumours, the disease. This was living.

'I'm sorry it's only soup and bread,' apologised Lizzie. 'They wanted to ease you in to our way of eating, nothing too rich. I snuck some butter on there for you though. It's harder to come by these days, but we do OK. And so should you.'

'Lizzie, this is perfect,' I stuttered, between gulps of soup and chunks of bread. 'I'm going to have to slow myself down or I'll be sick. This meal tastes of more than it is. It tastes of freedom.'

Lizzie glanced down at her feet, her skin flushing at the compliment the same way mine did when I was embarrassed.

'Do you mind staying while I finish?' I asked, sensing her awkwardness. 'I'd love to talk to you but I can't tear myself away from eating. I must look appalling - filthy and starving. I hope you don't mind?' Lizzie looked up, and smiled as our eyes connected.

'Of course I don't mind!' she beamed. 'I'd love to speak to you. I want to hear all about it. I only know what I'm told about Florivale, second-hand information, or stories which are long out of date. From the beginning, before things started to, well, change. Eat. Breathe. Then let's speak. I can always enjoy the lovely air in here while you enjoy the soup.'

She didn't need to say that twice. I methodically tore strips from the roll, buttered and dunked them into the soup, relishing every bite. Far too soon, the bread was gone, and not long after, my spoon hit the bottom of the bowl. I'd have to remember to save some bread to mop up the remaining liquid next time – it felt criminal not to be able to consume every last drop. I thanked Lizzie as she took the tray from me, feeling more myself than I had in days.

My hunger had shifted from an animalistic need for sustenance to an insatiable thirst for knowledge. It was time to talk.

I patted the end of the bed, an invitation for Lizzie to sit a little closer. I realised how soft the sheets were, and doubted they had been sterilised. They didn't have the crispness I was used to. I wasn't sure whether that was a good or a bad thing any more, but I figured if they went to the trouble of creating a tent of oxygen for me and monitored everything else, they'd be pretty careful not to give me infected bed linen.

'Thanks,' I started. 'For coming to speak to me, I mean. It's crazy being in here and I don't know where to begin, so maybe you could? Start, I mean. I think I won't know what my questions are until they walk into my head.' She looked at me, flummoxed, and I went on. 'Which means I'll probably interrupt you every five seconds. But I'll try. See! I'm burbling away at you already. Sorry. So, what's your story, Lizzie? How come you're in here? Or, more accurately, out here? And what is it like… out there?'

'I'm going to have to take it one question at a time, I think,' she said, laughing as she processed my questions. 'There are some things the Seniors think you're not ready to know yet, so we've got to sort of ease you out of your Florivale life and into this life, your real life. It's not all as bad as the water,' she said, covering her mouth nervously, the soft lines by her eyes dancing as she did.

'We're a Collective, like your Community, but here out of choice. There are about a hundred and fifty of us here. We're not the only group, but we pride ourselves on our democracy, our peaceful approach and our commitment to do the right thing, not just for ourselves, but for everyone. For the future. Because there is a risk that our future will be something unfathomable to anyone who remembers a time before it all started going badly. That was not long after Florivale was established. Your grandma would never have known how bad it got out here, but we've heard from Mike that she had her suspicions. As did he.'

'Yeah, how did Grandpa - I mean - Mike, get out? What happened? Was he busted out in an IsoPod like me?'

'Like I said, Victoria. One question at a time.'

'OK, OK! Call me Vic. I prefer it. I'm not some grand old queen in a history book, I'm just Vic. Vic is fine.'

'So. Vic it is. We're going to have to take

this all pretty slow.' It was going to be a long conversation at this rate. 'I think I was saying that we're the best community around and we're full of principles and morals et cetera.' She was relaxing into our conversation, the invisible rod of nerves removed from her back, allowing her to be more natural. A little slouched, conspiratorial.

'But the greatest thing about this place is the people. We only accept, and we only retain, the best people. And best doesn't mean strongest, although that doesn't hurt. It doesn't mean the kindest, although that doesn't hurt either. It means the best they can be. In whatever capacity that is. We see people living to their full potential as being essential to helping sort out this mess, to creating a real future.'

'So, what are you doing?' I asked. 'To sort the mess out? What exactly is the mess?!' Florivale was small and everything, but what were a hundred and fifty people going to achieve?

My monitor was beeping and Lizzie got up to check it. Apparently my heart rate was giving the game away and my calm façade was revealed to be a lie. It was all this new information. I did some careful Clem-style breathing, and when the beeping slowed, Lizzie carried on.

'You might have heard from the older people in Florivale, your Pioneers, that things had been getting bad out here. And, of course, you saw what your Grandma Sophie's notes said, too.' I made a mental note to find out how much she knew about the notes.

'Anyway, people were sick. They were getting worse. There was so much. Cancer, lung disease, heart disease, parasites. There was so much suffering – it was all going downhill, fast. Apart from the salaries of the doctors and the politicians, of course. Nobody knew what to do. So many people lost their lives because they had poor advice, or conflicting courses of treatment. Scores more died as medical provision became ever more expensive and only the rich, or those who sold everything they owned, could get the treatment they needed. Things were pretty bleak, when Minister Harte came up with her project, her baby. The Opportunity. You saw about the posters in the notes, right? But it got so much worse as time went on – for those outside Florivale, anyway.'

I nodded. 'Yes. I remember the announcement from the notes. But it's so different hearing it from someone out here. From someone who is still here and able to answer questions about it. The notes could have been pure fiction, but they weren't. It's almost unthinkable.'

'OK. So Harte comes up with her plan and spends a sum equivalent to years of free medical provision for the general public on creating Florivale.' Lizzie was exasperated at this, and then, just as quickly as her temper had flared, she had shaken it off. 'Like I said, it was her baby. The Pioneers got to escape their lives on the Outside, and all their problems, or at least, that's how it seemed, and move into this little corner of paradise. Somewhere that seemed to be a safe haven. From talking to Mike, I know just how bad things were for a lot of people. Debt, hard work and fewer jobs as technology made labour virtually redundant, fears for their safety, and for that of their children. It was a perfect storm. When the Value Life riots began, Harte had her PR moment. A call to arms for the nation's health. And that's where your grandparents, and their peers, came in.' She paused, seeing the anguish written across my brow. 'Sorry, Vic. You look like you're trying to remember every tiny detail, about to be interviewed on everything I say. Don't worry, we can take a break. I'll still be here to answer your questions. I can say all of this all over again.'

I shuffled forward a little. I couldn't process this fast enough. She was right. I wanted a note pad to write everything down so that I could pore over it later, like I did with the notes. I wanted to be able to parse every word for meaning, to weave detail into the bare bones that I understood so far. But what I wanted most was information. I urged her to carry on.

'OK. So, back to the plan. In come the Pioneers. Each one was carefully screened and selected to ensure they contained the best possible genetic combinations across the Community. Yes, I know, like cattle, picked out to be selectively bred into perfection. That's essentially what they were. Other tests checked for cancer markers, for early indications of susceptibility to illness. Stuff like that. Family histories were scrutinised and mental health was rigorously assessed. You see, Harte didn't want to have to let anyone from Florivale leave. Ever. It was to be her second world. She watched it like others watched TV, her own reality show playing out before her. Oh, TV is like a CompStream but from Before. I don't know if you'd have seen about those in the Community Centre.'

'I know what a TV is. I spent more time in the Community Centre and the Library than others. I like knowing things. Like Clem does.' My stomach dropped. 'Oh God. Clem. Do you know how Clem is? How my family is? And Josh?' My breath started to catch and my voice quavered. I was so worried for them, but I needed to know more about the wider picture before I could understand the details. I couldn't risk Lizzie stopping her story. I had to keep her with me.

'Vic, are you sure you want to carry on?' she asked. I nodded, although I wasn't quite sure. 'So, your family, and your friends, are… well, they're OK. Josh is still not great but we are monitoring him. He's not been hugely functional since his last T-Day. However, Clem is visibly disturbed. She has increased her running and her yoga and decreased all else. She is even failing to get her quota of sleep, she is trying to get sent to the IsoPods, but there's a crackdown on their use, since your departure. We think your disappearance may be responsible for that, and for Clem's reaction. You talked to her about the notes, and she's processing it all. Trying to connect the dots. She hasn't figured out the code yet. But, luckily, she's being given some latitude by the Carers, who interpret the changes in her behaviour as the manifestation of her grief at losing you.'

I realised that Clem was all alone, in there. Weighed down with the knowledge I'd given her about the notes, probably as angry as I was that we'd disagreed when we last spoke, and bewildered at my disappearance. I was a sister to her, and now I was gone. No confidante. No double act. Just gone. She'd have to balance her reactions to everything, try not to tell anyone about the notes, just in case I'd done what I'd set out to, and got out. She could hardly talk to Josh about it either, with Mrs. McLaine lurking in the corridors and Josh shutting us out. For a second, I wished I could be back in Florivale, not knowing any of this, doing my terrible attempts at yoga next to Clem. Or at Josh's bedside, doing anything in my power to make him laugh, to come back to himself. Lizzie's voice snapped me out of my daydream and back to my new reality.

'The announcement went out last week. They - I don't know how to say this - but I think I'm going to have to be blunt. They told all of Florivale over a Bulletin that you had drowned in the Lake. That you'd used your precocious, wilful ways to evade the Protectors and now the whole Community had to pay the price. You're the poster girl for how not to behave.' She looked up and saw the tears welling in my eyes. 'I'm so sorry. I should have stopped. I should slow down.'

'But, my parents,' I sobbed. 'What will happen to them? And Jack?' My throat tightened and I felt as though I had swallowed the Lake, submerged beneath undulating icy waters and unable to see the surface. 'The number of times I wished I could get Outside, leave them behind.' My chest racked with sobs, and I could feel nothing apart from the gentle pressure of Lizzie's warm hand on my back as I curled forward on my bedspread.

'I know, Vic,' she said, as she took my hand, the warmth of her palm seeping into mine. 'We all lose people. But you've lost everything, in one moment, with no fore-warning. And, as far as they know, they've lost you. But they haven't, and you haven't. You have us now. And we, together, can salvage something out of the scraps of the good life that was left behind. We can make it right again. But we need you, Vic. When the time is right, your loved ones will understand more about the truth. They don't even know it, but they need you too. But I don't think we should talk any more tonight. Your mind is flexing its muscles, and I don't want to strain it with too much to process. Grief is debilitating enough.' She stood and smoothed the covers over me, like mum used to.

'Sleep, Vic. You poor thing. Don't worry,' she said, as my eyelids fluttered with exhaustion. 'I'll stay here until after you fall asleep. You're not alone.'

I quietly fell into a stunned, deep sleep.

Just before I sank into the warm abyss of dreamlessness, I had a feeling of safety, of connection. Her hand on my back confirmed the honesty of her promise to stay with me. The world needed more of this.

Florivale needed to be woken up from its endless dream.

42

I woke early in the morning, my body deeply weighted into the be, compressed by the revelations of the night before. As I prised my sticky eyelids open, I realised I could see the other side of the room more clearly. Rubbing my eyes, in case this was an illusion I could dismiss with a brush of my hand, I realised that the fabrics draped on the wall were there, but in glorious technicolour. The tent was gone!

Regardless of the fact that the Outside air was reportedly so much worse than what I was used to, I felt free. I tentatively filled my lungs, waiting for something to catch, tighten, stick. But it was fine. I breathed again, and felt a smile dance across my lips.

The old medical monitor was still beeping at me every now and again, my odd companion. But the intravenous drip was gone! I went to take my first steps for a few days. I swung my legs around so they hung off the bed, snuck my bum forward, and the soles of my feet hit the coolness of the thin rug on the floor. The firm floorboards beneath. I pushed myself off the bed and stood on my own two feet, in the real world, for the first time. It felt good.

There was a hollowness in my chest, put there by the knowledge that Florivale was behind me, as were the people I loved – still trapped. They might never know that I was alive, that I wasn't quite wild enough to jump into the Lake. On reflection, I think they'd be entirely justified in thinking that I was. But with the hollowness I felt came my sense of responsibility. Clem, Josh, my family. I had a responsibility to them all. I needed to make the pain, the struggle, and the efforts of the people who'd brought me out of Florivale, worthwhile.

Gently walking away from my bed, I saw that the room was quite large. I reached the draped walls and peered behind the fabrics to see that three of the four sides of the room were painted beneath, each at differing levels of decay and peppered with peeling flakes. No tigers stalked across these walls. The air behind the drapes tasted damp, of wet stone, like the footpaths in Florivale after the rain. I let the drapes fall back into place, the room instantly jollier for their colour, for the way they masked the real walls. I understood why they were there now. On the remaining wall, adjacent to my bed, the fabric drapes concealed a large square of glass. A window. My heart fluttering at the prospect of my first glimpse of Outside, I wondered whether it would be full of shiny, empty tower blocks, a cityscape just like I'd seen in the books about Before. Perhaps the buildings would be falling down, like the Bulletins said, leaving shattered windows and loose bricks strewn across the pavements below? Or would I be in a countryside idyll out of a story-book, woodlands all around me, birds gently hopping from tree to tree?

I needn't have been excited. I pulled the drape aside and found the window was boarded up from the other side, and seemed to have been painted over with something translucent before the boards were nailed down. No light came through the cracks in the wood, and no light from within would reach the outside world when darkness fell. I rested my head against the glass, enjoying the cool smoothness against my forehead, watching the condensation forming cloudy patterns beneath my mouth as I breathed onto the pane.

As I stood there, for I don't know how long, I gradually became aware that someone was watching me. I turned and saw little Lexi just inside the door. A safe distance away, just in case I tried something. The kids out here are pretty switched on. I smiled and went to say hello, but she beat me to it.

'She's AWAKE!! Everyone, she's up! She's out of bed! I told you she would be up soon! I watched her! I knew! Come here, everyone!'

She yelled - at an impressive volume - as she hot-footed it out of the room and along what sounded like a long corridor. She reminded me of some of the kids from Florivale, such an excited little tattle-tale.

So much for a gentle morning. Footsteps began to beat their way towards me and, before long, into the room came four or five adults, Lizzie among them, with Lexi and Dom just about filling up the room as they squeezed their way to the front. Lizzie was first to speak.

'Bloody hell, guys,' she said as she lightly batted the kids back. 'Lexi, Heath, don't repeat that. It's a bad word. But really!' She looked at me apologetically, palms upward in acceptance that she couldn't corral the kids. 'She's only been here a few days, barely awake, and this is her first experience of us, piling into her room as soon as the tent is down, as soon as she's stood up. Give Vic some room.'

'But she's my friend,' said Lexi, pouting again. 'I want to play with her. I've been watching her the most while she sleeps. And finally, after ages, she isn't sleeping any more. Don't make me go away.'

'Nobody's going to make you go,' said Lizzie. 'But you need to give your new friend a bit of space because everything that you're used to is new to her.' Lizzie winked at me. 'You're going to have to help us teach her lots of things. It'll be fun. But you have to do what we say.' Lizzie turned to face me, stepping toward me as she spoke. Her tone deepened as she shifted her mode for speaking to me, instead of the children.

'Hi Vic. I'm so sorry we've bombarded you. But, I guess it was going to happen some time. With Mike on his way back from...' she paused, 'from, wherever, anyway. He's not here to remind us of his rules about swamping you., so upshot is - you're going to get a little crowded until he's back.'

I smiled nervously at the group. 'I guess I am.'

The introductions began, some of them having names I'd never heard before. I was never going to remember them, so I didn't even try. The usual questions, how old was I? Twenty. Had I really always lived in Florivale? Yes. Was I happy to have been liberated? I guessed so, I'd wished for it enough times. Did I miss Florivale? Yes and no. Did I like it here? I didn't know. I still didn't really know anything about where I was, who these people were, or why they'd got me out. Or even how. My bewilderment must have been written in bold capital letters across my forehead, because Lizzie silently lifted a hand, which had the unsettling but impressive effect of instantly silencing the crowd.

'Cool, isn't it. That's one of our rules here. Whoever has priority in a group at any given time gets to use the hand-raise to silence everyone. It's essential in our debates, when things can get a little heated.' She turned her back to me and faced the others.

'Right guys, you've had your first look at our very own Flori-born. She's pretty impressive. She's doing great. She'll be fully fledged and truly one of us very soon. You can harass her all you want then. But for now she needs you to zip it and let her work her way through what must be a whole catalogue of questions.'

There were disappointed grumblings from the crowd, but what Lizzie said, clearly went.

'Now get off and do your tasks for the day. I'll see you all at lunch.'

The group dissipated and shuffled reluctantly down the corridor and out of earshot. Lizzie came and sat on the edge of the bed, and beckoned me back from my spot near the wall with the window.

'Hey Vic. Sorry about that. Everyone's just so excited to see you. It's natural. You've become something of a legend already, and it's only been two and a half weeks.' I stopped mid-step on my way back over to sit next to her on the bed.

'Two and a half weeks? What?' How the hell was that possible?

'Yeah, your extraction and adjustment had completely taken it out of you. Saying that, you've defeated our estimates by over a week. Another reason you're becoming a bit of a celebrity. They'll stop staring so much once they've seen you a few times. Once they realise you're real, and that you're here to stay.'

Here to stay. There it was again. The hollowness, which came rushing at me again, out of nowhere.

'About that. Where exactly are we, Lizzie?' She paused, looked at the floorboards and cautiously ventured a glance at me.

'We're in England, just the same as Florivale. Same as your grandma Sophie and Mike came from. Same as your mum. A different part, of course, Florivale is quite a way from here. In a bit of the country which used to be called Kent. The whole site was acquired by the Ministry of Health years before they started moving people in there, giving them time to lay special water pipes with your sun protection already dissolved into the water for your showers. Filtration systems to ensure your drinking water was ultra-pure. Construction began, based on a careful plan, comprising modular homes which could be adapted based on whatever the Pioneers demanded as an incentive to move in. Anyway, like I say, that's kind of far away. South.' She pointed out the window in the direction of what I assume was south.

'We're further north. It's a bit colder here. You'll probably notice it, once you leave the building. By the way, we call this building the Base. Used to be a military barracks, but when government funding started to run out and things began to go wrong, this little place wasn't needed any more and troops were moved to more 'strategic', bigger bases. This area was where the important people had their offices. My favourite title so far is "Wing Commander". No idea what it means. Gibberish.'

'You'll notice there are rooms like this one all the way along the corridor of each block. We're in East block. My room is in a dorm a few corridors along. It's got an 'L' marked with ribbons across it. Girly and stupid, I know. But sometimes we all need something a little personalised to shake things up a little. Everything is so generic otherwise.' She had to catch her breath due to the pace of her speech, and reminded me for a moment of Clem in one of her Agitations.

'Ribbons,' I sighed, smiling at the thought. 'I get it. Everyone needs some outlet, some individuality. My friend Clem, she liked ribbons and coloured fabric. She was always desperate to improve her standard-issue clothing. Didn't work,' I smiled. I noticed Lizzie smile too, at the mention of Clem and seized the chance to ask more about her. 'Do you know Clem? About Clem? How is she?'

'I know about Clem. We know about all of the people in Florivale. Well, more about some than others. We're lucky to have had a few Techs get into Florivale as support operatives when things break down at the last minute and the Carers are too panicked, too terrified of having to report their failure to the Board, to use someone fully vetted. We've also had some Carers in there under cover, usually not for long. Your mother's wedding was one of those occasions. You might remember from that note you found, that things seemed strange that day. We were behind that. It failed of course, our attempt to get the Florivites to question authority. It's quite astonishing that you saw things so differently to the rest of them, to be frank.' She laughed at me, leaning so far forward with my mouth open in amazement. 'Wind your neck back in, Vic!' she laughed. 'How else did you think that stage image got to your CompStreams? Or the trail of metaphorical breadcrumbs which led you to the book, to the IsoPod.'

I put my hand up to my face, so that the reassuring softness of my cheeks could remind me that this was, in fact, reality.

'Were you... watching us? Really? The whole time?'

'Don't be alarmed. It was always for your good, for the greater good. But yes, we watched. Not all the time. But we kept tabs, we monitored who might be suitable for extraction, just like you. Your friend Clem seemed pretty likely too, but her tendency to panic made us think twice.' I glanced at her and mulled on this. I reasoned that Clem would not have coped well with extraction.

'You're not the only one, Vic. We're going to try to get more people out. But we have to be strategic. They're combing Florivale at this moment, looking for clues, interrogating staff. Good people, innocent people, are in a great deal of danger. The Board was not pleased to hear that one of its prime breeding and observational assets had been lost. That's you, by the way. You've caused quite a stir.'

'Hold on, a breeding and observational asset? What are you talking about? And I don't want to cause a stir. I never wanted that. I'm worried about the others, for everyone who's still stuck in there. If they're in danger, we're part of the reason why. I wished for this. I brought all of this about, and you helped. Right now, I don't care about the Carers, the Board, or the people behind this. If they're in danger, we have to get everyone out of Florivale!'

'Now is not the time, Vic. You have to trust me,' she looked at me, not meeting my eyes, hesitating as she measured my reaction before continuing. I figure she thought I might have been a little volatile. 'I think maybe that's enough for now. You're only just out of bed and you're already wanting to launch a full attack. I understand you're angry. But first, you need to learn some more about what life is really like out here, in the real world - before you get too carried away. There's more to it than the sanitised capsule you knew in Florivale. Which you always suspected, ever since the very first note. Clem is fine. She'll be safe for now. So are your family, and so is Josh. We're keeping a close watch on them.'

I knew she was right, but for a moment, I hated her. I asked her to leave me to my thoughts and went back to rest my head on the window pane, my only focus being the curling patterns of my breath upon it while I stewed on what she'd said and processed what I'd learnt so far. I needed to accelerate things. I needed to get them to tell me everything. Soon.

43

A while after Lizzie had left, someone came and explained that that I'd still need to be monitored and that I might need some supplemental injections in addition to the medication they put in my meals. Great. More unknown pharmaceuticals. Nevertheless, being free of that drip was worth any number of injections. I was beginning to have a great deal of empathy for Josh, hooked up to machines which pumped him full of mysterious substances and trapped in his bed after a bad T-Day.

The hours trickled by as I tried to make sense of the questions in my head. I rubbed where a new gauzy plaster was stuck to my hand, revelling in the free movement I was afforded now that the drip was gone. Some time during the late morning, there came a gentle knock on the door, and I instinctively knew it was Mike. Something about the percussion of his hand on the wood of the door already seemed familiar. I invited him in, where he found me sat on the floor in the corner of the room, my legs in the lotus position, an attempt to bring some order to the herd of thoughts stampeding through my mind.

'Hey Vic,' he said. 'I hear you had a fair few visitors in here this morning. I'm sorry. They mean well, and they don't get much excitement here. Well, not in the sense of anything new. And you're so new, and yet so familiar – we've known about you your whole life. You're kind of famous.'

I blushed, adjusted my legs and stood, walking over to the bed and beckoning him to sit alongside me. I was going to have to ask for some more chairs.

'I get it, I think. Well, actually I don't, but I'm trying. I just... I have so many questions. Every answer brings another one. It's exhausting.'

'I know, love. I know. It was the same for me when I got out – so much to learn about the developments Outside since we entered Florivale. I had so many people to thank, so many questions to ask about how they did it, and about what was going to come next. If learning everyone's names wasn't enough, I had to get my head round the new geography, the political shifts... the new dangers. So I figure you need to start getting some answers, sooner rather than later. I'll take you through what I can. You'll have to forgive me, though. I may be pretty spritely, but I'm seventy-three years old now, living on borrowed time and a breath or ten away from death – long overdue by today's mortality standards. So although I think I'm still pretty sharp, there will be bits I forget, details I omit. You'll just have to flag them to me as we go along, or get them filled in by someone else if you think of anything when I'm gone.' He smiled and winked, the flecks in his eyes catching in the overhead light.

I couldn't tell whether he was joking with his claims of elderly decline, or if there was some truth to it. I realised he was the oldest person I'd ever spoken to. What happened to the older people in Florivale? There must have been other Pioneers of the same age. Why didn't I see them around Florivale? And if they had died, where were the CompStream announcements? I'd seen a few, sure, but every family had to have had two Pioneers. There couldn't have been enough announcements for them all.

'Answers sound good to me. I'll try not to interrupt. But can you start by telling me where we are, and when I can leave this sodding room?' I asked. He laughed in reply. Pretty simple question, if you ask me. People out here laugh at the strangest things.

'Of course you can leave the room. Now that the tent is down and you're showing no risk signs, you can leave.'

At those words, the simple 'you can leave', I felt my shoulders drop an inch, not having realised the tension I was holding there. A taste of freedom – real freedom. I stretched my arms out wide, touching the void around me.

'So, Mike. Now that's cleared up, where are we? What is this place?'

He considered for a moment, as though he

were gathering his words from a cloud of fog. He spoke slowly, with measured and precise intonation.

'I guess we made this Collective out of who, and what, we could find. The riots, the disturbances, meant that the cities weren't what they started out as. As the poor became more disenfranchised, and as health declined, the cities narrowed, but the clusters that remained flourished – they became the preserve of the wealthy. Little enclaves of safety, better connected to utilities, healthcare professionals, airports. You name it, they've got it better in the city. Except space. Freedom from their stupid systems. Trust. The big stuff. That's the stuff we've got.'

'So, we have to make do here and there. We get electricity from our solar panels and any extra we can scrounge off their mainline supplies. That's one of the key benefits of having a bunch of engineers here at Base. We call them Techs. Water's similar. We collect and treat rain water, although the rising acidity levels are making that harder. The rest we siphon off from the mainlines into the cities. Things get more scarce; life becomes harder. Just one of the many reasons we need you, and why we need to readjust the imbalance. But we can achieve it - we can reset things. It's not right for such a minority to have so much, to use so many people so mindlessly, and for the rest of us to suffer.'

He paused, a shimmer in his eyes. I was certain he was reflecting on his own losses.

Sophie. Family. Everything.

'We can fill in the details later, as we go along. But the main headline for you is that life out here is hard. But it is real. Life in there is easy, if you like following orders – and I think we've established that you don't. But nobody in Florivale appreciates the terrible situation they're in. And that's where we, and you, come in. Our network has done excellent work in finding out as much as they can about the developments to the programme.

'Since Harte established Florivale, political unrest, rioting and the massive government deficit have meant her idyll never quite worked as planned. I'm sure she had some self-serving interests like all politicians but, unlike many of the others in here, I don't hold her wholly responsible for how things turned out. She may have unleashed a nightmare, but she did so thinking it to be a dream. Her personal dream was to leave behind a legacy of health. She just happened to be awfully short-sighted.' He took my hand, and with it, a deep breath. I braced myself.

'Vic, take your time to process what I'm about to say. Things changed. Florivale's purpose changed. Everyone in Florivale was a candidate for research. You kind of knew that I guess - all the tests, the Conditions. Looking for a cure, something for the greater good. But did you know that over time, you became available for hire? Rentable lab rats? For years now, Florivale's been owned by a private company, with a board of directors remunerated for leasing you at the highest price possible, with shareholders to answer to. Each of you is given a genericised name for use Outside. Something innocuous to reduce any feelings of guilt that an Investor might have, if they thought too much about what they were doing. When Florivale was established, there was at least a well-intentioned purpose. But the pound fell through the floor after the Value Life riots decimated the nation's workforce. Businesses collapsed as people fell ill, or quit their jobs in search of somewhere safer to live. The Government needed bailing out and Omniclin were the ones with the cash, ready to step in. Florivale was an asset they picked up for a song and used to become the most profitable company in the country. To Omniclin, and your personal Investors, you're not Victoria. You're AFSH-003.'

I shuddered, biting back the vomit induced by the sound of my true name. The name they gave me. He continued. He knew he had to.

'Have you noticed the addition of new Conditions over time? Or considered what's in the NutriVisor pouches, or anything else they give you in there? Take Josh, for example. Look at the increased effect of his transfusions, the addition of plasmoid. Things have been changing, accelerating his programme. Step by step, concern for your humanity ebbs away as one test leads to ten more. As one Investor bids higher for a unit in Florivale – that's what you're called, units - the higher the bid, the more unsettling the tests become. People want to get their money's worth from their investments.'

'But the worst lies ahead - for the next batch, and their children. The new Gen, the children of your Gen, are the first Florivale pure-borns – born of two Flori-borns, and with no connection to Outside. They're the first step in tailor-made research subjects. Which can be bought. And sold. Investors can even purchase and trade options on the future children of their preferred Florivale couple. Rights to units – that's you, Clem, Josh, any of you Florivites – are traded among people with a similar biometric profile. They rent or buy you so that they can test new drugs and treatments, with no risk to the commissioner. Because, of course, the unit takes all the risk. Your generation used to be the 'hot' investments, the first generation born in Florivale. But the pure-borns. Well. They're the most hotly anticipated options on the market. Extortionately expensive, far more than it would cost to use you.' He paused. 'Yes, Victoria Stone-Hunter. You're now a second-rate subject. Going cheap, by pure-born standards – although of course you still cost more than the Base operates on for a year. Well, it would, if we paid for anything instead of just stealing it. Why else do you think they make such a fuss over weddings in there? It's the carrot they dangle. A shower of attention and the chance to stand out for a day. Then you have to do your bit, create them a Flori-born or a pure-born to be auctioned behind the scenes to the highest-bidding Investors.'

I held up my hand to silence him. I didn't want to hear any more. This was disgusting. I felt sick.

How could one person buy another? How much of my life had been decided at the whim of one of these Investors? What the hell had they been putting in my food, my water, the IsoPods? I had always suspected there was something behind all of our Conditions, but I thought it was a Community-wide project, put together to see how everything interacts. Not a commoditised approach to medical testing.

No wonder everything was so regimented – it was mail-order medical research. It struck me: what were they doing to Josh, accelerating his transfusions? What did his Investors have planned for him? And how could I stop them?

My mind started to shut down and Mike left me in the labyrinth of my thoughts. I didn't want to speak to anyone for the rest of the day. I asked for the same tomato soup with bread and butter that Lizzie had brought me before, declining the invitation to eat with the Collective for the first time. I didn't know what to make of any of this. I wanted whatever comfort I could obtain, and took it from the repetition of the first 'real' meal I'd ever had.

Suddenly, the confines of this room didn't seem so bad. In here, I had relative control over who came in, what happened. What lay outside the Base seemed even worse. Out there, the streets were walked by the people lived who created Florivale, who transformed it into a living, breathing petri dish. And the remainder of them formed the terrified, permissive society which allowed it to happen. I'd never appreciated the scale of the operation, and kicked myself for being so slow to pick things up.

I got into my bed and pulled the worn blankets up to my shoulders, a cocoon from which I could let my mind meander. I'd asked Mike not to let anyone come in except for Lizzie, and to the Collective that I needed some more time to process the new information I'd received before I'd join them, but that I would be coming soon. I didn't want to offend anyone. I could imagine the disappointment of Lexi, Heath and Dom, the little scamps who'd made me smile, and reminded me of Jack and the other kids in Florivale. I ached when I thought of Jack. My stupid, adorable, little brother. Why hadn't I told him I loved him in those last few days? I couldn't remember the last time I had. I had been too busy focusing on the annoyances of daily life with a sibling. I made a reminder to myself never to take anything for granted again.

Understanding the history of what had created Florivale was nowhere near as pressing as the realisation that I had to help my friends, who had no idea of their destinies. Dark things had happened along the path leading up to now. But the future looked far more terrible from my new perspective. And the others, my friends. They were oblivious.

My mind turned to Josh, hooked up to all

those monitors, so isolated in his bed. What if he had been right about it all, the whole time? What if, when he said he felt like he was losing something of himself each T-Day, he was correct? It was the worst kind of vindication, and for once I'd have given anything to be wrong. I thought of every time Clem and I had teased him, and felt a knot of sickness building in my stomach. Sure, we couldn't have known he was right, but we never really explored it with him. When he closed his shell by shutting his eyes, we didn't fight to stay, or to prise more information from him. I don't know what we could have done to help, but we definitely could have done more than we did. Which was nothing.

His parents had never seemed to suffer to the same degree following a T-Day, and I had occasionally wondered whether they were in on some kind of secret. It was a thought too cruel, too evil, to bear. So I shut my mind to it, sealing it in a box and filing it on a shelf deep in the recesses of my consciousness. I brought my thoughts back to Josh, and to wondering how much time he had left before he lost any remaining sense of self. And, more worryingly, what the real purpose of the transfusions was. If someone had paid for him to be their subject, what nefarious purposes could they have for changing his very composition? Were they making him more like them, so they could use his blood, or worse, his organs? Or was it a test to see how much the human body and mind can be adjusted, how far it can be pushed?

What Mike had told me about the pure-borns rang true for me too. All the talk about marriage in Florivale, the fetishisation of bonding two Florivites. It began to add up. The profiling, the lavish expense and escalated status bestowed upon the 'happy' couple. They were becoming part of the production line, knowing nothing the whole while. They went willingly into a system they didn't know existed. They became immediately infatuated with people with whom they'd never seemed to share anything more than a casual friendship. It had never made sense, and I wished it still didn't. Sometimes, the truth is simply too ugly to be desired.

I realised that none of Clem's Conditions seemed anything like as severe as Josh's. She had to drink green tea, do yoga. So far, so boring. And she loved all that Hippy Mumbo Jumbo. So what was the benefit in someone buying her as a subject? Or was she just being primed in a 'normal' healthy state, waiting for an Investor to snap her up? A control element for the Opportunity? Or a fertile partner to breed more pure-borns? In which case, she would be woefully unprepared for whatever was in store, trusting and, most of the time, compliant. She'd need a Clem Agitation on a whole other scale to derail any plans they might have for her.

My parents seemed less at risk, from what Mike said. They were older, less pure. But who knows. Maybe their fertility had been one of the tests to get into Florivale. Maybe they were genetically matched as part of the plan to produce me and Jack. Now that their reproductive goal had been accomplished, would they be disposable, or would their purpose change? If it was so expensive to maintain Florivale, surely there had to be an end-game – why would they keep funding someone (although, I suppose to the Investors, they were 'something', rather than 'someone', coded up like computer parts), if they got no benefit. What would happen next?

And then there's Jack. My happy little moron brother, the person I'd felt so much frustration towards, for pretty much his whole life. My heart sank as I realised I needed him as my comic foil, my counterpart, my baby brother. I regretted my harsh words, the way I'd always dismissed him out of hand, never thinking there would be a time when I wouldn't see him. What did they have in store for Jack? Were my family the sheep on the wall? And did that make me the tiger? Part protector, part arbiter of chaos? Had my extraction set in train a series of events which would put them all in jeopardy?

Throughout the day, I heard occasional footsteps along the corridor outside, but had no desire to learn whose feet had made them. I heard voices, of both adults and children, and wondered whether Lexi, Dom and Heath were among them. I wondered whether the children out here were treated by society as genetically defective because they hadn't been 'designed' like the

Flori-born and the pure-born. Or perhaps the fact they had survived whatever medical crises had felled so many others marked them out as special. There was just too much to learn. I had to do something. I stared at the wall, watching the seconds tick by on the old-style analogue watch Mike had given me, now that my BioBand had been deactivated. I had to learn how to read the damn thing, but there was something comforting in the physicality of its movement, counteracting the nervous sickness building up inside me as I acknowledged that every second watching the clock was a second during which everyone in Florivale was at risk.

Lizzie brought my soup and bread, along with more salty butter. I felt cruel, sending her away when there was so much we both wanted to say to one another, but now was not the moment. I needed to process things, alone. Hopefully, she'd understand that.

I ate in silence, once again amazed at the depth of flavour in every bite. Before she left, Lizzie asked if I wanted something else and I was surprised to admit to myself that I didn't know what it could be, that I couldn't think of any foods I liked. Everything I'd ever eaten in Florivale was synthetic, processed, designed to be nutritionally perfect for my needs. Eating for pleasure was something completely different, with the exception of wedding celebrations, the thought of which now made me feel sick. I paused before I spread more butter on a chunk of bread and wondered if I'd gain weight, become obese like the people from Before. But I figured I'd run, I'd be healthy. Plus, what kind of society doesn't trust its own people to eat the right things in the right amounts – of course, there will be good days, and bad days, but it must even out over time, surely? That said, what I knew about society on the Outside didn't fill me with confidence.

My mind was wandering, avoiding the obvious and painful issues at hand. I traced back through my thoughts and it dawned on me that all I had to do was ask these questions. Ask as many people as would speak to me, so I could make up my own mind about the truth. Questions like how many other communities were there, and whether what had happened only affected England, or whether other countries were divided this way, the rich paying to maintain their crumbling health, while the poor lost everything. I didn't even know what year it was. Years weren't important in Florivale. Perhaps they weren't important anywhere, when it came down to it. We might mark the days off on a calendar, but another always follows. Time counts, time with loved ones, with friends. The way you count it is irrelevant.

Time passes. Some things stay the same. But others change.

44

I woke with a start the next morning. There was
no rap at the door, no sound at the boarded-up
window. In the void of silence came a sudden
moment of clarity. I had never had so much
control over my own destiny. I couldn't stare at
the face of a clock all day. I had to do something
for the people left behind, but I couldn't do it
alone. God knows how many people helped get
me, and Mike, out of there. But I was going to
have to ask them to do the unthinkable. To send
me back in.

I opened my bedroom door and saw the
corridor was much the same as my bedroom, the
walls draped in coloured fabric, some pieces
faded and frayed, with other, fresher pieces in
between. I followed along to the right, the
direction from which I thought I'd heard most of
the approaching footsteps coming. There were a
few other doors along the way, and I wondered
whether they were allocated for any others like
me, but I realised that was crazy. I knew I was
the only one they got out since Mike. I later
learnt that these were offices and meeting rooms,
and that the room I had been occupying was as
large as the dorms used to house four or five of
the Collective. It made me feel like a spoilt child,
moping in there for so long when I could have
eased the cramping for others.

Following no particular path, I descended the staircase at the end of the corridor and met the faint scent of cooking. This had to be the way down towards the kitchen, or maybe the dining room. Hopefully there would be people there. I was inwardly praying to find Lizzie among the first faces I saw.

The air was slightly cooler downstairs, and there was no breeze. I figured all of the windows were probably boarded up, and suspected this might be to keep the location secret from anyone who was not invited – or 'extracted' - in to the Base. I shuffled along the bare floors and found two doors at the end. A classic psychology puzzle – two closed doors and you have to pick one, not knowing what lies behind. I went for the one on the right, for no better reason than it felt like the right choice. No pun intended.

I knocked lightly, not knowing the etiquette here, and gently opened the door when there was no answer. A small group of adults were huddled closely around some papers which had been fanned out on the end of a table. I guess they hadn't heard my knock, because they hastily gathered up the papers and got to their feet. Each of them gave me an oddly reverential nod, which made me feel even more uncomfortable.

'Oh,' I stuttered. 'I'm sorry,' I said as I took a step back. 'I didn't mean to disturb you.'

I felt an odd recognition when I saw one

of the men in the group. Like something from a dream or from a session in the IsoPod, when real thoughts and dreams intermingle. I caught my breath as he stepped forward, and it was his voice that confirmed that I'd encountered him before. He wasn't a dream. Although, my word, did he look like one.

'Vic, you're up! I was really worrying about you. I mean, we all were. When Mike put the stop to any visits, even observationally, it shook us all.'

He laughed nervously and ran his large hands through his dark blonde hair, revealing as he looked up at me a pair of piercing green eyes. I was doomed. He stepped forward and rather formally held out his hand.

'I'm Alex. My mum's been helping look after you. She's called Elle. The bossy one. She's a former Carer who Mike got to switch sides when she saw how they treated Sophie. Sounds kind of snittish. But believe me, her heart's pure gold.'

Ah yes, I thought. The one who injected me. Maybe this Alex kid wasn't all that, with a mother so hell bent on medicating me into oblivion.

'Anyway,' he went on, 'we were just, um, discussing the, er, meal plans for when you were up and about. We heard from Lizzie so far, that you like tomatoes and butter. And we think we can show you a little more than that.'

The way he shifted on his feet gave him away completely, and I knew immediately that I had to see those papers. There was nothing on there about butter, that was for sure. Not to mention that these guys were all in the same dark clothing with a coloured stripe, but theirs was green. Not orange, like mine, or pink like Lizzie's. And I began to wonder whether those colours signified some sort of system. After all, the kids didn't have any colours on their clothing – kind of like they were waiting to decide. My train of thought was interrupted as one of the other men in the group came forward, one I didn't remember. He had a square jaw, and a light beard, which was clearly very carefully maintained. Beneath his face was a body which could have been hewn from marble, so broad and smoothly defined. He looked to be a few years older than Alex, who I guessed was a couple of years older than me. He introduced himself as Harrison and moved awkwardly around us out of the room, passing a nod to Alex and the others at the back of the room as he did so.

'Oh, shit! Of course. Vic, I'm so sorry, I keep forgetting to do such basic things. You don't know anyone really, do you?!' He turned to the others. 'Such a blast! Imagine not knowing the first thing and then some idiot like me starts chatting on about meal choices.' He turned those enticing eyes back to me. 'Vic, these are my team, well, my... er, we're friends and we work together.'

He swallowed deeply, and as his Adam's

apple bobbed in his throat, I smiled sweetly and plotted how I was going to infiltrate this group and get my hands on their paperwork. They were acting far too conspiratorially to be doing anything routine. He held out a hand, politely awaiting mine, and led me over to the others.

One, Graham, was shorter than the others, and a little plump, although I'd still wager he could beat most of the Protectors in a fight. He had kind brown eyes and squeezed my hand gently when he shook it. There was one woman in the group, who was not so accommodating. She had caramel skin, the most beautiful shade I'd ever seen. Her jet-black hair was scraped back into a ponytail, not a single strand out of place. When she smiled, there was no softness. When she shook my hand it was out of duty. She could barely let go of me quickly enough. She was called Bianca, and I immediately made a mental note to keep away from her if at all possible. Like the others, her body was toned and taught. She was slightly taller than me, and again, someone I wouldn't want to mess with, even though she had been nothing but polite - on the face of it.

I think that's something girls do much better than men. Project something which seems OK, but beneath which lies something distasteful, deceitful. Something mean. Like I'd seen in some of the girls from Florivale – sweetness and light as they say something cruel and heinous, laughing it off with a smile so people think you're crazy when you pull them up on it.

The final person in the group was a tall man with fiery red hair, who spoke in an accent I'd never heard before, but which Alex wasted no time in telling me was Scottish. The Scot was, ironically, called Scott, and put me back at ease with one line of his lilting introduction to himself. As we spoke, Scott, Alex, Graham and I moved out of the room, and I noticed I was being gently but effectively guided away from the papers which Bianca was pulling together and fastening into a folder. She slipped out through a door at the back of the room with the folder, while the others took me away.

'So, Vic, you can't put it off any longer. We're going to introduce you to everyone. No escape. You're our little showpiece now and we're going to love telling everyone how you just strolled in on us after being hidden away so long.' Graham was laughing as he spoke, gently bobbing along the corridor. Reaching a couple of large doors, he swung them open, undoubtedly for dramatic effect, and in doing so, introduced me to the dining hall.

We found ourselves at the top of a small flight of stairs down into a huge dining room. It was laid up long tables, and there must have been eighty people sat eating, with space for at least another thirty. More, if some people stood. I couldn't fathom eighty people eating in one room unless it was for a Florivale wedding! And it dawned upon me, that every single person in the room was staring up at me, their knives and forks limp on their plates, or dropped to the floor.

Alex stepped forward and took my hand possessively (I hoped), and raised it up with his own.

'Ladies and gentlemen of the Collective! This is Victoria Stone-Hunter. The first Flori-born to leave that hell and join us. She is our beacon of hope and,' he laughed, 'likely to be our healthiest new member of the Collective. I won't ask her to speak, not today, mostly because Mike would put me on plates duty for a month, but just take a moment. Observe her. She is the key. The future. She is our secret weapon.'

He stepped back towards me and dropped my hand, a wry smile fleeting across his face as he held my gaze for a moment too long.

I realised I might rather enjoy being part of the Collective.

Alex walked away, taking with him the unbelievable effect he had on my pulse, leaving my heart racing in his wake. I couldn't stand there endlessly staring at the void left behind him, plus I was ravenous, so I headed into the dining hall.

I made my way down the stairs and found a space a few seats away from a group who were sat eating, nobody I recognised among them. I decided that sitting a polite distance from them would allow them to break into conversation, if that's what they wanted to do, or equally to ignore me and carry on with whatever they were discussing. Truth be told, I was desperate to speak to as many people as I could, although I knew I'd have to be careful about how I did it until I'd got to the bottom of what everybody was like. I did not, for example, want to find myself on the wrong side of Bianca. Or Elle.

I wasn't quite sure how their food appeared - there wasn't anything like the NutriVisor pouch system, and everyone was just eating from mismatched, slightly worn-looking crockery and old metal plates. But each of them had a plate, so they must have come from somewhere. I decided I would just ask them, if nothing materialised in the next few minutes. It didn't. So I turned to face them and cleared my throat to speak.

'Hi. I'm, um, Victoria. I guess you probably saw that little welcome speech. Embarrassing.' Pretty lame introduction, huh? Anyway, they turned and smiled, so I can't have completely messed it up.

'Yes, hi Victoria. Or is it Vic?'

I nodded. We were getting good at this smiling and nodding business.

'Vic's fine. Better, in fact. I was just wondering whether you have to come at a certain time for food, or if they just bring it when you sit down? Sorry, everything here's so new, so different. It smells amazing, I can't even place what that scent might be. What is that?' I pointed at their plates of some headily spiced stew, with rice. Yes, even I, ignorant Flori-born though I was, could identify rice.

'You've never tried curry!?' exclaimed one of them, who later introduced himself as Greg. 'Well, that explains why you needed to be brought out. That might be one of the worst things they do to you lot in there!'

He chuckled to himself, highly amused at his own wit. Half-wit, I thought. But I had to remember to be nice. I was the new one, I needed all the help I could get.

'No, no I haven't,' I replied. 'But it smells wonderful. Where can I get some?'

A petite lady with dark red hair was sitting next to Greg and got to her feet. Reaching out her hand, she introduced herself as Rosa and offered to take me to the refectory, which was, she explained, the place to go for all of our meals.

'There are trays at the side,' she started, 'to put your plate and a drink on,' busily chatting as she walked me about the room. 'But it can get quite crowded in here, so most people just try to get themselves to their table as soon as they can, no tray, no spills. Over there are the cups and our water filter - nothing like what you're used to, I'm afraid, but at least it's less acidic than the rainwater!'

She prattled on as she led me around the

corner to a long silver counter, behind which I could see a couple of people bustling around in the kitchen, amazing smells and steam rising all around them. Rosa continued talking as she led me around by the elbow.

'And here's where you'll get your meals. No queue today, but it's a very different story when there's a gathering. My tip is to arrive in the queue right at the beginning, or to wait until about fifteen minutes have passed. Sure, the gannets ahead of you might be eating by the time you're served, but the chefs will probably have refilled the dishes by then, so you'll get a fresher portion.'

She winked conspiratorially as I took it all in. I couldn't believe the scale of the operation, and wondered whether Grandma Sophie's dream of a large kitchen and entertaining a crowd had stemmed from the impersonal alternative of queuing like this for food back before she took up the Opportunity. A loud rumble from my stomach roused me from my reverie, and I blushed at Rosa's raised eyebrows.

'Sounds to me like we'd better get you some madras pronto!' She turned to the counter and started waving embarrassingly, intending to get the attention of a chef. When that didn't work, she resorted to a more direct approach.

'Oi! ROB!' she yelled, at which a stocky man, aged about thirty and with the same kindness in his face as Lizzie, turned to us. He gasped and flung a cloth over his shoulder as he scurried to the serving hatch.

'Victoria! It's you! Just like they said!'

He looked at Rosa, clearly excited to have the newbie at his kitchen, on his shift.

'Rosa, they all said she was a stunner, but Christ!' He looked at me and shifted on his feet. 'Er, Vic, what I meant to say was, that you're very welcome here and we are so glad to have you with us. And, if I may say,' at this point he blushed, 'you are possibly the most beautiful person I have ever seen. Lizzie was right.'

He awkwardly turned around, as if to regain what little composure he had. Gesticulating towards the steaming pans lined up on a large cooker against the back wall, he announced the meal of the day was a curry, with rice and pickles. He turned back and smiled with pride, not realising that I had no idea what this was, as I smiled and nodded at him.

'OK. Sounds great,' I said.

Rosa piped up, obviously bored that this part of the conversation wasn't directed at her. 'You'll get pretty bored of it soon enough. Nothing easier than a curry when catering for the Collective, is there Rob?' she laughed to herself, pleased with her slight.

I thought she sounded spiteful and I wanted to leap to his defence. It really did smell wonderful.

'Rob, thank you. I'll take some of everything if that's OK. I'm so excited to taste everything out here!'

He beamed with pride as he slopped a ladle of each of rice and a deep red stew, filled with chunks of peppers, potato, courgette, tomatoes and onions, onto my plate. With an unexpectedly delicate hand, he added a sprinkle of what I later learnt were chili seeds - nobody warned me about those. Suffice to say I did not care at all what the water tasted like while my mouth was on fire. I also had a small spoon of a sticky, sweet chutney and a bitter pickle. I thanked him and headed back to my table with Rosa, to re-join her small group, and a couple of others who had come in to the hall in the meantime.

I sat down, and realised nobody else was eating, and therefore, that they'd be watching me. It felt a bit weird, but I was so famished and intrigued by the smells encapsulated in the vapours steaming from my plate that I decided I didn't care. With a sense of ceremony, I loaded up a fork with some of the rice, some of the curry, and a little of each of the chutney and pickle.

I could not describe the beauty of those flavours and give them justice. I had reached culinary heaven, and so far I'd only had tomato soup, bircher muesli for my breakfasts and a curry. What else could this incredible kitchen deliver?!

It dawned on me that this was my life now, if I stayed. Not that I knew where else I'd go. There were so many people to meet, the Robs, the Rosas, the inimitable Alex. I was sure there was definitely only one of him.

I was making connections with these people, knitting myself into the Collective. And not idly or without purpose. I needed to talk to the key people who got me out, and who could get my family, Josh, Clem, everyone in fact, out of Florivale and its warped programme. It still made me shudder to think of our 'unit' names. And of Josh, being replaced cell by cell, transfusion by transfusion.

Josh, with his acerbic tongue, always the ideal counterpart to Clem. How he could be immediately silenced with any threat of a T-Day. People he had never met exercised absolute control over the very blood in his veins. People whose existence he had probably never contemplated. We just thought it was part of the search for a Cure. We lapped it up, feeling proud to be part of something which would benefit others. What a bunch of idiots. I knew that, if my suspicions were correct, things weren't going to be too easy in Florivale following my disappearance, and were probably going to get significantly worse.

I wanted to ask Mike how we could help them, but I knew his judgment would be clouded by affection and his desire to protect me from the worst. Which was all very nice and everything, but not what I needed. I needed the truth, and a plan. I thought Lizzie would be as good an informant as any, at least for the initial phase of my questions. She usually popped in during the evenings, after dinner service and any meetings were done, to check in and see how I was getting on.

That night, true to form, there came a gentle knock at the door. I shouted that she should come in, and Lizzie folded herself around the door and into the room, as though apologetic for her presence. With a crinkle-eyed smile, she came over and sat next to me on the space I patted on the bed.

'Lizzie,' I sighed. 'They have to move me out of here and free up some space in the building. I'm fine now. I'm breathing your air, drinking your water, eating your amazing food. And look! I'm still alive!' I was embarrassed at my special treatment, and told her so. Lizzie brushed at the air with her hand.

'No, Vic. Everything in good time. We're actually going to have to work out your sleeping arrangements once we know more about your Role. Everyone has to have one, I'm afraid, and I think there'd be a mutiny if you didn't take one too.'

My bewildered look must have said it all.

'Roles,' she continued. 'You know. Jobs? Duties? Take me, for example. I'm a Chef. There are a bunch of us, well, five at the moment, to be precise. We take turns to keep everyone fed. Given we try and keep our location secret, for security reasons, and the general scarcity of food out here, you can imagine it's not the easiest job. Sure, it's not the most glamorous either, but I'm also less likely to get attacked, have my cover blown, or generally face any more risk than nicking my thumb with a paring knife. Which would, at the end of the day, be my own stupid fault anyway.' She laughed, and I saw her relax. 'There's Rob, who I know you met. He likes you! In the kitchen with him today were Mac and Bea. Mac's a bit of a bohemian, always wanting to mix things up with his crazy twists on recipes. We have to rein him in sometimes. That being said, his Chinese-style egg-drop soup is one of the top meals we do in here. So, sometimes crazy has its place. Bea is this lovely, really chilled little flower. I'm not sure she could do many other Roles - she's too delicate. And not hugely bright. She's generally the one measuring things and peeling vegetables. Like I said, sweet, but maybe not the wisest.'

I was amazed at the delineation of responsibilities to suit personalities within the Base. 'How do Roles get defined then?' I asked. 'Do you get assigned one by a vote, pick a name from a hat, do a test, or what?'

'Generally speaking,' said Lizzie, 'people know what they want to do, and it usually suits them pretty well.' She paused, and pulled herself further back onto the bed. 'But sometimes, well, it necessarily work straight away. And there are some Roles you can't pick. You get selected for those. Libs, basically. And Seniors.'

Once again, my baffled expression prompted Lizzie to give me a little more to go on than Community jargon. I thought Florivale was bad!

She laughed. 'Sorry, Vic. The Libs are the guys who got you out. It's short for Liberators. They're our small unit of brave, strong, and slightly unhinged individuals. They know what the corporation will do if they get caught, and still they fly in the face of everything Omniclin stands for.' She stopped short when she saw the horror in my face. But she misread my reaction to the name of our oppressors. She thought it was just the first time I'd heard of it, and I couldn't find the words to tell her I already knew about them.

'OK,' she went on. 'I'll use less jargon. Omniclin means Omniclin Limited. That's the reason you're here, specifically. They run Florivale now, after buying it off the government for nothing when things really went wrong and the government was broke. It's Omniclin's Board, their shareholders, who decide the fate of everyone in Florivale. So if I refer to the company, what I mean is Omniclin. They operate away from the stock market, partially because it's completely corrupt these days, but, more importantly, because they have limited filing and disclosure requirements by staying private. Clever bastards. That approach, and their rigorous confidentiality requirements for new members and Investors, is what made it all -

everything they're doing right now - possible. Obviously there are other companies like it in other cities, but Omniclin are the biggest, and the worst. We also think there are similar operations in other countries.'

I didn't like the sound of Omniclin one bit. In fact, I knew immediately I had to put a stop to it. Make them pay for what they've done. But I did like the sound of the Liberators. They must have been the ones who got me out.

'So, have I met any Libs? And are there Libs working in Florivale, under cover? Otherwise how could they have got me from the Isopod and out here?'

'Slow down Vic! One question at a time! Yes, you know some Libs. Yes, they got you out. But that's a story for another time. Way too complex for you just now – you need a framework first or you'll never make sense of it.' The assumption that I couldn't handle the truth was really starting to wind me up. I let her continue, stowing away my frustration for another time. I needed Lizzie to keep talking. 'And yes, you didn't ask it, but you're only human, so you couldn't have failed to observe him. Alex is a Lib. A very promising, but quite scary one. He has almost no regard for his own safety – when he has a goal to achieve, it's always the mission first and everything else, including safety, second.' She paused, a smile curling at the edge of her lips. 'Although, I did see him checking in on you rather more than I'd have expected. And he refers to you a few times a day more than is normal. So I'd say he's noticed you too,' she said, laughing as she watched the blush spread across my cheeks.

'So there are Chefs and Libs. Opposite ends of the spectrum really, but both vitally important. All the Roles are. Of course, there are some tasks we all have to do. For ourselves, and for each other. Everyone has to make their beds up, ensure their possessions are secure and tidy, for the good of everyone in the dorms. We have a small team of Domestics. They're the ones who make sure this crappy building doesn't fall apart and who improve and fix things as needed. They work a lot with the Techs. They're the technical whizzkids who work on computers, cables and so on. The Domestics deal with any issues to the property maintenance, fix tiles, board windows etc. If there's a flood, while we all chip in, it's the Domestics and the Techs who lead the show. There is nothing about this place they don't know. They worked with the Libs to make sure the IsoPod escape would work outside of Florivale, and it's the Domestics who set up your air tent and this room.'

I made a mental note to respect the Domestics. I had a lot to thank them for. Lizzie went on, yawning and stretching as though she wasn't imparting something fascinating. I guessed that, to her, this was all pretty banal. But this was a whole new way to govern a group. I was so intrigued.

'Then you have the Eds - that's the Educators, pretty straightforward. They're usually pretty calm. You'd have to be, to be able to handle the likes of Lexi and Heath every day! So what have I just explained… Libs, Chefs, Eds, Domestics, Techs. There are some other Roles too, like the Seniors. Take Mike. He's the leader of the Seniors. Most of them also have a Role, but some of them are just Seniors. It's a full time job. We vote on most matters, but the Seniors get a casting vote. They have the history on everything. They're a pretty cool bunch, actually. Oh, Meds. We have Meds too. They're like your Carers, but here we call them Meds – and their job here is ten times harder than it would be in Florivale. The joke usually goes that our Meds don't care what it takes, or how much it hurts to fix you, because they'll do it anyway.' She rubbed the side of her jaw. 'Though I have to say it's not that funny when you're the one getting a tooth pulled out with only some home-brewed alcohol to ease the pain. It gets like that when we're coming up to needing a supply run.'

'They're pretty exciting, but highly dangerous. Typically, a bunch of Libs come up with a plan, pass it by the Seniors and then co-opt anyone else they need from the specialist teams who are needed for the supplies in question. So, if it's a predominantly medical run, the Meds. Sometimes, one of us Chefs has to go. For food additives, preservatives etc. But that's pretty rare. I've only been on one. And I couldn't stand to go again. Rob usually does it now. God knows Bea would be utterly useless. I couldn't face all those tunnels. The silence. The constant terror. The darkness.'

Tunnels and darkness. Not concepts I

would ever be happy with. But it did explain how things were moved around undetected, and brought to this boarded-up old building. Bea told me these barracks used to house massive suites of offices, which is why there are so many rooms and the big kitchen and dining hall, into which the troops used to come every afternoon for their lunch. I asked what kind of work they would have done, which could have been anything, considering how little I knew. I remember being told that office work was what the majority of the population did, Before. Financial industries like banks, big businesses selling things to other businesses and other people, their lawyers, their accountants. Or charities, working from offices on reports and plans to help the less fortunate. Bea laughed at that part and said there were probably a thousand people working in one bank for each person working on charity projects. She said there was more pencil-pushing than action in the military these days, and laughed, which I thought was odd. Surely it was better for there to be more writing than there was violence.

Lizzie didn't know much about the detail, just that the Base was outside of a big city, in some suburban area. When the riots escalated and public health declined even further, there was an exodus of people desperate to leave the suburbs. They had to choose between hiding in the cities, hoping to avail themselves of electricity, services, food and the last few jobs working for the rich, or taking their chances by living off the land in the countryside, praying the whole time that they didn't get sick. She explained the hospitals were all but impossible to reach from the countryside, with most medical professionals following the money into the shrinking cities, where the last of the wealth endured. And where the assholes who paid for Florivale spent their days happily gambling away the lives of Florivites as they decided between test methods.

It all spurred me on. Why should our Meds be limited to the few Carers we had convinced to leave Florivale? People who, in doing so, we had compelled to leave behind all that they held familiar and start a new life of subterfuge. And why should we sneak about in tunnels, only to appear and take our chances in the daylight when absolutely and strictly necessary?

I was getting cabin fever. I had explored the many corridors of the building, wondering whose former office I was in at any given time, and what they might have done as they sat at their desk. I'd told Mike I was going stir crazy, that I needed to feel my legs move, to develop their strength. One look at Bianca's physique was all I needed to confirm that I'd lost most of my muscle tone. I'd noticed after a shower - no aroma steams out here, unfortunately - that the toned line down the middle of my stomach was fading, and my bum was sagging where it had previously stood proud. My arms were prone to wobbling when I moved too fast, and I didn't like it. I hated the thought that I couldn't run away from someone if I needed to, and the realisation that I couldn't attack knowing I would win.

Mike had laughed, and patted my shoulder as he told me he thought I had nothing to worry about, but that he understood. He took me to what was called the gym. It's like Outside's version of the FitHub, although obviously all the equipment is much shabbier, and a lot older. It's got a few beaten-up looking treadmills and some other basic fitness equipment. You can't get personalised calorie and heart rate information because there are no BioBands. I still look for mine on my wrist every day; I'd never realised that I found it a source of comfort. It was also my daily tormentor. I'm weird - go figure.

Anyway, you can insert your height, weight and age into the machines and they will do an estimated calorie output, which is better than nothing. Next to the treadmills there are some fake stairs, which you're meant to just climb, endlessly, with no end in sight. Frankly, I can't think of anything worse. There is a rudimentary cross trainer in each corner, and weights machines are dotted around the room at random. I don't think the people who tend to use those are that great at putting the weights away. The whole room had the cloying smell of stale sweat, but I didn't mind once I'd put on the sports clothes Lizzie had given me and hit the treadmill.

As the familiar, addictive, pounding sensation

built in my legs each day, I pictured the fibres of my thigh and calf muscles thickening, binding. With every ragged breath when I pushed myself to the limit, I inhaled determination and strength, and exhaled anger at the system which was failing everyone I loved. At the blindness of the Omniclin Investors. At my own short-sightedness and the unbearableness of knowing my family and friends were stuck there. Even the people I didn't like needed saving. Melanie and the like. That was saying something, considering how many times I had wanted to shove them into the Lake, knowing they wouldn't be able to swim.

As I ran, I wondered whether there was any open water out here that I could swim in, which wouldn't be too polluted or too visible to malicious eyes. Being land-bound struck me as a really stupid idea for a girl who had spent her whole life wishing she could escape an island under nothing but her own power. Which is, no doubt, why learning to swim had been forbidden and the Lake perimeter was out of bounds.

I made sure I worked out in the gym every day, even if only for a shorter session. Some days I'd run, others I'd cross-train, others I'd do weights. I still wasn't inclined to use what I called the Pointless Stepper. As the days went past, I felt my old strength coming back. During my cool-downs, I tried hard to remember all the stretches Clem would have gotten me into, almost certainly getting them wrong. I missed her laughing at my inflexibility. I missed her laughter, full stop. I'd have put up with a hundred Clem Agitations a day, if it meant I could have her with me, someone who knew what I was going through and who understood how completely alien everything was, now that the Flori-veil had been lifted. I smirked at my own pun. Come on! That was a good one.

Occasionally I'd see someone else in the gym, although it was never that busy when I went. Most of the time, it was one of the Libs, showing off their strength with weights, laughing together at their prowess compared with everyone else. Perhaps some of the people here didn't work out at all. I couldn't imagine anything more unbearable, more frustrating, than being stuck in my own floppy, weak body. I wanted to be poised and ready to react at all times.

As I ran, it became clear to me that the only Role I wanted was that of a Lib. I lacked the knowledge to be a Med, to teach, or to cook - although Lizzie had offered to teach me. More truthfully, I lacked the desire. But I craved adventure and getting out of the Base to see what was left behind of the England I'd seen in photos and videos.

Which is, of course, precisely why that is not what I got. I was assigned the Role of a Domestic.

45

Day one of being a Domestic started with meeting the team. I'd get a full tour of the building later, which, I have to admit, was pretty great. Finally I got to see how all the corridors and doorways fit together – connecting areas I knew with others I didn't.

But first, the team. Whilst there isn't technically a 'boss' or a leader, it's clear that the Seniors in each Role call the shots. We have two Seniors. First is the formidable Grace, five foot nine, although six foot two if you count her mane. She has dark skin, and a strong body, honed through years of work. The second is Dan. Dan's about the same height as Grace - excluding the hair - and for every iota of her sass, Dan is mellow and calm. Dan's got thinning brown hair, blue-grey eyes and a soft voice. Dan is something of a cross between a Tech and a Domestic. Something of a liaison to make sure it all ticks over. What he can't tell you about wiring or some gadget or gizmo isn't worth knowing. Grace told me this, and Dan deflected her compliment by clarifying that he's no good on the new programming stuff, on the computers and so on. That's why he's aligned into the Domestic Role – he works with his hands, on real things, things that he can see. This got a proud little cheer from the group which had gathered around me when I was introduced to

Grace and Dan. In turn, they all introduced themselves. A few stood out more than the others, but I knew I'd learn everyone's names within a few days.

There was a tall guy called Pat. For Patrick. He had sandy hair, a bit like Alex's, but not as shiny. He seems pretty nice and I'd wager he's next in the line of command after Dan and Grace. He looked strong and his words clearly carried weight with the group. Grace referred to him as the King of Cabling, to much laughter. As I was smiling and nodding at this, with absolutely no idea what they were talking about, a girl, Ella, came up and explained that the nickname was a joke. Pat had once been working his way through a supply tunnel to hook up a cable to the external utility grid, and got his foot caught in the cables, leading him to panic, using up all the oxygen in his section of tunnel. He was found passed out when the rest of the team noticed the cable wasn't unspooling from where they'd set up base. Oh, how they all laughed. Hilarious.

Tunnelling was never going to be my thing. Being in that small a space, for a period of time, is not an option. That's one thing the IsoPod has taught me with absolute certainty.

Ella's about my age, maybe a year or two either side. She's got dark hair, like me, but shorter and cut into a shaggy cropped style, like a boy's hair that's grown out. She's always brushing is back behind her ears, only for it to fall right back into place in front of her eyes as soon as she moves her hand. I don't know why she doesn't get some kind of grip or grow it out a bit longe. Maybe she thinks it's cute or something. Her specialism is planning. She can sketch out a plan in no time. I've seen. She can point out each cable, power point, drain, tile. You name it, she knows it. I asked her how she learnt all this stuff.

'You seen Lexi?' she asked. I nodded. 'Lexi's older than I was when I came in here. My parents got sick and died. I was wandering the streets of the city like a lost little lamb and Grace's team saw me out there whilst on a supply run. They brought me in. This building's all I've ever had to call my home. It started out as my way to fill my time, while I still missed my parents with an actual, physical pain. But then I realised I had a real talent for this stuff, for the details. It distracted me from the darker thoughts. So I took to mapping things out, labelling them really neatly. I didn't have the brains to be a Tech, or the balls to be a Lib, so they put me in here. With my skills, if a tile flies off, we know how would be quickest to get to it and replace it. If a gutter cracks, I can work out immediately where we can take another one from, to use as a spare until the Libs do their next supply run and find us a nice, nearly-new one from another building.'

She said this so matter-of-factly, glossing smoothly past the part where she lost both her parents. It brought a new rush of my own pain, of longing for my family. Jack would have loved weaselling his way around this building, learning all about it. I doubt he'd have had Ella's brains, but he'd have been happy. And it was anyone's guess what they were doing to him in there right now.

'You alright, Vic? I'm sorry, I know it's pretty boring. Anyway, come over here and meet Flo and Tom.'

With that, Ella led me by the arm across to where another pair were studiously going through a pile of old trash. Bits of metal, plastic, fabric. Scraps everywhere.

'We're doing inventory from the last supply run. You going to join us?' asked the guy, who I correctly assumed to be Tom.

'Sure,' I said, still reeling from the sudden emotion of thinking of Jack. 'What do you need me to do? Are we literally just moving everything into piles by category? So, say, plastics, metals, fabrics, others?' I saw dried food remnants on some of the items and recoiled. 'Do we even keep the dirty stuff?'

Tom and Flo caught each other's eye for a moment and burst out laughing. When the hilarity subsided, Flo held up both her hands, in mock supplication.

'Sorry, little Flori-born. We're in the real world here. And what we've got isn't the best, isn't the finest. But it's sure as heck all we've got. So yes, we take the dirty stuff. And yes, first job for a newbie is always to sort. So if you make four piles, we can go through and work out if those dumbass Libs actually got what we wanted, or just scavenged any old thing and threw it in a bag.'

This was the first time I'd felt a bristling uncomfortableness since Bianca pushed past me when I met Alex and his friends going over the papers. Flo seemed to be putting on a bit of a show, but I was immediately on guard. Bravado could be dangerous. And it's one hell of a giveaway, like a flare telling you there's something more than meets the eye.

'OK, Flo,' chipped in Tom. 'That's enough. Sorry, Vic, Flo gets a little anxious when we have someone new join us. Lots of people don't take much pride in being a Domestic, and with all the attention you've been getting, we all kind of assumed you'd be given a Role with a little more profile. Like educating people about Florivale. Or, maybe, if you're as amazing as they say, being a Lib.' He paused. He must have seen my eyes light up.

'Oh, that's it! No way! You wanted to be a Lib!' A raucous laugh escaped him. 'Sorry, Vic. Nobody gets to pick Lib. You get picked. Or you don't get Lib. But whatever Role you're allocated to, it's 90 per cent likely to be the one you stay in. So, my guess is that your best job right now is to get sorting. Enjoy.'

Tom and Flo stood up to go and speak with Grace. As I started sifting through the enormous pile of dirty junk, I could feel their eyes on me, their silent judgment. I was going to remain calm, taking on a Clem-like sense of zen as I did this menial task. It wasn't that I thought I was above this Role. I could see its importance. But I didn't know how it was going to fit into my ultimate game plan of getting back into Florivale. I kept quiet. I categorised random bits of junk all the way to lunch.

The bell sounded and everyone dropped what they were working on and headed over to the dining hall. The smells coming from it were something I'd never experienced before. Almost sweet, definitely smoky. Turned out today we were having baked sweet potatoes topped with a rich tomato and soya-protein chili. Everyone else grumbled that this was a store-cupboard meal for when the real food ran out. I thought it was delicious. Bea came over and sat with me, providing a nice change of scene. It dawned on me that all the Chefs seemed pretty chilled. Clem would definitely have been one. She'd have been friends with Bea, this little bubbling blonde – tiny, like an imp.

'I can't believe you got Domestic,' she said, rolling her eyes. 'I put in a special request for you to come and be with me and Lizzie, in the kitchen. Fat lot of good that did. Sure, chefs get burns, but at least we don't have to sort through rubbish. Let me guess, they got you doing inventory?'

I nodded. 'Bullseye.' I thought, what the hell, I'll ask. 'So, what's the score with Flo? Is she really a massive bitch, or does she just give that impression with her scraped-back bitchy quiff hair?'

Bea snorted and spat out a glob of deep-orange sweet potato as she laughed. It was pretty disgusting, but I couldn't help laughing in response.

'Oh my god, Vic, be quiet! Did she pull that whole badass thing on you?' She laughed, more quietly this time. 'She's actually a bit of a pussycat. She's pretty proud of being a Domestic, and has been asked to go with the Libs on more supply runs than anyone else of her age. What she doesn't know about making things work in here, and what's needed to improve things, isn't worth knowing. I think she's also got a thing for Tom, so watch out for that. But give her time. She needs to establish that she's the boss, then she'll chill a bit and let you into her circle of trust. She has to. You're going to be something important to the Collective and everyone knows it.'

'I'm not sure about being important. I don't want to be. But I do want to be involved. I don't have an issue with my Role, but I feel like I can do something with more, well, more impact. I don't see how I can change anything if all I'm doing is sorting plastic from metal.'

Bea put her hand on mine. 'You're doing something important alright. You're here, aren't you? You solved the riddle in Florivale, that Shakespeare thing. You survived the journey out and the transition. You're proof it can be done. And who knows Florivale like the little rebel we busted out? Nobody.' She lowered her voice further. 'You're the most important thing we have. And think outside the box, Vic. Maybe you're in with the Domestics for safety. And I'm not just thinking about yours.'

After dinner, Mike came to see me. He looked exhausted, the bags beneath his eyes a faded purple. He said he'd wanted to check in, while we had some privacy and some more time, before my duties fully kicked in. He'd heard about my Role, and he was proud.

'Nobody should ever underestimate the importance of each cog in this machine,' he said. 'Every single one of us has an input – a slight misalignment can throw everything off. And if we're talking about cogs, having you arrive has to be something like the Industrial Revolution. You know, from Before. Sure, there'll be the Luddites, those who can't accept the change of direction or acceleration towards the future and want to smash everything up. But the future always wins out in the end. There's a new age dawning. I can feel it.'

'I don't feel much,' I said. 'Just this inertia. What difference can I make while I'm sifting filthy junk?'

'You can learn, Vic. Everyone has to start with the basics. As a Domestic, you'll get to take it all in. Out of all of us, you're the one with the eyes to truly see what's happening, what needs to be done differently. You're a creature of both worlds.'

Before he left, he held my hand and told me about Grandma Sophie when she'd been about my age. Wilful. Strong. Frustrating in the extreme. And truly magnificent. He said he saw her in me, every day, and knew she would be cheering me on, ever supportive in everything I did.

46

I was assigned a dorm the next day. I guess they'd decided I'd monopolised my previous accommodation for long enough.

Lizzie was in there, and Bea, the two people I'd most wanted to share with. Unfortunately, the final person was Bianca. Not that I'd seen her by the time I went to bed. But I'd noticed her equipment laid out on her shelf, hooks and cables, a sleek black backpack, and her clothes perfectly folded in her section of the cupboard. No mess. No fuss.

When we got back after dinner, I saw that Lizzie and Bea had laid out some new clothes for me, and had given me a few essentials to call my own - a beaten up hairbrush, some clean underwear, and a new toothbrush. I was exhausted, so I hugged them both in thanks, picked up my clean towel, still crunchy from the wash, and headed down the corridor to the showers.

I enjoyed the sensation of the warm water running down my body, soothing the cramps my legs from my run and literally washing away the dirt of my day's work. As I waited for the suds to disappear from my hair, which was getting pretty long, I heard the tinny rasp of voices, whispering. I knew they couldn't be in the bathroom with me, or I'd be able to hear more. But I caught a hint of Bianca's voice, and another, lower tone. A man's voice. Desperate to know what they were saying, but not wanting to get caught, I was torn between (a) the discreet wastefulness of leaving the shower running, and (b) turning the water off so I'd have a better chance of catching more of their conversation before they realised I was listening.

As quietly as I could, I reached for the towel and wrapped myself in it. Taking a tentative step towards the door, I held my breath so as to keep everything in my cubicle as quiet as I physically could. I caught a fragment of whispered, stressed exchange.

'She's never going to be one of us, Gareth.' That snappy enunciation simply had to be Bianca.

'She is, and you damn well know it,' came the hushed reply. 'Have you seen her in the gym? Have you watched how alert she is every time she speaks to someone? Her ears practically pricked up at the mention of Outside. She's perfect for it. And she's perfect for the extraction.'

There was a pause, and I could almost feel his face at the other side of the wall, listening out for me. There was an exhausted sigh. 'This discussion isn't over, Gareth. It's not just about us, or what we think. You know he'll object.'

A few light footsteps padded away. Just as I turned to take a step back from my listening spot, to make sense of what I'd just heard, came another whisper.

'I hope you heard that, Vic. I know you're listening. You're going to become one of us. Whether she, or he likes it, I don't care. There'll be some sort of test, some sort of time. But we'll all be watching. And I know you'll nail it.'

His own footsteps faded away, and I clutched my towel. If the junk-sorters were the sheep, the Libs were the tigers. And now, maybe I could really join them. I just had to figure out what to do to make it there. And how to pass whatever these tests might be, whenever that might happen. And who 'he' was. Simple.

I was dealing with too many unknowns. First was this man, the one who wanted to stand between me and the Role I knew was my destiny. My first guess was Mike. I was going to have to speak to him about that.

As part of my orientation, Flo told me about the alarms. If an alarm sounded, with a low but persistent tone, everybody had to drop what they were doing and immediately get into Defend and Deflect mode. Apparently the Libs were unbearable when excluded from taking control of this so, although it was technically a Domestics job, Grace had conceded long ago that it was right for the Libs to be part of managing the process. I was told there would be a drill at some point, and that my main job during it would be to make sure that nobody took it as a joke, that everyone did what they were meant to do.

'Everyone has to learn to just do it, by instinct,' said Flo. 'No questions. Military style. That way, when we have the added elements of terror and panic thrown in, at least the basics will have become automatic. So, the principles of Defend and Deflect are essentially these: one; lights out. This means getting all doors and windows shut. Any light escaping them is to be prevented and any cracks covered, assuming this can be done within ninety seconds. Two; keep low. All movements are to be low-level, to prevent identification of our location due to visibility. Three; quiet. It's imperative that everyone can hear the commands without us having to shout over a panicking crowd. Doesn't sound like it, but that's usually one of the hardest parts. Four; Collective down. Everyone except the Defend and Deflect assault teams have to get to the ground floor and into the basement, if it's clear. Five; Assault to the top. Pretty obvious, but the assault teams head to the roof, via the weaponry room. And, you know. Defend. Deflect. Assault.'

I was agog. My heart raced at the mere idea of the adrenaline that would course through my veins in the event of an alarm being sounded, one which wasn't a drill. I paused, processing it all. 'And how many of these alarms have been raised in, say the past two years? Ones which aren't drills?' I asked.

'Oh, about ten or twelve,' said Flo. 'Yeah, I'd say one every couple of months on average. Sometimes they do it twice in a week, try to sniff us out and capture anyone they can. It's always grim when it comes to the re-count. We go over the numbers remaining after a raid. If we're lucky, we lose nobody, or maybe just one or two. When we're unlucky, it's been as many as seven.' Her breath seemed to catch in her throat. 'It's always awful.'

'And how many practice runs would you say you do?'

'I reckon once a month pretty steadily. More if we get intel about an attack. One was actually scheduled for the week after you'd been extracted. It was delayed on the grounds we couldn't protect you from the panic, and on the assumption we'd need you strong and recovered for the inevitable rush of raids once it was discovered you were gone and assumed that we were involved. Assumed correctly, of course.' She fiddled with a drape, which was hanging from the wall. 'So we must be due one any time now. Obviously we don't get told when they're scheduled, but you'll know because a test alarm has the same low, persistent tone, but interspersed with a double 'tapping' sound every few seconds. The real one doesn't have the taps. It's like something inside you, a noise you have to shake out of your ear. It can make it hard to remember what you have to do. But try to stick to the five headline points and the rest will follow. One, lights out. Two, keep low. Three, quiet. Four, Collective down. Five, Assault up. I doubt you'll ever have to know about five. But I guess it helps if you can work out why a few people are going the wrong way. Just repeat the mantra of five and you'll get there.'

I was determined to be part of Defend and Deflect. I wanted to know about part five. And I wanted to make Omniclin pay for what they had done, were still doing, in Florivale. But, more immediately, I needed to know about the weapon room and the raids.

'What do the raiders do with the people they take?' I asked. 'I mean, do you even know? Do you ever hear from them again?'

Flo looked at the ground, and then up to the middle distance, where her gaze held. 'It's hard to say. Mostly, we think our people are taken alive for a reason. Torture to extract information, perhaps. But, more likely, we think they want more healthy bodies. To the Investors, some disease-free DNA is worth far more than any retribution for insurrection against the system.' She looked back at me, angry tears in her eyes. I realised she must have known people who'd been taken. She gulped back her emotions and continued.

'They won't say anything about us, I'm sure of it. We all left the official system for a reason, burnt our bridges before coming here. But the ones they capture will not have had an easy ride. Think about your friend Josh.'

My heart pounded at the mention of his name. She continued, words pouring from her like venom from a cobra's fang.

'Our latest reports indicate they've accelerated his program further and have managed to change his blood type completely.

The DNA adjustments they're doing have already changed the colour of his eyes to those of his Investor. Can you believe it?'

I choked down the bitter bile that was rising in my throat and wiped my sweaty palms on my trousers.

'And what's worse,' she continued, 'is that Josh is going through this in a permissive environment. It's an accepted aspect of his Condition. One his bitch of a mother can't even see is going too far. For as long as she receives preferential treatment and gets to stay queen bee in Florivale, she won't question it. Any of it. And they know that.'

I was rendered mute by the mention of my friend and the sad vindication of being proved right about his mother. It was unthinkable. Flo went on.

'If you think that's bad, just think about the difference between him and our Collective members. Ours are captured from a rebellious group. A group which has been criminalised for breaking laws they did not vote into enactment. For stealing the electricity upon which the system has made us depend. Food which we can no longer grow because of their urbanisation of the landscape, all for profit when the going was good. For water which is safe to drink, after their pollution turned the rain into acid. Our friends, these "criminals", don't need to be tricked into complying with any tests. They are disposable. They can be treated as sub-human.'

'Their bodies escaped the disease which afflicted the others, the dead, the rich who fund Florivale. If you ask me, or any logical mind, they and not the pure-borns, are the ones who hold the key to health. And catching us doesn't require expensive programs like Florivale. Oh no. Once one of the Collective, or anyone from any of the other groups like us, is caught, they are the property of the person who caught them. Like bounty hunters, there are those who capture and trade us to the highest bidder. That bidder might be someone from the authorities, and they might want to interrogate us. But more likely it's a shareholder or an Investor from Omniclin, or something like it. Someone with the same sick leanings and the self-convinced theory that their disgusting experiments will further a superior human race. A race impervious to disease, created by a people impervious to morals.'

'That, Vic, is the true horror of the alarms. It's a game to them. A race to create the perfectly healthy human. A blueprint for their own medical treatments, to be cloned, wounded, murdered - to be used however the highest bidder wishes.'

I was no longer sure I wanted to experience an alarm. But I knew I would. And I knew it would be soon.

47

What Flo had said about the raids never strayed far from my mind. I'd find myself applying what she'd told me while I learnt about my Role. I'd be sanding down a rusted old piece of metal so it could be used for repairs, and wonder how it could be used as a weapon. I'd cover up a crack in a window so it excluded all light, and just before the task was complete, find myself peering through that very crack. I was desperate to see something outside, a sniper point, another building. Any point of reference. Trying not to be slow in my work, I berated myself, although I couldn't help doing all the time. On my tours of the Base, I'd think about whether there was a better escape route, or consider how best to do step four, Collective down, if, say, there was a fire a floor below us. My senses were on constantly high alert, and I must have looked like either a lazy daydreamer or seriously disturbed. I wasn't sure which impression I preferred.

The aspect of my Role that I came to prefer, as my tasks became slightly more varied, was working with the Chefs to pick fruit and veg from the Ponics. The Ponics are these vast chambers filled with SunLamps, in which we grew as much fruit and veg as possible. Some things didn't really work well down there, so they seem more exotic – like oranges. For some reason, they don't like the SunLamps. So things like that had to be stolen on supply runs. But the majority of our every-day food came from down there.

We had masses of soya beans, peas, and essentially any kind of bean the planters can get their hands on. The Chefs are always going on about the amazing value of plant protein and the Domestics love the way that legumes put nutrients back into the soil, where the other vegetables just suck them right out. Safe to say, they all love a bean. The planters were gathered from the Domestics and the Chefs, usually taking rotational shifts to make sure we didn't just end up with what one person thinks is delicious or, if you got a lazy person on shift during planting, easy to cultivate.

My first trip to the Ponics was with Rob, who was kind of bashful the whole time, but whose eyes lit up when he saw the bountiful crop of bell peppers.

'Vic! Look at these! Beautiful, plump little things!' He was caressing a pepper like a lover. I kid you not. 'These contain all the flavour and vitamin C a man could dream of! And they're perfectly ripe for picking. Come and help me. Oh Vic, think of the ratatouille!'

The plants gave off a warm, heady scent as I plucked the peppers from the stalks and put them into a basket – far less reverently than Rob was doing. He was running through the names of recipes I'd never heard of, like an incantation. Rob was most definitely in his happy place. We then continued our walk around the Ponics room, deep at the bottom of the Base, a floor below the gym. There were ripe tomatoes, straining at their skins. A dark room at the side contained no SunLamps, but row upon row of densely packed mushrooms of every variety imaginable. Rob told me with glee how they grew so quickly in some phases of their development that, if you came down at night and crouched near the planters, you could hear them squeak as they grew.

There was another side room, which I wanted to go into, but found the door locked. Rob heard me struggling with the handle, and came over.

'Don't go in there, Vic. We haven't sorted that room out yet.'

'What's to sort out? A few errant mushrooms growing from the floorboards?' I joked.

'No, Vic,' he said. 'We used to keep livestock in there. Some chickens for eggs, and a couple of pigs. One of the former members of the Collective went a little, frankly, crazy, and decided it was not for us to decide whether to eat an animal and that it was cruel to keep them in pens and hutches. Don't look at me like that! I know you're a lifelong vegetarian, but they had better lives in here than they would have done out there. We looked after them really well. It was the kids' favourite part of the day to collect the eggs and watch the pigs potter around. But Hank put a stop to that.'

'Oh my god. What did he do? Hold on, I don't think I've met Hank, have I?' I asked.

'No. and you won't. He was ejected from the Collective. He let his own principles and a moment of over-zealousness jeopardise the food source of the Collective, and there was a risk he'd draw attention to our presence with his crazy behaviour. He's no longer welcome here. He killed them all. The smell of their blood has only just faded away.' His eyes were brimming with tears.

'Do you know where he is now?' I asked, wondering whether the tears were for Hank, for the pigs, or for the fact bacon was no longer on the menu.

'I don't. Once someone is ejected, they are ex-communicated. We are forbidden from speaking to them. It's all for the good if the Collective, and I understand that, but Hank wasn't cruel. He'd just had a rough time lately and something snapped. I reasoned with the Seniors to let him stay, to give him some form of punishment and an education programme, but to them, the damage was done. Basically, if you put the Collective at risk, you're out. It's the only way this place works. But it makes me sad. It's like, I get it – but it doesn't stop my heart breaking every time I think of him out there. I don't even know if he's alive.'

I didn't know how to respond. 'I'm sorry I rattled the door handle, Rob.' I said, in a low tone that I hoped was soothing. 'Come on, why don't you show me what's planted in those rows at the end.' I guided him away from the ominous locked door.

'Potatoes,' Rob muttered. 'One of our main crops. They grow in the root system, you see, so it's quite tempting to dig them up when they first get all bushy. But that's no good for anyone. You have to wait for the good things. Good things never come easily.'

And we were off. Rob told me about all

the fruit and veg until I could have pretty much written a book on them. Hank seemed to have been put far from his mind, but it left a bitter taste in my mouth. Nobody spoke of infractions in the Collective. Nobody discussed any consequences to misbehaving. Things like that made it feel oddly familiar. Some things in here were ominously like life in Florivale.

48

I started to become familiar with the meals, the timings, the chit chat between team members. They called it banter, but couldn't tell me why, or what the word meant. Grace continued to govern the group with her iron fist, although in a velvet glove, and the frostiness Flo had initially put out began to fade as she realised I was a normal person and wasn't any form of threat to her, or Tom.

I was sitting with Tom one day, trying to understand why everyone went down corridor B when there was an alarm, rather than alternating routes, so we became familiar with them all, just in case any particular one was blocked. Tom was having none of it, because 'it's always been this way,' and I was getting angry because he couldn't explain why that was. He sounded like a born-and-bred Florivite. Grace came over, having heard the increasing urgency and frustration in our exchange.

'Now, now, you two. What's causing so much fuss over here? We can't concentrate on our work because we're too nosy and I want to hear about whatever's got Tom so caught up.' She laughed, although there was a line of seriousness beneath her smile. 'We kind of expect some hot-headedness from Vic, after all we heard about her life before the extraction, but this is most unlike you, Tom.' She turned to him, with a benevolent but steely gaze.

'Vic's wanting to change the corridor routing. Thinks she can just turn up and change everything. She doesn't get that it's so familiar now, and that's what makes it safe. We repeat the drills until they are second nature.'

I chipped in. 'Look, I get the second nature thing. I really do. But what I think is worth at least considering is that corridor B could get shut off, say by a fire, or a new line of attack from outside. We'd be stuck, walking into the jaws of danger. If we have some alternatives, any intel we have could be used to minimise that risk and get people safe in other ways. We should be able to identify any weak points from sentry reports, or from building surveys, and issue a new type of alarm, so people know which route to take.'

'But that's so much work Vic. Who's going to do it, huh? Me? You? You're crazy if you think we've got all the time in the world to go making new systems and...'

Grace cut him off with a single glare and the raising of a flat palm into the air. This was her signal. Silence was required. She paused, considering the options.

'Tom. I hear you. I hear your concerns and to some extent, I share them. But Vic, I also hear you.' She paused, taking time to look slowly at each of us. 'Tom, do you not think that a new person's perspective, that of a complete outsider to our ways, someone who has come from a system of absolute control and oppression - and had her eyes opened in the most unimaginable way, might have some valuable new thoughts to bring us?'

Tom pouted. But he did not object. Grace gave him a moment, but as no comments came, she continued.

'I think this is something to raise at our next general meeting. Something on which the Community should vote, with weighted votes to the Libs and the Domestics, considering it's our duty to ensure safety when there is an alarm, and it's also us who will have to do the additional work to implement any changes. And I'll have no more argument, from either of you. Vic, don't be proud. Tom, don't act wounded. The best thing you can do as a person is to allow jealousy and anger to slip away when they no longer serve you. That is how we survive. Live by this.'

She lowered her arm from the air, and as Tom turned away, she winked at me. She mouthed the words 'good job' and quietly glided back across the room to return to her task.

That evening in the dining hall, Mike stood up, tapping his spoon against his glass for attention. Grace must have proposed the motion. The room calmed, and I could taste the excitement of having made a useful suggestion, of starting to repay the Collective for having me here.

'Everyone, listen up. We have a motion.'

A hushed silence filled the room, and Lizzie jabbed me in the side with her elbow, whispering. 'This must be yours!' I smiled, blushing and nervous in case everyone shared Tom's views. Mike continued.

'This evening's motion is a matter of security and safety, and therefore of utmost importance to us all. It has been proposed by a Domestic that our evacuation methods could be revised, so that following an alarm, corridor B is not the only escape option.'

There were a few mutterings around the room. I held my breath a little too long, and realised I'd turn blue unless I quit. I allowed myself a breath. A tiny one.

'The headline pros and cons of this motion are simple. Pros are that we would have viable alternatives if, for example, corridor B were blocked, aflame, or susceptible to invasion by our attackers. Cons are the obvious. It would mean more work for all of us to learn the new routines, but in particular, more work for the Libs and the Domestics, who would need to devise the alternative escape routes and train us all in using them.'

Mike brought his hands together and silently looked across the room. It felt like he looked into the eyes of every single person there, and when he met mine, I felt a pulse of reassurance. I don't know how he did that, whether the connection was some crazy DNA thing or, more likely, a Mike thing. I snapped out of it when he spoke again.

'And so, we must come to a vote. Any questions before I ask you to do the usual?'

There was a pause, some more muttering. But nobody spoke. Clearly, whatever they muttered did not carry any conviction, either way. Mike waited a few minutes longer.

'OK, then. You know the score. We vote with our feet, as usual. However, as Grace rightly requested, in this vote, the Libs and the Domestics will have a weighted vote, to reflect the additional work and risk they would take on if this motion were to be passed. Each Lib or

Domestic shall stand at the front of the applicable voting group – either pro or con. Pros shall stand to my right, and cons to my left. We will count the votes excluding Libs or Doms and then separately add their weighted votes before establishing whether the motion was passed or rejected. Of course, as always, abstinence is an option.' There were some titters at that, although I wasn't sure quite why. 'Anyone wishing to abstain should stand at the back of the hall, clearly separate from each voting group. Let's make this as quick as possible so we can all move on to some dessert. I hear the last scouting mission got hold of dried raspberries.'

I felt sick with nerves and couldn't believe how casual Mike's tone was, when this was something so important to me. Amid the scraping of chairs and general chatter, I caught the odd phrase, moaning about having to vote, or about extra work, or even about there always special privileges to the Domestics or the Libs. The uncomfortable hint of dissent, or dissatisfaction. Stangely, it made me glad. I wanted people to be angry, to have their own voices. But I also wanted them to agree with me. I know. I'm complicated.

I made my way over to the line of people voting pro, scanning the room as I did, in order to try and work out how many were headed in each direction. I recognised most of the faces now, even though I didn't know everyone's names. I was pleased to see that Lexi and the other kids had come to my side. And Graham. Lizzie too. I noticed how the Seniors held back, as if not wishing to sway the rest. The movements of the gathered Collective seemed pretty equal for a while, and then, with an almost imperceptible movement, I saw Alex step to the right, to my side. All but two of the Libs followed him. One abstained. Bianca voted against me. I mean, against the motion. I held my breath again, suddenly conscious of my body, of the increased muscle tone since my gym visits, my whole physical being becoming taut at the proximity of Alex. His broad shoulders and proud chest. I tried not to look at him - I knew I'd blush. I still hated that I couldn't stop that.

Grace moved over to Mike's right. To my side. Mike winked at me. And suddenly, it was clear. By a large majority, my motion had been passed, and I had won.

I smiled, and looked up, catching a grin from Alex as I did. He mouthed at me, 'great work,' and I could hear his voice in my head as clearly as though he was speaking out loud, his tone mellifluous and deep. I blushed and looked back down immediately. I felt Mike's hand gently touch my shoulder and turned to face him.

'Great job, Vic-a-nic. I knew you'd shape things up around here. Nepotism wasn't even required!'

I spent the rest of the evening on a cloud of excitement, wondering when the planning would commence. I'd already started visualising the new routes, the potential issues to overcome, even the new alarm tones. I thought Ella could create maps for us all, each of the escape routes colour coded for ease of reference in a panic. I could barely sleep with excitement and I realised this was the life I wanted. Out here, I could make a difference. I could keep people safe. In Florivale, I'd never have fitted in. I'd only ever have been a danger, an inconvenience. And having Alex around certainly didn't hurt.

Tom didn't talk to me the next day. I don't think he took Grace's advice on board, about letting things go.

49

After finishing my day's work, I headed to the gym to work out some of my frustration towards Tom, and my excited, nervous energy about the changes to the evacuation routes. In my skin-fitting gym attire, I noticed I was getting back into my old form, taut and toned, lean and strong. Finally, things were getting back to normal for me. Well, as normal as you can be when you're suddenly stolen away from everything you knew and supplanted into a new society with completely different accommodation, rules, people and fears. Yep. This was the new normal.

I filled up my water bottle, making sure the filter at the top was properly screwed in. It was revolting when you forgot to filter it, and the last thing you needed when you were hammering the treadmill was to choke, drowning in a gulp of foul water. That would be such a lame way to go. I got onto my favourite treadmill, third in from the left hand side. It sounds stupid, but this one is directly beneath the main SunLamp in the gym, so it feels like you're bathing in pure light as you run, fortifying your bones with vitamin D as your muscles develop – pretty efficient, right? There's also something that feels angelic about the way the SunLamp glints from your hair and skin when a beam hits you directly. Plus, you know, health reasons.

I plugged in my height, weight and gender and cranked the settings up to a fast jog so I could warm up for the first few minutes. Lizzie had given me her most treasured item, a small music player, which had thousands of old songs on it, and I was working my way through them. It was pretty amazing, but the bloody thing needed charging all the time, so if there was no solar power, the music ran out. It was forbidden to use energy siphoned off the grid for personal devices. Most of the songs were even older than Grandpa Mike, who told me to get straight to the 1960s and 1970s sections for the real gems. Turns out I'm a Bowie fan. As I finished my warm up and started to really run, I whacked on 'Rebel Rebel' and zoned out, losing myself far more effectively than I had in any of Clem's yoga tutorials. Being still and silent just isn't for everyone.

I didn't hear anyone come in, but had that prickling sensation up my neck, the heat of someone's eyes watching you from an unseen location. I kept running, looking straight ahead at the map of the old city of London, which had been the centre of Before, and was now the key stronghold of the rich, sick bastards who thought they could, buy, sell or capture others for personal interest or financial gain. Consumed by anger, I didn't envy whoever was sneaking up on me, the target for my next outburst.

Suddenly, Bowie was ripped from my mind, the earphones snapped away by someone else's hands.

'Hey! Bloody hell, Vic, come back to the

real world!' It was Alex. 'I've been stood over there watching you, waiting for you to realise you weren't alone. I was there for a while. You looked, well, terrifying! I certainly won't try to outrun you any time soon.'

I looked up at him, pleased at the idea of being terrifying to the strongest, fastest-looking man I'd ever seen.

'How often do you run like that?' he asked.

'I try to do it every day. Sometimes I swap some of my session out for weights or cross training just to shake it up.' I realised I was suddenly blushing through my sweat-drenched forehead. 'But, you know, I don't run at that pace for long. I'm a sprinter, not a distance girl. I like about five to ten kilometres.'

'You're not even out of breath, are you?'

'I guess not. Maybe I wasn't pushing enough.' Note to self. Push myself harder.

Alex paused, and stepped back slightly, taking me in. I stood motionless before him, torn between pride at the body I'd created and anxiety at what he might think of it. In Florivale it hadn't been like this. I'd always figured someone would be selected for me to marry and we would just go along with it and procreate, hoping to get along in the meantime. Out here, things were different. All the couples in the Collective had chosen one another - which was a deeply thrilling prospect. And, simultaneously, absolutely horrifying.

Alex ran his hand through his hair, golden strands catching the light against the darker blonde. 'You're quite something, Vic. I hadn't really believed you'd be this different. This new.

But you're everything we need. And your motion to shake up the routes when an alarm sounds, that's just the start. I know you'll change much bigger things.' His eyes flicked to mine. 'Don't look at me like that! Don't dismiss what I'm saying,' he said, laughing as he spoke.

'It wasn't anything massive, Alex. I don't even know how you know it was my motion. I just said what I thought made sense. If I'm honest, it seemed kind of obvious.'

'That's exactly it, Vic. Your perspective is exactly what we're lacking. What we need.' He laughed. 'Doesn't hurt that you're also the granddaughter of our favourite Senior, and the first Flori-born we extracted, either.' His laughter stopped, and a steely intensity filled his eyes. 'And that's why we're going to need you to help us get more Florivites out. We need your unique point of view. You know Florivale. You know us. You've survived both.'

This was what I had wanted to hear. I'd been silently burning with fury for so long, so desperate to get everyone I could out of that overgrown laboratory. So I couldn't understand why I was hesitant, why I was afraid. I gathered my thoughts and calmed my breathing.

When?' I asked.

'Soon, Vic. Really soon. But we need you trained up first. I need to get you selected as a Lib to get onto the extraction missions. Then you'll get trained up, come on some of our supply runs. The basics. I'll have a few political hurdles to deal with first...'

'Bianca?' I asked, cutting him off.

He smiled from one side of his mouth, the informal way which feels like it's only ever directed at me, like he's never smiled at anyone else. 'You could say that. She's not that bad. She's... ah. She's protective. Not a fan of change. But she believes in extraction more than most of the rest of us. That's why she cares so much.'

'Doesn't seem like it,' I said.

'Can't you see?' he asked, suddenly exasperated. 'Your extraction was so hard-won, so long in the planning, and so reliant on you being as brilliant as we thought you would be, that she can't face the risk of anything going wrong. Of you being injured. She didn't even want you dormed. She wanted you set up in a safe, private room like the most special person Out here. Because, to her, you are that precious.' His eyes dropped to the floor. 'And it's not just her who feels that way.'

Stunned. That's the word. That Bianca thought I was precious ran contrary to everything I'd seen or believed. And yet, phrased the way Alex had put it, it made sense. I knew I'd have done anything to protect something I believed in that much. That must have been why she voted against the changes I'd suggested. She must have known I'd have to be involved. Alex side-smiled again. 'You're pretty special, Vic.'

He took my sweaty hand and I immediately wished I'd had some warning, some time to wipe the sweat away. There was a fuzziness to our connection, like we held more than each other's hands. And I knew immediately that he held the key to unlocking some secret about who I was that. This man, with whom I'd shared a handful of words on a handful of days and yet to whom I felt inextricably bonded. I could say nothing, but I didn't need to. Our eyes met, and our gaze held for a moment too long. But rather than being flushed with pleasure, I was terrified. I didn't know how to navigate these waters. To me, it felt terrifying. As though, by being this close, staring into the darkness within my flecked irises, he could see directly into my soul. Something even I couldn't see. I couldn't bear it, and I had to look away.

I broke the spell. We parted hands and awkwardness took over me once again. Alex checked over his shoulder to make sure we were alone. Just before he walked away, he leaned in, very close. I could feel his breath brushing the tiny hairs at the nape of my neck and longed to turn my face up, to meet his lips. But I knew I wouldn't. Not now.

'Keep doing what you're doing, Vic. There'll be some kind of test soon. I can't tell you what it will be, because I don't know. But be alert, be ready.'

And then he was gone. The tinny sound from the headphones on the floor told me the 1970s were still going strong, and I gathered them up, untangling the cables as I tried to untangle my thoughts. How was I meant to get ready for something I knew nothing about? And what on earth had just happened with Alex?

I got back onto the treadmill and worked out I had another three kilometres to go if I wanted to get to eight. I couldn't face doing weights, which required too much time stuck in the confines of my own mind. Too much time dreaming of becoming a Lib, or of thinking about the curve of Alex's arms. So I cranked up the music and ran as fast as I could, on as high an incline as the machine allowed. I wanted to sweat out my confusion, and exhaust myself to the point where sleep would creep over me without warning once my head hit the pillow.

I dreamt of Florivale that night. I was at home, and different Florivites kept arriving at the house. They were coming for my wake, but I was there. It made no sense. I opened the door to them, but they said nothing to me. I showed them to the kitchen, where my family sat, red-eyed and exhausted, people cooing around them like a flock of birds around a picnic, each desperate for its own crumb. I spoke, but nobody heard my voice.

50

Something was wrong.

I was pulled from my bed, any sound I might have made blocked by a hand holding a fabric mask close against my mouth. The others in my dorm were still asleep, and there was nothing I could do to rouse them. How could they sleep through this? Group of morons! I did my best. I kicked, scratched, bit. But nothing caught. My limbs were jammed tight into the group of people who had grabbed me from my bed and slipped me through the door and into the corridor as though I was no heavier than one of Lexi's dolls. The Investors must have assembled a team to recover their asset. Me. AFSH-003. I wouldn't go quietly. I would take down everyone, everything, possible in my path.

I was dropped, abruptly, onto what felt like a medical bed. Someone crept next up from behind me, lowered themselves so I could feel their breath on my ear, and spoke.

'You're coming with us. On tonight's supply run.'

Relief flooded my body as I separated nightmare from reality. But I still couldn't understand their methods. Why would they feel the need to bring me to the brink of terror to get me to go with them? The hand holding the mask to my face gently pulled away, hesitating to see whether I'd scream before fully withdrawing. I coughed.

'What are you doing!?' I spat the words out. 'Why would you that? Why couldn't you have just woken me and asked me? You know I'd have come – it's all I've wanted since I found out what a Lib was!' Anger clouded my judgment and I wanted to tell them where they could stick their Role. Luckily, for once, I refrained.

I saw Alex in the group and resented him immediately. I was humiliated. My terror must have been palpable. I had been a hair's breadth away from wetting myself, like a scared child, and I was furious that they'd put me in that position.

'Can't you see, Vic?' he asked. 'We had to get you out secretly, or they'd never have let you come.'

'I'm getting tired of being asked what I can and can't see. Everything here is new to me, and you know that. I'm trying, and I think I'm coping pretty damn well.' I was so consumed with anger, I struggled to keep the words in order and my voice down. 'And what do you mean they'd never let me come? Who was going to stop you? Lizzie? Bea? Dream on!'

Bianca came forward and crouched down, close enough that I could see the pores of her skin, feel her breath lifting the tiny hairs on my cheek. A softness I'd never seen before came over her, and she lowered her voice to a gentle hum.

'Vic, it's not Bea, or Lizzie we're worried about. It's the Seniors. It's Mike. He'd never have let you come. Think about it. Hell, I didn't want you coming, not after all we've done to get you safe. But I can see it in you. A ferocity, a compulsion to fight back. You need to save them as much as I needed to save you. You want to make things right.'

I had no idea what Bianca was atoning for, but I realised this was not the appropriate forum in which to ask prying questions.

'Damn right I want to fight,' I snapped. 'But how does a supply run constitute fighting?'

'Let's just say this is a different kind of supply run. Unsanctioned by the Seniors. This is where you prove your ingenuity. We need you to help us out, without anyone knowing.'

'But why? I don't understand. Why couldn't you just not tell them I was coming and get their approval anyway?'

'We need to be able to evade our own systems to make sure we can evade systems out there. To outwit our attackers. The people who would gladly steal us away and turn us into test subjects. People who would tear families apart without another thought.' At this, Bianca's voice started to crack.

I think I was beginning to understand why she was so desperate to save people, to liberate Florivites.

'Vic. It doesn't stop with Florivale,' she said. 'Yes, you're special. But you're not the only one. Being exceptional doesn't mean you're the only one worth taking a risk for. I know you agree.'

I looked at Bianca as an unspoken understanding passed between us. I didn't need to think about this.

'Count me in.'

As I got to my feet, I checked out the group. In

addition to Alex and Bianca were Graham, Pat, Harrison and a Lib I'd seen but never met. Alex introduced him to me as Adam. From the Domestics, we had Sylvie, who I'd been on a shift with a few days before, and Tom, which surprised me. He was the first to speak.

'Look Vic, maybe you were right about shaking up the alarm drills. I'm cool now. We're cool now,' he said, glancing about the group for approval and getting little. They clearly didn't think he'd gone far enough. He paused, and looked pleadingly at me. 'I hope?' I relented.

'Of course, Tom. I just hope you can now see that I was only suggesting something I thought might make us safer. I didn't mean to throw more work your way.'

'Nah, I was just in a dreadful mood,' he said. 'You know when nothing seems to be going your way. Anyway, I get it and I agree with you. Bygones etc. So let's move on. Plus, if I were averse to extra work, I wouldn't have signed up for this secret supply run, for which, I'd note, we won't get any credit from the Seniors.'

'And a shit-ton of grief from them if anything goes wrong,' said Graham. 'So let's quit chatting and make our plan.'

Everyone nodded and gravitated towards Bianca, who was unrolling a sheaf of large pieces of paper. She must be key in planning these missions and I figured they were something similar to the papers I'd glimpsed when I first walked in on the Libs. When I'd first seen Alex, whose presence made me feel like I was standing on an electrical conductor. I had to keep reminding my brain to stop buzzing. To focus.

'Right guys. Different drill today. We

need the Domestics with us to help us find specific defensive and repair materials. We need some medical supplies too. On the left of each of these sheets, and programmed into the PalmScreens Graham's going to hand to you, is a list of what we need. As you'll see, there's a lot. We want to fortify the sentry points, bolster our barricades and make sure each of us is sufficiently armed.' She paused and looked about the room.

'Of course, the easiest way to arm ourselves is to take weapons from an attacker but, with no intel of anyone seeking to intrude or based in our vicinity, we can't rely on that. Also, it's ridiculously dangerous. Which is probably why it's the Libs' favourite method.' She grinned at this, perfect sharp teeth peeking out from her lips as she smiled.

'Which brings us to today. No Domestic is to be separated from the Lib they are assigned to accompany. Tom, you're with me. Sylvie, you're with Graham. Adam and Alex, you've got Vic. No offence Vic, but you'll need two. You're new.' I nodded. 'So that leaves Harrison and Pat to monitor our progress and float between me and Graham as required. Any issues?' None were voiced. Alex stepped forward to speak.

'Tonight has to be about stealth,' he started. 'Nobody but us knows about this plan, and we don't want the Seniors knowing, or they'll slow us down, change things. We may need to innovate and we hope Vic can help us there. But, most importantly, we need to stay safe. There's no hope for those left behind if we go missing. Today is not the day to act like a hero.'

I could hear every beat of my heart, stirring me to take my place, move forward and get Outside.

'So where do we start?' I asked.

Alex stepped forward and indicated that we needed to huddle in closer. 'We need to leave the building, silently,' he said. 'Through the roof at the top of the office section, was our plan. That way, we can ride the old window washing carts down the side of the building, or use the external fire escape stairs if there are any problems. That will reduce footfall inside and keep the noise down. Unless, of course, anyone prefers the tunnels?'

He hesitated, and looked directly at me, smiling from the side of his face in that perfect way. 'And anyway, there's no rush like the feeling of freefalling in the carts. It'd be rude to deny Vic that privilege.'

Murmurs of assent passed around the room and it was clearly decided. We were using the roof. I'd be going up, out. Really Outside. For the first time in my life, I'd be outside a fabricated environment. It was all I could do to keep myself from running to the roof.

'From the ground - and don't worry Vic, we'll get you down safely – we'll disperse. Our best bet for plastics is the defunct NovCorp building over to the west. Bianca, you good to take that one?'

'Sure thing. I hate those bastards anyway.'

'Good on you. Graham, you're on metals. So you need to head a few streets to the south, to the skeleton buildings. The ones which never got finished. It's really tough work, so make sure you pick your metals carefully and keep the heat cutters as quiet as possible.'

'Got it, boss,' said Graham, as he winked and mock-saluted.

'Adam and Vic, you're with me. We need to get stuff for the Meds. This isn't something we can easily acquire. Hence we may be needing Vic's ingenuity, although hopefully there'll be no surprises. This is more of a training run for you, Vic. But obviously, if you see anything you think we should factor in to our protocols, let us know. We've got to head to one of the less reputable pharmaceutical offices, or one of their labs, and see what's left. That is, if there's anything at all. Our Meds are running low on pretty much everything and due to the lockdown in Florivale, any operatives inside the unit are maxed out trying to stay alive and evade detection. We can count out any chance of them sneaking anything out from under the Carers' noses. So the three of us are going west.'

The mention of a lockdown in Florivale had me frozen. I couldn't think straight, instantly visualising my family held captive in their home. Clem trapped somewhere. Josh stuck in his bed being transfused, injected, or subjected to any other disgusting treatment the Investors devised.

'Vic,' came a voice through the terrible vision. 'Vic, is that OK with you? We head west and steal a bunch of old drugs from those dickheads?'

It was Adam, right in front of me, holding my hands in his as though I were lost and needed leading. Perhaps I did.

'Yes,' I said as I snapped out of it. I had to.

'Yes, that's fine. But what's the lockdown? Are they hurt? I need to know!' I could feel the quavering of my panicked voice, and hated how weak it made me sound.

Alex cut in. 'I'm sorry, Vic. We don't have time right now. Short story is that the Florivites don't know much about why, but things are changing. Controls are tightening. We're not able to get our people in or out any more. Suspicion is everywhere among the Carers, Protectors and so on. And things will escalate. Florivale may have been told that you drowned in the Lake, but many of them question whether even you would be that stupid.' Adam and Alex both smirked at that.

'We have to get supplies so we can survive while we prepare to attack the authorities,' said Adam. 'We need to take down Omniclin. But remember the first step is the supplies. And we need you to help us achieve that first step.'

He had a point. I had to do this. I shook the image of Florivale under siege from my mind, but it caught at the corners, leaving a ghostly overlay over everything I had to accomplish.

'Let's kit up,' said Bianca. 'Vic, come with me and we'll get your assault suit.'

I liked the sound of that. She indicated to a door at the back of the room, and opened it to reveal a cavernous space, incongruous with the small room we'd just been in. Every wall was lined with custom-made weapons of every type imaginable. I recognised some of the Protectors' stun guns, some with modifications and others exactly in the same state they had been when they were presumably stolen. There were knives, guns, sprays, small round things that looked like Lizzie's portable speakers, but which I suspected were something far more sinister. Hanging on a rail to the right were a handful of black suits, sleek carbon fibre glinting across the breastplates.

'Pretty cool, huh?'

'Yep. Pretty damn cool. Which one's for me?' I asked.

Bianca pulled one from the rack and held it against me. 'They've done a perfect job,' she said as admired the new suit. 'No scuffs. Pristine. Of course, it won't be after an hour, so enjoy it for now.'

The suit was made out of one smooth piece, with different materials for each area. Dense, elasticated fabric ran the whole length of the garment, and a thick gold zip ran down its side. Each leg had a carbon fibre panel down the front and back, with an ingenious gel-filled section underneath the solid cap over each knee. The arms followed the same design. The front featured a breastplate, which had a series of armadillo-like joins from the upper ribs to the hip, allowing for free movement. The back was similar, although the whole thing was made of those armadillo sections.

'The zip's the weakest part,' said Bianca, running her finger absentmindedly along the golden metal teeth. 'But metal's the only way to stop it catching. There's a flap of the same bulletproof fabric which lines the whole piece, tucked just inside. That needs to be placed beneath the zip, so make sure you don't leave it folded back by accident.' She grimaced and gripped the suit tighter, her white knuckles giving her away. 'We learnt that the hard way.'

I gulped at that, but I was still desperate to try on my suit. My new exoskeleton. As she handed it to me I noticed it was no heavier than my casual clothes, and I couldn't fathom how that could have been done.

'Here's your mask, said Bianca officiously. 'That's for the toxins and the sprays. They'll use anything against us, so we always have to be prepared. Frankly, I'd rather they just killed me than used MindFog. At least that way it would all be over quicker.'

She passed me a black balaclava-style mask, which would cover my whole head and face. The front had a cut-away section for my eyes, and there was a grille of some kind in front of my mouth. She saw me looking at it in horror.

'Yep, the mouthpiece filters everything. MindFog, toxins, even Graham's farts,' she laughed. 'The mask is one of our best bits of tech. Of course, you'll need some goggles too.'

She moved along the shelves, slowing every now and again to consider which item might be best. She selected some goggles from a box, all of which looked the same to me. They had black frames, which covered both eyes, and a black head strap. The lens was green and the glass contained a mishmash of tiny wires that I stared at in bafflement.

'The goggles are where it gets really fun,' Bianca said. 'They can tell us everything. Projected distances, intruders, comms from the others in the team. You'll get used to the microwires and you'll stop noticing them after a while.' I personally doubted that, but she went on. 'For now, I'll leave you to suit up.' She looked at me, awe-struck and laden with my equipment. 'You've got five minutes. Remember what I said about the flap under the zip. And don't worry,' she paused. 'I'll keep Alex out of here while you change.'

I felt my blushing skin and wished she'd leave a little quicker and stop scouring my face for my reaction to his name. Was I that obvious? I turned from her and lay the goggles and mask gently on a shelf, wondering how best to get into the suit. Whip my current clothing off as quickly as possible and get straight in, I figured. That way I could work out the details and the zips once I wasn't naked. I was acutely aware that Alex was on the other side of the door.

I pulled it on, surprised at how cool and smooth the inside of the fabric felt, like a second skin. I left the mask and goggles off, not wanting to look like an idiot if everyone else put theirs on at the last minute. I came out of the room and saw that I needn't have worried. Everyone was already fully kitted out, masks and all.

'Well, look at you,' said Bianca. 'One of the best fitting suits I think we've ever accomplished.' She strode over, her eyes slightly obscured by the lens in her mask, tucked my hair into the back of my suit, and helped me pull my mask over my head.

'The trick is to tie your hair in a low ponytail at the nape of the neck, or a braid, and tuck it in before you put the mask on. Bloody nightmare otherwise.'

I nodded my thanks at her and she pulled the mask over my face, adjusted it, checked I could breathe and see, and strapped the goggles around my eyes. I gasped.

'The colours! How is it all in colour? The lens is green!?'

Everybody laughed, and Alex stepped forward. 'We told you the goggles were cool. Click the button by your right ear a few times, have a play with them.'

I did, and translucent but perfectly clear information became visible at the left hand side of my lens. I clicked it again and different information appeared at the top of the screen, clicked once more, and new information showed on the right.

'This is amazing!' I exclaimed. 'But how does it tie in with our PalmStreams?'

'It's all the same info. Saves you needing to use your hands. Once the goggles have recognised your retinas, you'll be able to double blink for the same effect as clicking the button. It won't work for a few minutes yet, but once it does, all you need to do is blink twice, very quickly, and it'll click through in the same sequence. It's also voice activated, so say left screen, top screen, right screen, and it'll shift. But that's no good when you're trying to be silent, so I wouldn't rely on it.'

I was fascinated. By clicking through using the button, I worked out that the left of the screen was a sort of projected map, which showed in miniature, three-dimensional form, what lay ahead. The curve of a corridor, an obstacle beyond. Top of the screen was comms, for the team. Updates, information, locations. The right side looked like a weapon inventory, showing how many bullets were left, how long the batteries in the system would work for, and so on. This was seriously cool.

'So what weapons do I get?' I asked.

Everyone laughed, hysterically. Apparently, I was quite the comedian these days. As he regained his composure, Graham was the first to speak.

'You don't, Vic. Not just yet. Your suit contains your defensive kit, but you won't get assault kit until you're fully briefed and trained. Nobody gets assault kit on their first run. So. Right pocket contains two FlashBursts. Little black balls. Click the top, chuck them at your opponent and run like hell while they stagger around, blinded.' I gasped.

'Temporarily, of course.' He indicated to my left pockets. 'Left pockets contain MindFog. It's a canister of spray which, if inhaled, causes extreme confusion and disorientation. You might recognise some of the sensation, if you're ever unlucky enough to be at the wrong end of a can. We used low doses in your IsoPod when we busted you out. I think you'll remember the nausea in particular. Multiply that eighty times or so and you'll be somewhere close to the sensation of a minor MindFog inhalation.'

I remembered. I made a mental note never to leave the mask off. I was going to need the mouthpiece.

'Your suit is your key defence. Bulletproof, heatproof, flameproof, waterproof. Lightweight. Padded supports for key landing areas – knees, elbows, palms. The built-in boots have both mechanical and gel shock absorbers. You'll love it.' I nodded, admiring my gloved hands as I turned them about in front of me.

'But remember. Every piece of kit we have

is obsolete, by Omniclin standards, or made out of something discarded by the establishment. Their fabrics will be better than ours. Their goggles will be better than ours. But we can, and will, beat them. We've evaded them pretty well so far. Largely by the skin of our teeth and the seat of our shiny black pants!' He slapped his bum and winked, ever the class clown.

Alex interjected. 'Yep, OK guys, suits are great, weapons, got it. We have to go. Someone will notice otherwise. Let's get up to the roof.'

Without another word, we moved as a unit into the corridor and through the door at the end, into the darkness of a stairwell I'd thought was only used for emergency access between the floors. The stairs were eroded, the bannisters long gone. And it was, of course, pitch black. Which is where the goggles came into their own. I could see everything, as clear as if it were midday. We hastily sped up, the shock absorbers in our boots absorbing more sound than I'd have believed possible if you told me. My breath was the loudest thing in the corridor.

I was behind Adam when we stopped, quite suddenly. Our almost-silent ascent was over, and everyone's excitement at the prospect of getting Outside had become palpable. The air hung thick with anticipation.

A flash of text across my goggles showed I had a comm from Bianca, who was at the front.

'ARMED. OPENING IN FIVE SECS.'

Another came straight in from Alex and I realised I had no idea how they actually wrote the messages, especially this fast.

'LET'S DO THIS.'

A cool sensation ran over my suit and I realised the shift in temperature was my first feeling of the night air since I'd left Florivale. The roof hatch was open, but no light had yet hit us. We moved up, pressed into a dense pack. Suddenly, I was on the cusp. I climbed a few rungs of the ladder towards the hatch. My head was exposed, but all I could see were the boots of the others. A handrail ran over the lip at either side of the opening and, when I saw a gap in the people out on top, I hauled myself over onto the rough concrete of the flat roof. I steeled myself and rose to my feet with my eyes pressed shut.

I took my first look at reality.

51

The night sky was a deep purple-grey. I later learnt this was a scar in the atmosphere from pollutants, which had largely been excluded from Florivale's airspace at enormous expense. The stars of a Florivale night sky were mere projections, no more real than the nightscapes on the films in the Community Centre. There were no stars out here either, just an ugly wash of filth across the horizon. I'm learning that the truth isn't necessarily beautiful.

Buildings appeared to have sprouted all around us, some gone to waste following the exodus from the towns and cities, others clearly inhabited by workers and residents, the last remaining few who were part of the establishment but who, due to being too poor, or too greedy, remained out here at the coal face of the human struggle. Not protected in the central cities. Half-crumbled walls gave way to streets riddled with plaster and stone. Other buildings were punctuated by lit windows, within which the remaining people worked, slept, and tried to survive whichever circumstances they'd been dealt.

There was nothing uniform to this place. Unlike Florivale, where each building had a clear purpose, being municipal or residential, each with its own landscaped garden, out here it was chaos. Tall buildings towered over squat blocks of concrete. Roads and utility lines carved their way through the landscape, which ceded to their priority.

I breathed in the cloying air, filtered through my mask. I was disappointed to learn that what I'd yearned for whilst in Florivale was nothing but an artificial dream. But at the same time, exhilarated that I was free. Sure, it wasn't the kind of freedom I'd dreamed of. It wasn't the landscape Grandma Sophie had told us about from her childhood. There were no stars or hedgerows here. But it was the new reality, and I was part of it.

'That's enough, dreamer,' came Alex's voice. 'Over here. We're going in this cart.'

I crossed the roof to where he and Adam waited, by the edge of the building. I guessed we must be about fifteen floors up, based on the floor plans I'd been learning as part of my Role. I peered over the edge. I couldn't help it. Clem would just lose her mind at this! But I couldn't. I was struggling to contain my excitement, but also desperate to look calm and collected in front of Alex. He nudged me gently in the rib.

'You ready for our little ride, Vic?' I nodded. 'It's pretty simple,' he explained. 'You stand in the cart with us. You can hold on if you want. To me or the cart.' He winked, and I looked away. 'Adam pulls some levers. We go down. Fast. Got it?'

I nodded.

'OK, guys,' said Adam. 'Here. We. Go!'

With a lurch, the bottom of my stomach dropped out and the city rushed above me as we whistled to a stop a few feet from the ground. It could only have taken seconds. It was silent.

'Shit, Alex, that new lubricant Bianca nicked for us really worked!' exclaimed Adam. 'Straight down, no squeaks. Nice.'

A message flashed across the top of my goggles.

'NICE WORK BIANCA GREAT LUBE.'

'THANKS, IDIOT. GET GOING. BACK TO BASE WITHIN THIRTY PLEASE. NOBODY CAN KNOW WE'RE GONE.'

'GOT IT. SEE YOU IN TWENTY FIVE. IF YOU THINK YOU CAN DO IT.'

'YOU'RE ON.'

Alex signalled for us to join him as he leapt from the cart, and we headed off at street level, our goggles illuminating everything to perfect daylight conditions and mapping out the terrain ahead. The feeling of omniscience was amazing. My stomach lurched again when I realised the blurry spots moving in some of the buildings were people within. People who could harm us. Knowing this fact was the perfect incentive to keep quiet as we stepped past crumbled bricks and burnt-out plants, frazzled by the acid rain but still fighting their way through cracks in the pavement. Clever, tenacious little things.

'OLD LAB AHEAD LEFT. LET'S TRY.'

'GOT IT.'

It was pretty frustrating not to be able to type back. So I just followed, trying to keep calm. We were going to steal things from people who wanted to hurt us. And it felt good. Scratch that. It felt amazing.

We continued in silence, the messages across my goggles slowing as each of us acknowledged that this was the time for intense concentration, to evade detection. Being captured was not an option. Alex was in front of me, Adam behind. After a while, Alex began to slow, before crouching down to the ground. We did the same, careful to keep out of the line of sight from the windows in the low building ahead.

'RIGHT THIS IS IT. WE GO TO THE DOOR ON THE RIGHT. KEEP LOW. STAY OUTSIDE UNTIL I MOVE IN. GIVE ME THREE SECONDS AND FOLLOW.'

'ROGER.'

Mute, without any understanding of how to operate the messaging system, I accepted that I'd just have to follow orders. This time.

As Alex approached the door, his lean body lengthened against the door frame and his hand moved towards the handle. It hovered there, just a moment. He slipped a thin metal card through the space between the door and the frame, and I noticed a red light emanating from it, creating a warm glow. It must have somehow melted the lock, or decoded it, if it was electronic. Because in one smooth, silent movement, he was in.

Adam was facing me, on the opposite side of the external door frame. He held up his fingers and slowly indicated for me to go through, one, two, three. I didn't manage to breathe the whole time.

He pointed in, and I gulped in what I realised might be my last breath as I swung myself round the doorframe and immediately down to the ground once I was a couple of paces inside. Just like Alex had done. He was crouched four or five paces ahead. All as planned. I felt the air move as Adam slipped in behind me after another three seconds.

My eyes didn't need to adjust to the light conditions, due to the goggles. It was still weird.

'ANYTHING?'

'NOTHING.'

'GOOD. SEE THE CUPBOARDS AT THE FAR END? THE DOOR IS AJAR. I SAY I TRY IT AND YOU COVER ME. OK?'

'ROGER.'

I wondered, as I had done before, who this Roger was, and what he had to do with anything. But I wasn't about to breach our carefully constructed silence to ask.

Alex moved forward, lupine in his movements, stalking his way towards the cupboards and racking at the end of the room. They seemed to contain pots and jars of tablets, some full, and some half empty. Some unopened boxes, which I guessed might be the ultimate goal. Reaching the end, he paused, waiting. There was no noise other than our stilted breathing. He rose to his full height and glanced at each label before committing to any particular item.

'GREAT STUFF HERE GUYS.'

He reached into the pocket at the back of his suit, just underneath where the curve of his bum met his muscular thighs. From it he drew a small piece of gossamer-thin fabric, silvery-black through my goggles. As it unravelled, it became capacious beyond reasonable expectation. Every single bottle or jar Alex picked from the racks fit in. It simply seemed to morph to whatever size and shape was needed to accommodate it all.

He was methodical in his selections. I

realised he must have an inventory of sorts on his goggles, or some reference as to which substances we needed, because he was taking his time. I'd expected more of a smash-and-grab approach after jumping off the top of a building to get here – but what did I know? It was hard to fight the mounting nerves that built in my gut and rose to form beads of sweat on my forehead. We'd been in the same place so long, exposed but determined to return laden with essentials. Adam was visibly scanning every perimeter, every point of entry. I felt safe in my spot between him and Alex, who turned and nodded. Adam caught the signal, while I was mid-daydream.

'ALREADY?'

'BACK TO BASE.'

'ROGER. VIC, FOLLOW ME. SAME AS BEFORE YOU DON'T LEAVE UNTIL THREE SECONDS AFTER I STEP THROUGH THE DOOR. NOD IF YOU CAN READ THIS.'

I nodded. Adam made off slowly towards the door, creeping low on his hands and knees as Alex had done, before stretching out to his full height along the door frame. I joined just behind him before allowing myself another breath.

A few seconds passed while Adam scanned what lay beyond the closed door, during which time Alex unfurled himself at the opposite side of the door frame. He nodded, and I noticed that the bag now strapped to his back and somehow re-formed into a fluid, ergonomic shape, no edges or lumps.

Adam slipped through the door. This time, Alex used his fingers to count me out, and when he reached number three I stepped over the threshold and back onto the streets. I took two paces forward and crouched down like I'd been told. Another three seconds and Alex was behind me. They were so slick, so well-practised.

We crept back through the streets, taking a different route to the one we had on the way here, careful not to leave any tracks. In the silence, my pounding heartbeat sounded to my terrified ears like the footfall of giants. Being exposed was almost worse than being in a tunnel, I decided.

We reached the main building, which held the entrance to the Base. I took my first proper look at it. It was half crumbled away, pieces of the façade rotting or chipped down to the underlying structure. They had done a spectacular job of concealing it. Nothing suggesting it was any more occupied than the barren streets in which it stood. There were ground-level windows along the floor, and as I scanned them I realised the window carts had gone. I looked up at Alex and Adam for reassurance. How were we going to get back up?

'THE CARTS. SHOULD HAVE TOLD YOU. NO CARTS UPWARDS. TOO SLOW. NOISY.'

'YOU'RE GONNA HAVE TO COME BACK IN THROUGH THE TUNNEL.'

The absolute last thing I wanted was to go into any sort of enclosed space after the IsoPod. But I knew there was no option. I had to be brave, be the tiger. Not the sheep.

'THIS WAY. EYES DOWN.'

Adam led this time, Alex following behind me. We crept two streets away from the first building, and into another. If you could call it a building. It was a crumbling edifice. It looked bombed-out, like something from an old wartime movie in the Community Centre. We stepped over mounds of rubble and crossed what was clearly once a large atrium with beautiful plasterwork alcoves carved into it, now falling into ruin. On the other side, there was a hint of movement in one of them, at the bottom of the wall. I realised I'd seen the top of Bianca's head as it slipped into the darkness beyond. I couldn't mistake her poise, even fully masked. A message came in.

'BEAT YOU GUYS. SUCKERS.'

Alex shrugged off the playful insult and motioned for me to follow Bianca and her team into that darkness. I did, and found myself working down a small flight of stone stairs, much newer and better maintained than the rest of the building, only accessible through this uninhabitable, crumbling frontage. Very clever. Down the steps, the air turned cooler and I followed whichever person was directly in front until we stopped.

'YOU KNOW THE DRILL. ONE BY ONE DOWN THE HOLE. TAKE THE PASSAGE TO THE LEFT THIS TIME AND DON'T STOP UNTIL YOU'RE IN THE BUILDING. NO RUNNING. ALEX I MEAN YOU.'

I felt him laugh behind me, tantalising as his chest raised and lowered so close to me. We moved forward slowly and I waited with trepidation as those in front of me popped down through a hole in the ground, which had been covered by a massive stone. A stone which appeared to have been tossed aside like a feather. I needed to ask about that. My money was on Graham being the only one strong enough.

Eventually I was in front of the hole, only a couple of people left behind me, by the sound of the footfall. I held my breath, crouched down close to the lip of the opening, just as I had seen those before me do, and flung myself in. I hadn't expected to fall far, but I'd put it at eight feet, enough to hurt when you landed without knowing your terrain. But I felt almost nothing. No pain, just the recognition of something solid underfoot. There had barely been a sound. This suit was incredible.

I paced along, following the others at a fast and silent walk, until we reached a metal door, which was open and ready for each of us to slip through. We arrived into the gym, in the basement of our building. Harrison was the last to join us. He pulled the outer metal door shut, then the inner door, and concealed it with a piece of internal wall partitioning. I had never even noticed that. I wondered whether all the Domestics knew it was here. I doubted it, but I wasn't quite sure why.

'GREAT JOB GUYS ALL RETURNED AND ONLY TWENTY SEVEN MINUTES.'

People started pulling off their goggles and masks, an elated grin plastered across each face. They patted one another's backs in celebration, mine included. I stood like an idiot, not knowing who to hug or what to say, but overcome by exhilaration. Without saying a word, they swarmed in around me, and lifted me above their heads. My blushing was incontrollable, but I let myself go. I enjoyed it. I relished their acceptance.

After a few seconds of being hoisted around among the group, they lowered me to the ground, and Bianca stepped forward. I was still reeling from the spinning as I felt a pair of hands gently take my shoulders.

'A brilliant first supply run. Silent, effective, quick to learn.' She smiled. They all smiled.

'You've made the grade, Vic. You're a Lib now.'

52

I grinned as I woke the next morning, remembering the exhilaration of the night before. Relishing my achievement. I didn't feel tired at all. Elated, yes. Delighted, defnitely - anything but tired. I was a Lib now. A Lib! We'd celebrated, trying to keep quiet, in the gym. We had some contraband alcohol that Pat had smuggled in from the stores – usually reserved for special occasions. Collective-wide things like births and funerals. But he figured we deserved it; this was the birth of a new phase of my life. Pat was pretty fun. The alcohol was pretty revolting. I genuinely don't know why they got excited about that part.

It struck me that I didn't know if my new position meant I was no longer a Domestic, or whether the Roles overlapped, but I could ask Grace about that. Or Mike. Or Alex. Or, in fact, any of the other Libs. Now it was official.

I already longed again for the feeling of being Outside, and back in the window cart, adrenaline coursing through my veins as we hurtled towards the ground. I didn't want to get out of bed and deal with the realities of daily life. Staying in bed meant I could hold onto my delight without having to share it with anyone. At the same time, I wanted to leap up and tell Lizzie all about it, about how successful had been. I went with the second option.

Nobody was in the room, which was odd, but I guessed perhaps I'd overslept after the exploits of the night before. I got out of bed, pulled my towel from my sparsely-populated shelf and headed for the shower, where I could relive the memories of the night before in silence. No amount of scrubbing would wash the smile from my face.

Heading down the corridor, it struck me again that nobody was around, which was unusual. Even if everyone went to the dining hall at the same time for breakfast, which never happened, there would usually be some stragglers, or people coming off night shifts, wandering around the corridors. I checked the time and I definitely wasn't late – I'd never been late for a shift and didn't want to start being tardy now, after such an accomplished first supply run.

I'd have a quick shower and get downstairs for some of Lizzie's overnight oats to kick-start the day. How she made such gargantuan quantities every evening and yet each pot felt specially crafted for the recipient, I'll never know.

The shower block was completely empty. This was just getting weirder. I pulled the door shut behind me and flicked the power switch to start the hot water. I'd learned the hard – and cold - way just how important that switch was. As the warm water began to flow over my shoulders and drenched its way through my thick hair, I smiled to myself, proud of everything I'd achieved the night before.

I was even more determined to get out there again, and more than that, to get fully weapon-trained. I wanted to assault, not just Defend and Deflect. And I wanted to really, directly help the people of Florivale – get them out and give them a taste of the real world. A world where a BioBand didn't tell them what to do, where they were trusted to look after their own bodies. A world where everyone had a real purpose, a community in which everyone contributed and, in doing so, gained so much more than they did in a society where everything was handed to them. Somewhere that each morsel of food wasn't attached to unseen strings. A place where nobody, not a single person, could force experiments, tests, Conditions or marriage on you for financial or empirical gain.

I finished my shower and left the small nub of AllSoap, which somehow simultaneously served as a creamy lather to wash your body and clothes with, and a cleansing and conditioning hair treatment, on the shelf in the cubicle. Wrapping the rough towel around me, I buffed myself dry, leaving pink marks where I rubbed a little too hard in my haste.

I stepped into my towel slippers and made my way across to a changing cubicle, and got into my usual trouser suit, dark navy with its stripes down the side. I dropped my wet towel into the disposal unit for cleaning and jogged back to my room to comb the tangles from my hair and put on my day shoes, soft black trainers made of leather and fabric and which fit like a glove.

Grinning to myself as I remembered the feeling of bursting through the door on the count of three, of having Alex there with me and earning Bianca's approval, I sauntered down the corridor to the dining hall. Half way along, suddenly reached out and pulled me into a side room.

'Vic,' said Bianca, 'you can't go down there.' She was ashen faced, eyes wide. I'd never seen her look like this.

'What do you mean? I haven't had anything to eat yet, of course I have to go down there. You know me, if I don't eat, I don't function!' I said, laughing. 'I get so angry when I'm hungry!'

'Something's happened. Something I, I mean, we, need to tell you. Before you go in to the dining hall.'

I stopped laughing. I noticed Alex sitting behind her, in a chair in a dimly-lit corner, with his head in his hands. Grace stepped forwards from the gloom and Bianca took a pace back towards Alex. He wouldn't look at me, no matter how much I willed him to. Surely he could feel my eyes burning into him? Grace placed her palm on top of mine.

'Victoria. Please sit down,' she said, her eyes as wide as Bianca's had been as she led me to sit on one of a few chairs in the corner opposite Alex, behind the door.

'I need you to try to remain calm, which I know you can do, if you really try.' She paused. 'Can you do that for me, for us?'

I nodded, swallowing the enormous lump in my throat and clenching my jaw to steel myself for whatever she had to say. I must have done something wrong on the supply run, forgotten something, made too much noise. Maybe I wasn't a Lib, after all. I'd already lost the respect I'd just earned. I stood waiting, as the crushing feeling took over.

'Vic. Your grandfather is dead.'

53

'There's no easy way to say this,' said Grace, her voice floating over me but hovering slightly away, not quite able to penetrate my shock.

A tear slipped from her eye and rushed down her cheek, plunging to the floor below. I watched the pattern as it spread, tiny fronds of saline escaping the perfect droplet from which they'd been released. She carried on but I heard only odd words, concepts, phrases. I brought myself back into the present by force of will. I cut across her as she spoke.

'But when? How? Was he sick?' I asked, trying to hold back the tears which were threatening to breach my eyelids.

'Some time after the supply run. Yes. I know about that now,' she said. 'You know you put yourself, and all of us in danger. We'll discuss it later. But Mike is more important right now. We think it happened between three and four a.m. We've been trying to work out more but it's very difficult. He'd not been sick since before he went into Florivale, and even then he faked the illness that got him out.'

'So, you're saying it could be another faked illness? He could be OK?' I asked as I parsed her face for any sign. Alex and Bianca still wouldn't look at me.

'No, Vic. I'm afraid we know he has faked nothing. We have... we have his body.' Her slow reply was echoed by the slow raising of her eyes to mine, where she held my gaze with an intensity of grief I'd rarely seen matched.

'His life was taken,' she continued. 'Someone on the Outside was leaving a clear message to us to desist from our efforts to undermine them. To give up the fight. They took our strength. Our true leader. Mike. Your grandfather. The man who started everything.'

Her voice caught and she sobbed, her grief finally audible. I realised I'd never seen more than a firm but fair kindness from this woman, who seemed to weigh every word before speaking. She was a pillar of strength, crumbling to dust at the morning's events.

'No. Nobody can take from me the last connection I had to my family. Nobody can do that.' I said, my breath calm as rage replaced my shock. I brought my heart rate down, using one of Clem's breathing techniques. I needed clarity. Panic would not help me now. 'This isn't over. They can't do this to us.'

'Shhhh, sweet girl,' Grace interjected, squeezing my hands to snap me out of my denial.

'I'm not a girl,' I snapped, pulling my hands away. 'I'm not sweet. I'm furious. This act cannot go unpunished.'

'OK, Victoria. I hear you. I respect you.'

'I don't give a shit about respect! Get angry! Be angry! You're meant to be a Senior, a leader. And here you are – acting like a sodding automaton!' I screamed. I could barely believe the words as they ripped from my throat. Grace didn't flinch. She simply continued, as though nothing had been said. I thank her for that clemency now.

'We don't know much at this point,' she said. 'But what we know is this. Mike, as you know, had his own room here. Usually, he's up at first SunLamp, so to speak, so we tend to see him when we arrive in the Senior committee room, sitting with his breakfast. But,' she paused, gathering her thoughts and stemming the flow of her tears. 'We didn't see him this morning. So Rob and I went to check on him. Mike's been quite distracted since your arrival and we thought maybe he'd been up all night again, working things through. You know, planning like he always is. New schemes for the Ponics. Work rotations. You name it.'

She stopped, clearly not wanting to go on. I pitied her. But more than that, I needed her to stay strong and tell me everything. She cleared her throat and I watched another tear splash onto the ground.

'He was just lying there, as though he was asleep,' she said. 'But there was nothing left. He was gone, like a waxwork model of him had been left there as a decoy. He was just not there. Departed. The skin on his face had taken a glossy sheen, unreal. The life had flown from his eyes. His flesh was already cold by the time we found him. But his soul was free.'

Her voice quaked to the point where she stopped speaking. She looked at me, a plea in her eyes, but I wouldn't relent in my quest for the truth. I needed it all, and I needed it now. Before emotion took over and while I could still hold the lurch of my stomach at bay.

'It wasn't until we pulled back the bedsheets that we saw what they had done,' she said, regaining control of her voice. 'They'd used some sort of heat rod, cauterising as it went through him. To stem the bleeding. To trick us. To delay our discovery of their crime.' She gulped back a lump in her throat. 'You could see straight through his torso to the bedsheet beneath.'

She broke down, sobs racking her body. Stoic Grace, felled by grief.

Alex stepped forward. 'Vic,' he said. 'You need time. You need to process. Hold this anger back. Bide your time. Brew your fury, leave it preserved for the people who deserve it. At the right time.' He stopped speaking as he swallowed back a tear of his own. 'Grief will pass, but you must experience it first,' he said, as he stroked my hair.

'Grief won't get him back,' I snapped. I glared up at all of them, the tigress inside rearing. 'I need answers. We need to regroup. They won't expect instant retaliation.'

I noticed that Bianca was smiling at me from her chair in the corner.

She stood and walked towards me. We understood each other. Someone must have been taken from her.

'This is a clear message to us, Vic,' she said. 'Think about it. They usually want to test on us, not kill us. Even the old ones, like Mike, have value. He probably has more value as a research asset than most of us, given he was a Pioneer in Florivale, managed to escape the Community and had adjusted back to a life here in even worse conditions than those he and the other Pioneers fled. And, aside from all that, he survived. If anything, he would have been their best source of intel about us, so it makes even less sense to kill him. He was our leader, the only one who could defeat the collective fear and unify us. That's why we're called the Collective, by the way. Grace, I don't mean to offend, but you know it was all him.' Grace bowed her head in acknowledgment. 'He had something. A charisma, an otherness that none of us have. They took that from us when they took his life. Just as we took you from them. Because you have his qualities. Stubborn as a Stone, ruthless as a Hunter. This murder was a message. There's no doubt about it.' She looked up at Grace, who nodded, apparently unable to speak.

'Vic, in Mike's bed, in his limp hand, was a note.' Bianca looked up at me, put her arm around my shoulder.

'It was based on a line from Shakespeare. Just like the code Mike used to get you out. They know, Vic. They know it was us who got you out.'

'What was the line?' My voice was mechanical, my mind predicting what it might have said.

'From As You Like It, we think. The same play as he used for the code which led you to the IsoPod. Someone's seen it. They're checking up on us, probably to make sure we don't liberate anyone else. We think they changed the words from the original text a bit. It said:

"Bring her, dead or living,
Within this twelve days or turn thou no more
To seek a living in our territory"

'We think they've changed it from twelve months to twelve days. And we know the original line referred to "bring him," not "bring her". We think it's about you, Vic.'

I knew my own line on vengeance from Shakespeare, from trawling through the records in the Community centre one idle afternoon. Think therefore on revenge and cease to weep. I took a breath, collected my thoughts. Thoughts centred entirely around revenge.

'I'm going to the dining room,' I said. My voice was flat. I'd stripped it of emotion. I guessed that's where everyone would have congregated, trying to make sense of the unjustness of it all. Trying to work out what happened next.

'Anyone coming with me?'

I hastened down the corridor, wiping a disobedient tear from my cheek and pulling my damp hair away from my forehead. I needed to be able to see everyone clearly. I hurled myself from the room, so fast that nobody could slow my progress, even if they wanted to. I suspect they did not dare. I found myself, as I had during my introduction into the Collective, at the entrance to the dining hall.

As I reached the double doors, I allowed my pace to slow slightly as I brought order to my erratic thoughts. I threw the doors open.

Unlike last time, the room was absolutely packed. No seat was left unfilled. No standing room remained. And not a single person spoke. Each of them looked up at me, many of their faces marked with tears. I ached when I saw that, a hollowness blooming in my chest in the spot where thoughts of Mike used to fill with joy. It spurred me on. We had all been robbed when they took him.

'People of the Collective. Friends. I know I haven't addressed you before. I may not have the right. I've never wished to, nor have I had cause to,' I started, focusing on keeping my breath level, my tone unimpeachable.

'But today is a terrible day. A day we will all remember for the rest of our lives, be that a few short days, or many long years.'

I felt Alex, Grace and Bianca come and stand behind me, which spurred me to continue.

'Something has been stolen from us. Someone. A life. We are under threat. Danger is nothing new to us, in here. But a direct attack, straight into the heart of the Base, undetected and without warning is not a threat with which we are familiar. Nor should we be. They have taken from us, this mournful day, a man who was better than each of us. Better than all of us.

They killed him in his sleep, cowards lurking in the shadows to kill an old man. They didn't give him a chance to fight. And they left a message – one that referred to me. I am the one whose arrival brought this chaos to your door. I am the one they want back, dead or alive. So if you want to give me up, that's your choice. But I know there are some who will stand with me.'

Alex, Bianca and Grace stepped forward, Alex and Bianca each taking one of my hands and raising them to the ceiling – unified in our solemnity and determination, our differences connected by a common thread. The thread of survival against all of the odds. The thread that brings freedom.

Silently, but for the scraping of metal chair legs against floor tiles, people began to stand.

Lizzie and Flo were among the first. Tom followed, Graham and all of the Libs. A ripple went through the room and wordlessly, they stood. Dom, Heath and Lexi climbed on their chairs to bring them to the same height as the adults, and the other kids followed suit.

I paused, hesitating at bringing harm to the doorstep of these innocent children. But the wolves already surrounded the flock. We had no choice but to fight to protect ourselves, and them.

'They will rue the day they came for us,' I bellowed. 'Things are going to change. And we are going to be the catalyst of that change. There will be no vote. If you don't want to join us, you are welcome to leave. But if you remain in this building after two hours, you're part of the new order. An order which doesn't hide in the shadows, but charges out and takes back what belongs to it. A new order of freedom.'

A cheer ran through the dining hall, sound booming through the rafters. Remaining quiet, keeping our secret, was no longer a priority. They knew we were here. They'd probably known for some time, peering at us from the dark city. We no longer cared. We were proud. We were loud.

We were not split by greed. We were not isolated by ailing health, nor torn apart by senseless cruelty. We were united. United in valuing human life and human spirit above all else. This was our true strength, something no amount of force or brutality could take from us. The things they did to Josh, to Mike, to all of us, were coming to an end.

Now, all I had to attend to was the small matter of making our plan. A plan everyone in the Collective would stand behind, that they would follow with unfaltering dedication.

A plan which would overcome the lockdown of Florivale and bring Omniclin to its knees. With no time to do it, no weapons training and dwindling supplies.

Perfect.

54

Victoria

If you're reading this, it's happened. I've suspected for a while that it was coming. Of course, I can't tell you how they did it. I don't know yet, of course, how it all came to an end for me, but I guess you know by now. Macabre to think of the options.

There are more people involved than we knew about. Collusion from within the Collective. I am saddened that I haven't had time to establish whether the intelligence fed to those Outside, Omniclin among them, was provided by someone from the Base, or from one of our eyes in Florivale. I thought everyone shared our ideals.

A lot can change when you're under threat.

It falls to you to unite the free. You'll only get one shot. It should start with Florivale. We know the history there; they have weak spots.

Speak to the Libs. Alex is key. He told me he'd take you on a supply run as a trial for the Libs and I am confident you'll have already flown through it by the time you read this. I knew all about that, of course – whatever they might have thought. He's a good person. And his mother, too, although I know you don't like her much. I can't say more in case this is found before you're meant to see it. But find Alex as soon as you can.

Victoria Stone-Hunter. AFSH-003. Whatever name you choose to go by, you're the medicine this world needs. Too long have we cowed in the shadows, dreaming of doing something, of doing anything more dramatic than a supply run. For too long have we waited to attack.

You're new. You're different. You're compelled to strike out, born for the Role.

Galvanise the Collective. Galvanise the free. But remember to mete out forgiveness alongside your vengeance. Vengeance alone brings only pain.

I'm happy to be the catalyst for something drastic. Something I know you can lead. Sophie would have been so proud of you. Remember what she wrote, all those years ago. "We are all here for life. Cherish freedom." That was her mantra. We must protect it. Don't waste any tears on me. I'll be with her now, where I truly belong. I can let go now that you're here.

With eternal love, your Grandfather, and your greatest believer.

M x

I only wish I could have seen you do it.

55

With finding that note came the seal on my fate. I'd do whatever it took to change things.

There was no other way.

www.ingramcontent.com/pod-product-compliance
Lightning Source LLC
Chambersburg PA
CBHW021223060726
47590CB00005B/1618